TRIGGER POINT

TRIGGER POINT

Above the Rain Collective
2022

Above the Rain Collective
abovetheraincollective@gmail.com
North Georgia, USA

Contributing Editor: J.A. Sexton

Publisher's note:

ISBN: 978-1-7377970-4-3

First Printing September 2022

julietrose.author@gmail.com
authorjulietrose.com

Cover graphics and interior formatting by J.A. Sexton
Above the Rain logo artwork by Bee Freitag, text by Jack Freitag
Cover photos from top to bottom: Tatjana Posavec (top), Stefan Schweihofer (middle), Spike Summers (bottom)

To the Deaf Community: Thank you for sharing your culture and experience.

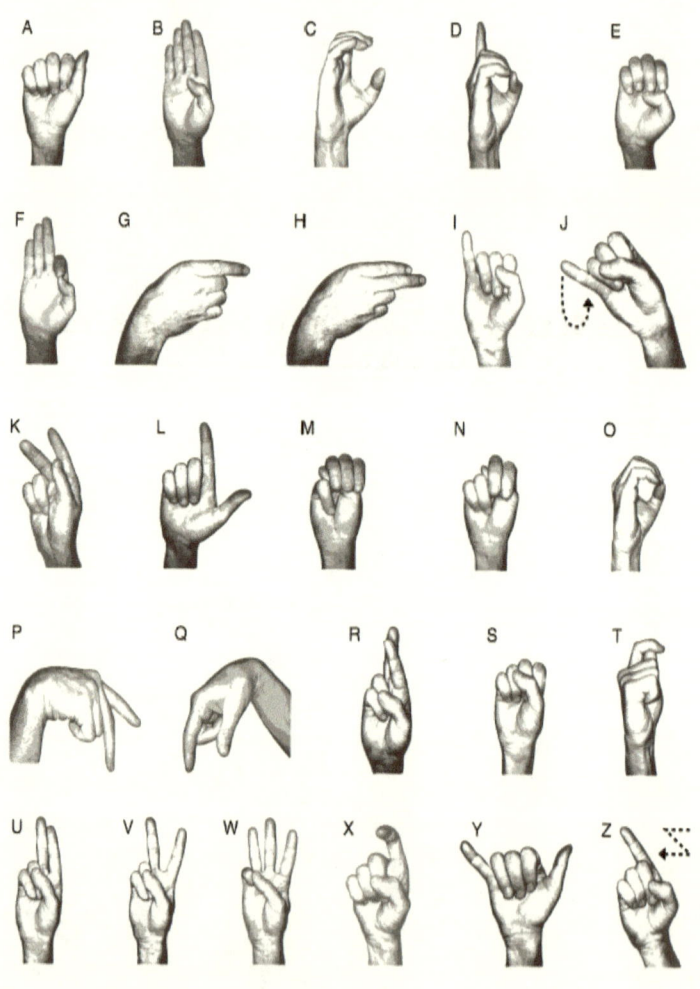

A note from the author

I wanted to touch on some points in my experience writing this novel. In no way am I an expert on American Sign Language. I took a class when in school and over the years have worked on adding to what I learned. However, a deaf preschooler could put me to shame. American Sign Language is not a translation from English, but rather its own language. Its own culture. In writing this story, I had to attempt to interpret from ASL to the written word so the reader could understand the emotion being conveyed by the characters. Anyone familiar with ASL knows that hand signs are only one small part of the full communication. Body language and facial expression are equal parts of the complete sign. ASL is an interactive language. Not being able to show that completely, I needed to be creative in my interpretation. In doing this, I had to work outside of the parameters of true ASL for clarity and eliminated contractions in those interactions to create a mental difference for the reader. I also did the first letter in each chapter from the sign language alphabet to introduce the idea.

Watching people communicate through sign language is a beautiful thing. I highly recommend learning even the basics of ASL and personally believe it should be taught in schools starting at a young age. ASL could be used in many areas to heighten communication across the board. To start, I am including the sign language alphabet on the adjacent page. Learning ASL can be a lot of fun and can be used in many circumstances!

Thank you!

Prologue

ot everyone can be saved. It's the grim reality of Search and Rescue. The alert comes in and units mobilize quickly. If they know where the person is, chances are higher for survival. If they don't, it's literally a race against the clock. In the case of an avalanche, there are about eighteen solid minutes to find the person, thirty on a good day. After that, the chances of survival drop substantially. Trained dogs can cover the same amount of area in minutes it takes humans hours, or even days, to cover in a search. To the dogs, it's a fun game of finding the buried scent. They can be thrown off the scent by the smell of other humans in the snow, but a good handler can get them on track again immediately. In the case of an avalanche, dogs are still an invisible victim's best chance of being found.

The thing is, people don't always understand how dangerous that sheen of untouched snow can be. How a fresh snowfall over older, thawing snow can be a death trap. They see the allure of cutting through it on their snowmobiles or

snowboards; not taking in one wrong impact, one rev of the engine, one simple turn, can bring it all crashing down. By the time they see it coming, it's too late; they can't outrun it. They were just out there for the day. They didn't bring survival gear, they don't know how to get themselves out.

It's the college students snowboarding on semester break. The couple skiing on their honeymoon. The father, bringing his young children out to snowmobile on the weekend. It's those who don't understand the delicate nature of the mountain. How the silent, white expanse can turn into a roaring monster, chasing them down to swallow them up in one fell swoop. Search and Rescue, though, they know. They know the mountains and their secrets. Knowing doesn't always matter. Warning people isn't always heeded. A beautiful day can turn into disaster in a matter of minutes... time is everything.

The alert comes in, teams head out on skis, snowmobiles, and on foot. Dogs are prepped, excited and ready for the chase. Their handler, understanding the reality of the situation, keeps them in check, keeps them focused. The handler knows they may not be out there to save anyone. The term search and rescue is a misnomer. Sometimes it's search and recovery. Either way, the dogs don't care. They're doing their job and they're good at it. They'll be rewarded for their hard work, they'll be praised and sleep well at night.

It's the humans, those that have to dig out what the dogs find, who'll carry the emotional toll. It's the humans who'll be haunted at night. They're the ones who'll rescue the college student but only recover his best friend. Who'll recover the body of the young woman on her honeymoon, then have to break the news to her new husband who was saved. They'll be the ones to

first touch the cold, dead hand of the child, who trusted her father would keep her safe and knew what he was doing. They're the ones who stay stoic in the face of the public, but behind closed doors fall apart and question if they're even making a difference. If they have canine companions, the dogs will comfort them, though they'll know not what for. The dogs just know their person is hurting and ultimately want to make them happy.

The next call will come and the team will load up to do it all over again. Again and again, until their souls break and they can't face another call. Some will retire, some will lose their lives in the line of duty, and some will end it to shut off the demons they can no longer run from. The dogs though, they'll continue going until their bones no longer keep up or until their handlers can no longer lead them.

Only then, will they stop the chase.

1

---

he triage station was restocked and organized since the last patient, one of the Search and Rescue Team, had left. Just a couple of stitches from a slip on the ice. It'd been a few days since an actual call had come through, so other than training and patrols coming and going out, base camp had been pretty quiet. Not that Zoey minded, it was always feast or famine out there. She was in her final paramedic intern rotation with the Mountaintop Search and Rescue, or SAR for short, in the Beartooth Mountain Range in Montana. Mostly volunteers with a few paid staff who were experts in the field. They'd just lost their SAR dog handler, who'd decided it was time to retire and take his dogs farther south. A new dog handler with two dogs was due to arrive from a team in Colorado any time now.

Zoey was glad the new handler was experienced as they were deep into the season, avalanches were a regular enough occurrence. They hadn't had one in weeks, which meant they were due. The dogs made all the difference in time, and often in

life or death. From what she'd heard, this handler, Micah Byrne, had one older very well-trained dog and another he was a year into training. She just hoped they didn't get a call before he arrived and got his bearings. A search without dogs slowed the whole process down. The mountains out the window of the triage tent looked so calm and serene. They'd had a fresh snow which gave an aura of stability. It was deceiving as before the snow, they'd had a few unseasonably warm days starting a melt, creating a slick, fragile layer underneath. The team was on edge, knowing this made things ripe for avalanches.

The ski patrol came in from their rounds, making their way to the warming tent attached to the triage tent. Kyle, the oldest and most experienced of the group, came in and grabbed coffee, followed by Megan and Jake, two of the newer volunteers. Most volunteers lasted a season and moved on, so it was a constant state of training.

"Hey, Zo, pretty quiet?" Kyle asked while making notes on a clipboard he hung on the wall.

"Beyond quiet, not that I'm complaining," Zoey replied and plopped down next to Jake on their makeshift couch, constructed from a cot and some waterproof pillows. "How's it looking out there?"

"About what we expected. Sink right in at spots," Megan said as she filled her coffee cup.

"Did the warnings go out?" Zoey fiddled with the zipper of her coat. Even in the army surplus tent, it was chilly despite the wood stove.

"Yeah, I notified local authorities about the danger. Not that it'll matter. We'll just need to be ready." Kyle shook his head with frustration.

They had a warning system, but like with fire danger in the warmer months, people just didn't listen. Everyone was on their own agenda, thinking they were immune to danger. Bad things happened to other people. Jake ran his hand through his light brown hair and glanced at Zoey, his eyes about the same color as his hair. Jake was in his early twenties and had a boyish, good-natured way about him.

"Do you know when the new handler is coming?" he asked.

They were all anxious for Micah's arrival, ready for a complete team again. Zoey shook her head. It was supposed to be today, she thought, but it was afternoon and he hadn't arrived yet. Maybe he'd been delayed.

"He should be here before nightfall," Kyle replied, sipping his coffee.

"Is he staying at base camp?" Zoey asked.

Not everyone did, however, the closer the handler was to the action, the better. They typically lived in a one-room cabin at base camp.

"From what I understand, he will. His cabin is set and ready to go for when he arrives. I don't know much about him, except he's been doing this for around ten or so years in Colorado. Oh, and he's deaf," Kyle added as if that bit of news wasn't important.

Zoey and Jake glanced at each other in astonishment. The handler was deaf? He must use hand signals for the dogs, but how would they all communicate with each other? Zoey had learned how to fingerspell in school but would need to brush up on that as she hadn't used it in years. She thought she knew a few words like thank you, mother, and father... that was about it.

"Wait, the dogs are deaf or the dude is deaf?" Megan asked unceremoniously.

"Micah the handler is deaf. Obviously, this shouldn't be an issue since he's successfully been doing Search and Rescue for years. Right?" Kyle's voice had a hard edge to it. While he understood their surprise, he didn't want this to degrade into gossip and doubt.

They'd simply need to learn to adapt. They needed a handler and this was who was coming. Zoey nodded, considering it. She could at least spell out words to start. Maybe she could pick up some basics. Quickly. Being a paramedic, she needed to be able to communicate with everyone on the team. They could figure it out face to face. It was radio communication she was worried about. Everyone had walkies and while they had cell phones, too, service was not reliable this far out. Maybe they could use a form of morse code. She was getting ahead of herself, though. She needed to meet Micah first and see where they were at.

It didn't take much longer for that to happen. An old, beat-up, blue pickup truck pulled up about an hour later and parked by the tents. Two dogs jumped out of the front, running around the truck happily. One was a larger Retriever-Saint Bernard Mix, the other was younger, a Border Collie-Beagle mix. The younger one was sniffing its surroundings while the larger one came back, patiently waiting for its owner by the driver's side door. The door swung open and a lean guy about early thirties got out. He had mid-neck length red hair, with a short, dark red beard, and was signaling to the dogs who immediately came to his side. He grabbed a pack out of the back of the truck and walked toward the tents.

Zoey went out to greet him, to show him where his cabin was, so he could put his things away. She was nervous and didn't want to make a fool of herself. She'd never directly interacted with someone that was deaf and didn't want to offend him with her lack of sign language knowledge. She opened the door and stepped out, instantly drawn in by his greenish-gray eyes. He smiled, creating crinkles around his eyes.

"Hello, my name is Zoey," she painstakingly signed to him. "I know how to fingerspell."

He broke out in a big grin and nodded. She felt stupid for saying she knew the alphabet but didn't want him to think she was fluent. As if *that* wasn't already apparent.

He motioned to his mouth with two fingers and mouthed the words. "I read lips."

"Oh! You can read lips?"

He bobbed his head, smiling. She waved him inside the tent and showed him the triage area and warming area.

"I'm a paramedic. Well, doing an internship. So, if you get any bumps or bruises..." She laughed awkwardly and made sure to keep her head up, facing him. "Over here is our break room of sorts."

He looked at her and put his hand on his chest, then tapped his first two fingers from each hand together in front of him and fingerspelled Micah. Zoey figured out he was saying, "my name is Micah". He motioned to the large dog, spelling out Chef, then to the younger dog, and spelled out Trek. Then pointed to Chef, making the letter C and touched his ear, then to Trek to make the letter T and wiggled the letter Y in front of his face.

Their nicknames.

"You are Micah, that dog is Chef, and the other is Trek?" Zoey asked, hoping she understood correctly.

He nodded his head in acknowledgment. Zoey knew she'd already introduced herself but wanted to do it correctly. She put her hand on her chest, then tapped her fingers together like he'd done and fingerspelled her name. He laughed, sliding his left hand across his right hand, then put his hands in fists with his pointer fingers up, moving his left hand towards his right hand. Zoey turned her head, trying to figure out what he was saying.

"I don't understand."

He fingerspelled, "nice to meet you," then repeated the hand motions. Nice to meet you. Zoey mimicked the motion. They didn't get very far, but she was determined to learn what she could. She led him to his cabin and showed him inside. He set his pack down and motioned thank you, putting his hand to his chin and moving it away from him. That one she knew. She thought she knew *you are welcome* and tried putting her open hand, thumb first to her chest.

He grinned and spelled out, "not bad."

"We're glad to have you here, Micah. Trek and Chef, too! I'll let Kyle know you've arrived. Reach out if you need anything. It's been quiet the last couple of weeks, which means it won't be soon. Kyle will fill you in more, you can go out on patrol with him in the morning."

She signed, "nice to meet you," again and waved as she left the tent. As she headed back to the triage tent, she let out the anxiety she was holding inside her. He seemed nice and she didn't think she'd come across too daft. She caught her reflection in the stainless steel of the coffee maker, embarrassed to see her

cheeks so flushed. She pushed her dark hair out of her face and stared closer, her deep brown eyes peering back from her reflection. Hopefully, he didn't notice how flustered she was. Not only did she feel like she'd been dropped off in an unfamiliar country, he was also very striking to boot. Meeting his stone-colored eyes so much had gotten her a little off-kilter.

She settled into a cot to read for a bit. Two paramedics rotated shifts and she covered that night. She saw Kyle head over to Micah's cabin and go inside. Hopefully, he was better at communicating than she was. They had an early patrol in the morning. That was if no calls came through before then. She began to doze off and decided to run to the bathhouse before it got too late. Micah was out with the dogs, letting them sniff around and get used to the area. She paused on her way back to the tent, watching them. He was in a long johns shirt and jeans, his muscular outline apparent. The dogs intently watched his face and hand motions, understanding what he was communicating. He knelt and rubbed each one of their faces, motioning to go back to the cabin. The dogs disappeared inside as he turned to see her watching him. He waved and went inside.

Zoey slipped back into the tent and under the covers. The previous handler had been in his late forties and not terribly friendly. He was good at his job and barked commands at his dogs like he was in the military. He and Zoey were pleasant with each other, but she'd always felt like she was under the stern eye of her father. He was loud and commanding.

Micah was the opposite. He and his dogs had a silent language they used to communicate. A simple flick of his wrist and Trek and Chef knew exactly what he meant. What he needed. She considered how this would affect Search and Rescue.

Would they be more in tune, not having orders shouted at them? Could they sense changes quicker? She didn't know but was fascinated by the process. She hoped Micah wouldn't mind if she observed training sessions to get a better understanding of his process.

As she drifted off, she wondered what made him come to SAR. To be a dog handler in an environment that was already unforgiving to those with all of their senses. Then she thought about how dogs can rapidly find a person completely submerged under the snow, mainly just using one of their senses. The more she thought about it, the more it seemed to add up. She didn't comprehend how it worked but clearly, it did. Her last thought before she fell asleep, was what it was like to be trapped in pitch dark if one was deaf, and she pushed away the fear it bubbled up in her.

2

he following morning, Zoey peered out and saw Kyle and Micah getting their skis on as Trek and Chef bounded around them, unable to contain their excitement. Kyle was talking and gesturing out towards the mountain tops. Micah had clearly told him he could read lips and was nodding, his eyes intent on Kyle's face. He glanced to where Kyle was pointing, placing his hand over his eyes to shield the glare. He slipped goggles over his eyes and they headed out on patrol. Both had radios on their packs and inflatable vests on. Zoey watched them disappear over the hill and turned back to the tent. It was Thursday, her relief was coming in a couple of hours. She didn't need to be back until the following Saturday afternoon.

The other medical person, Brandon, covered her days off while she interned. She was offered a paid position once her internship was up, but it was lower paying than what she could get in the cities as an ambulance EMT. She wasn't sure what she wanted to do. She still had two months left on her internship, up

mid-March, to figure it out. SAR was generally lighter-paced overall. Outside of the skier's body they recovered the prior month, and a suspected suicide when she first started, she hadn't dealt with too much death.

EMTs in the city faced a lot more, and she wasn't sure she was ready for that yet. If she did accept the position in SAR, it came with a small cabin, like Micah's. No previous interns had accepted, so they were leaning pretty heavily on her to accept. Only Kyle, the handler, and one paramedic were full-time paid employees. Everyone else was either volunteers or interns and part-timers in heavier seasons. In off-seasons, it was just those three, plus volunteers. Sometimes just the three. They each had access to a one-room cabin with a wood stove and fed off the main generator. Each cabin had a propane stove. They shared a small bathhouse with a shower and toilet. It wasn't glamorous, but the ones who chose the life were usually very driven. Volunteers covered days off, except for the handler who had to depend on other SAR handlers to cover calls if they wanted time off. They always made sure at least one of the full-timers was on at all times.

Brandon drove up and came into the tent. Zoey was hoping to communicate with Micah before heading out to the room she rented in town on her off days. She checked the time and figured they should be coming in from patrol in a couple of hours. She weighed waiting around but the idea of a hot shower and soft bed drew her away. She filled in Brandon on any happenings, then headed out. The drive off the mountain into town was peaceful, a few snowmobiles passing her on the road down. Hopefully, they'd seen the warnings and knew what they were doing.

Zoey swung by the bookstore to see if they carried any books on sign language. There was a basic one for ASL and she felt that was a good place to start. She checked out and drove to her place, which was an apartment with four other people. Luckily, most were at class and she was able to get right into a hot shower. They had the bathhouse at base camp, but to preserve the generator it only got lukewarm and they limited showers to under five minutes.

After the shower, she climbed into her bed and opened the sign language book. She practiced the alphabet over and over, realizing she'd been doing the letters p and h wrong all along. Micah hadn't pointed it out. She got down greetings such as, *how are you?* and *hello. Hello* was easy enough, just a wave from the side of her head. *How are you?* was a little more difficult putting her hand to her chest in a loose fist with her thumb pointing to her chest, then rotating her hand outwards with her thumbs up, followed by extending her pointer finger. She tried to think of what would be the most critical signs to learn in an emergency. She made a list of questions she might need to ask. Allergies? Where does it hurt? What happened? Pain scale? She'd need to work with Micah on these in case he got injured or they had a deaf rescue case.

By Saturday, she felt like she had a decent grasp on the basics like greetings, alphabet, and simple questions. She realized she wouldn't necessarily understand him replying, so she practiced in the mirror to see what it appeared like coming back at her. It was rough and awkward but the overall motions seemed right. She practiced questions and their responses, so she could see how they appeared from both sides. No matter what, she felt like a toddler trying to sign.

She headed to the mountain early, hoping to catch Micah before the beginning of her shift. When she arrived, he was out in a snow-covered field, working with the dogs. He must've buried things the day before because while the field was a clear sheet of snow, making nothing visible, the dogs were intent on what was out there. He signaled them to wait for his command and they sat on their haunches, watching him. Chef was calm and patient, Trek was wiggling in his seat. Micah raised his hand and gave them the command to search.

Like bullets, they were off. Within less than a minute, both had found the scent and were digging. Chef came up first with a blue piece of fabric, followed seconds later by Trek who played a little tug of war with Micah before giving up his scrap. Both pieces of fabric had been buried multiple feet deep but were no issue for the dogs to find.

Micah turned to see Zoey approaching and waved hello. She waved back and signed, "How are you?"

He signed back, "Good, you?"

She replied, "Good." She paused trying to remember how to ask if he could teach her sign language. Flustered, she finally fingerspelled it.

He looked at her thoughtfully and rubbed his bearded chin. He signed, "yes," then asked her what she wanted to learn.

She shook her head, laughing, then spelled, "everything."

He shrugged and nodded. He waved her over to the dogs, then showed her how to get them to sit and stay. She copied his hand motions as the dogs looked from her back to him. He then spelled out the word, "chase," showing her the sign for it by rotating his left hand with his thumb up towards his

other hand, which was closed with the thumb up. On command, the dogs took off and began searching for a scent. Zoey laughed and tried the sign. Micah moved her hand in the correct motion and she tried again. He smiled, giving her a thumbs up. The dogs, not finding the scent, circled back around and he signed for them to stay.

Zoey eyed him from the side, watching him with the dogs. He was rubbing snow on them, grinning. He glanced up at her, meeting her eyes for a second, his sage-gray eyes twinkling. He had a broad, open smile and light freckles that almost matched his auburn hair. She couldn't deny he was very attractive and looked away, blushing. He didn't seem to notice, then stood up.

"When?" he signed. He was asking when she wanted to meet to learn.

Her answer was going to be painfully long, attempting to explain her schedule in sign, so she met his eyes and said, "How about Monday through Thursday at nine in the morning?"

"Sounds good," he replied in sign, mouthing the words back to her.

She signed it back to him. It was time to relieve Brandon, so she waved goodbye and headed for the triage tent.

Brandon was reading a book and smiled when she came in. "Hey, Zoey. Not too much going on over the past couple of days. We had a call Friday night for a lost skier but they were coming down when we headed up, so we guided them the rest of the way. A snowmobiler was stuck and we dug them out. That's about it. I saw you with the new handler, Micah. Seems like a nice guy."

24

"Yeah. Hey, how are you communicating with him when on a call or patrol?" She'd forgotten to find out how that was going.

"He stays pretty much to his own but there is a sheet of code signals we can send back and forth on the desk over there."

Zoey walked over and saw a list of messages in morse code. The radios had a light on them and when a button was pushed the light would illuminate. The codes were basic and they could send coordinates that way as well. She'd study those while it was quiet and ask Micah if they could practice those, so they were on the same page.

Brandon headed out and Zoey tidied up the space. She went out to scoop snow for the coffee maker and was caught by the beauty of the mountains as the sun glinted off them. She was born and raised in the area. Her mother was originally from Guam and her father from Montana, they met when he was in the military. They'd lived on a farm outside of town with Zoey and her brothers and sister growing up.

They were a close family, but she'd grown up familiar with the stares of people in the area who weren't comfortable with "her kind", as she heard them say when they thought she couldn't hear. Her *kind* being brown people, or in general not white people. She had dark brown hair and mocha eyes, her skin a light shade of caramel. All of the kids were different, anywhere between both parents' traits. Her older brother and sister had moved away to be in a more diverse area, leaving just her and her younger brother to help her parents out. Zoey loved the mountains and didn't want to leave. Her brother, Charlie, was in his last year of college, and being the baby by far, five years younger than her, had seemed to find a new generation who

didn't care about the color of someone's skin. He had a good group of friends and snowboarded every chance he could get.

She scooped the snow into a pitcher, pressing it down as hard as she could, so it would make a full pot. As she turned to go back inside, she caught a glimpse of Micah standing at his cabin door, watching her. Their eyes met, then he blushed and glanced away, staring off to the mountains with his hands in his back pockets.

Zoey couldn't be a hundred percent certain, but at the moment their eyes met, she was almost positive she saw admiration in his eyes. She went back into the tent and set the pitcher down to let the snow melt. She glanced out the plastic tent window and saw Micah looking at the flap she'd just entered, with a soft smile on his face. She felt her cheeks get hot and she shook it off.

However, she knew what she saw.

3

 he next day, a call finally came in. Three skiers were caught in an avalanche. One injured but made it out, the other two buried, one visible, one not. This was where the team came alive. Within minutes of the alert coming through, the team was loaded on snowmobiles and speeding toward the scene. They packed shovels, wore inflatable vests, had their radios and skis, in case they needed to move on foot if the ground couldn't handle the weight of the snowmobile. They all had basic first aid kits and training to get the rescued to the triage station at base camp.

Trek and Chef were more than ready to go, barking as Micah loaded the snowmobile. Zoey stayed back to tend to the injured as they came in and to prepare them for transport if it became necessary. The team consisting of Kyle, Megan, Jake, Micah, and the dogs, were off towards the site while Zoey prepped the triage area. It'd been over a week, which was rare, but everyone was always ready to go at the drop of a hat.

Thirty minutes later, Megan brought back the injured, but safe, skier and headed back out to the rescue site. Zoey brought the girl in and got her on a cot, checking her vitals. Other than a dislocated shoulder, her vitals were good and she sat quietly, pale but alert. Zoey tried to get her comfortable, recognizing she'd need to get the shoulder at least stabilized.

"Hey, I'm Zoey, I'll be taking care of you until we can get you transported to the hospital. I think we should wait to set the shoulder until you get there, but I'm going to wrap it to take some of the weight and pain off, okay?"

The girl tipped her head, staring out of the tent. "Are my friends going to be alright?"

Zoey knew better than to conjecture without knowing how deep they'd been buried or how quickly the team would be able to get to them. "The Search and Rescue team is out there now doing their best. They're experienced and will do what they can to help your friends. Try to rest your arm and warm up."

Zoey heard the radio crackle and stepped out of hearing range as she answered. It was Kyle. One victim was unconscious, the other was conscious but had an extremely low body temperature. They got them both out and were on their way back to the camp. Zoey touched base with the ambulance coming from the hospital, they'd be there just a couple of minutes after the team got back with the patients. She prepped blankets to warm both victims.

As soon as she saw the team coming over the hill, she ran out to meet them. They immediately brought the guys in and Zoey started to strip off their wet clothing to get warm blankets over them. Two males about mid-twenties, with no obvious injuries outside of one being unconscious and the other shaking

badly. The girl came over to them and watched as the team stabilized the patients. The ambulances came over the hill and the two EMTs were inside in a flash. They transported the patients to the ambulance, the unconscious male in one and the conscious male and female in the other. Zoey followed them out, filling them in on their vitals and the female's condition. Once the ambulances left, she headed back into the warming tent for coffee and to settle her nerves. No matter how many times they dealt with this, it always felt like the first time.

Kyle handed her a cup of coffee and sat on the cot couch. They chatted about the rescue as they always did to work out the stress. The female had been sitting in the snow and pointed when they came up, but the dogs were already on it. Chef found the unconscious victim and Trek went to the conscious one. They were already digging by the time the team drew their shovels out. Within minutes, they were down to the victim's level and were pulling them out. They weren't sure if the unconscious guy had gotten hit in the head, knocking him unconscious, or if his body temperature had dropped too quickly, causing him to slip into deep shock. Either way, time was of the essence.

Kyle got up and radioed the ambulance driver for an update. The girl and conscious guy were okay, stable and talking normally. The unconscious guy's temp was staying low but they were at the hospital, transporting him into emergency and likely up to ICU. They'd call with an update as soon as they knew something. Kyle thanked them and sat back down, sighing. It was hard to let go until there were answers.

Micah was outside playing with the dogs to use up their pent-up energy. Zoey brought him a cup of coffee. He took it and signed thank you. The dogs were wagging their tails and

running back and forth, jumping over each other. Zoey liked watching them play. It brought a lightness to what they had to deal with. Micah signaled to them and they ran up to him. He walked over and opened the cabin door. They ran in and settled by the wood stove. Micah motioned in, his eyebrows raised to see if Zoey wanted to come in. She nodded and followed him into the cabin. The cabins were small but had a full-size bed, a small couch by the wood stove, a table with two chairs, a kitchenette with an icebox, a standing propane stove, and a couple of cabinets. It was cozy for one and the dogs had a bed right by the wood stove.

Zoey sat on the couch and signed, "How are you?"

Micah shrugged. He responded, "Good."

Zoey looked at his face. "I guess you are used to it now?"

Micah shook his head, then signed, "Never."

Zoey nodded. She guessed not. She signed *never* to try and remember it. Micah came over and sat on the couch next to her.

He set his coffee down. "Are you alright?"

Zoey didn't know the signs directly but could read the expression on his face and coordinating hand movements. Some didn't need interpretation. She bobbed her head and gave a small smile. "Yeah, I guess I don't have to deal with the hard part. By the time patients come to me, it's pretty clear what direction needs to be taken with them. Plus, if it's bad, the ambulance is usually here in a flash."

Micah thought about what she said and smiled. He signed, "Still hard."

Zoey couldn't disagree with that. No matter how many times they dealt with victims who might not make it, it never

became easier. Everyone wanted the best outcome. She leaned back on the couch. Micah got up and grabbed a couple of sodas out of the icebox, handing one to her. Trek, curious to see if there was anything for him, came over and nudged her hand. She petted him and laughed. He was thin and lanky, still growing into his body. His amber eyes stared at her to see if she was going to give him anything. Then he moved to Micah, who'd sat back down. Micah petted him and gave him the hand motion for bed. Defeated, Trek went and laid back down on top of Chef, who hadn't budged. Trek gave them big, sad eyes and sighed heavily. Zoey chuckled and sipped her soda.

They chatted using a mixture of the alphabet, and signs Micah showed her. He also kept a pad and pen nearby to write out what he was signing if they got hung up. Zoey responded by saying words and either spelling them out or signing if she thought she knew them. It was overwhelming, but Micah never acted impatient or frustrated. She learned he was born in New Mexico, but put up for adoption in Colorado when his young parents realized he was deaf. He didn't blame them, they wanted a better life for him, or so he'd been told. He'd been adopted by a couple familiar with the deaf world, which made growing up easier. They were hearing and had a hearing son, however, were fluent in ASL. He went to public school but found himself angry and frustrated most of the time. He got into a lot of fights, eventually finishing out schooling at home.

He'd always loved dogs, and as a kid began training them, using hand signals for basic commands. After graduating, he did wilderness survival training and from there started training his dogs in Search and Rescue, volunteering on weekends. Before long, he was offered a full-time job and had

been doing it ever since. Chef was his third dog and Trek his fourth. His original dogs had aged and passed on. He'd only been training Trek for a little over a year and Chef was six years old. Both were rescues.

Zoey explained she was from the area, and how growing up being biracial had been a challenge in the farming community. She told him about her older siblings moving away and her younger brother, Charlie, going to school and snowboarding. Micah motioned to his own snowboard leaning against the wall and signed, "awesome." He asked where her mother and father were from. She signed mother and fingerspelled Guam, then signed father and here. He nodded and reached out to touch her dark hair.

He signed, "beautiful," which made her blush and look away.

Chef interrupted at this point and Micah got up to feed them. Zoey watched him move around the cabin, feeling warmed by his compliment. He was striking. She'd always thought of herself as plain since in school, boys were more interested in the blond, light-eyed girls. The white girls. That a guy who looked like Micah would even take notice of her was surprising and disconcerting, to say the least. She'd noticed him as soon as he'd set foot out of the truck, his red hair and stone eyes so unique and mesmerizing. She put her bottle down and stood up. Micah turned, meeting her eyes. She motioned to the door and went to head out. He touched her arm, signing something she didn't understand. She cocked her head, confused, and he spelled it out.

"I am glad you are here, Zoey. I like you."

Zoey didn't know how to reply and chuckled awkwardly. She went to step out, tripping over her own feet, and

fell into the snow. Micah came out and gave her a hand up, laughing. She brushed the snow off her clothes and met his eyes.

"Sorry, that was stupid. You're nice, too, Micah. I look forward to getting to know you better," she stammered.

He smiled at her in the way he was smiling the day she disappeared into the tent. She didn't know what to make of what he'd said or how to respond to it. He liked her? What did that mean? She found herself staring at him a little too long and flushed. She turned and waved a quick goodbye, escaping to the triage tent. Kyle was wrapping up a call and nodded in her direction.

"The unconscious guy is going to make it. They're getting his body temp up and he is starting to respond to certain stimuli. They ran a cat scan and it appears he took a blow to the head, maybe a rock caught up in the snow. No major internal bleeding, so it may just take some time. Docs say the prognosis is good."

Zoey breathed out a sigh of relief. "That's good to hear. Another successful day."

Just as she said that, an alert came in. Flipped over snowmobile, injuries reported. Kyle threw his hands in the air and began putting on snow gear. The thing about quiet weeks was the universe had a certain amount of accidents that were supposed to happen and if they didn't happen spread out, they'd come in all clumped together. Jake came in and grabbed his pack and a donut off the table, grinning at Zoey.

"No rest for the wicked," he said as he ducked out the door.

Megan was already on her snowmobile and the three of them headed out. The dogs weren't needed this round since it

wasn't an avalanche or a lost person. Zoey stepped out to watch the snowmobiles ascend the mountain and glanced over to see Micah watching as well. She waved at him, spelling out, "flipped snowmobile." He nodded. The dogs were behind him, seeming hopeful, but he shooed them back inside. Zoey waved, "hey," at him to get his attention and he stopped to look at her.

"The unconscious guy from the avalanche is going to pull through!" she yelled in his direction, signing the few words she knew. She felt stupid for yelling but shook it off.

He watched her lips and gave her a thumbs up, signing, "good." Then he went back into his cabin, much to the disappointment of Trek and Chef, who were more than ready for the next adventure.

Zoey went into the triage tent, snagged a cup of coffee on her way, then listened out for the crackle of the radio and the snowmobiles coming back over the hill with the injured.

4

he next few weeks were busy as they rolled into February. Zoey decided to take the full-time position once her internship was up. Kyle was thrilled to hear it and offered her a cabin early if she wanted to move in prior to the position start date. She considered it and decided saving money on renting a room would be the smarter decision. She gave her roommates a couple weeks' notice and moved her paltry amount of belongings to the cabin, which was situated between Kyle's and Micah's. She'd miss super hot showers, but not having to drive up and down the mountain or sleep on the triage cot would be a nice change.

The cabins were set in a semicircle with a large fire pit in the center. Occasionally when the weather allowed, volunteers would pitch their tents on the other side, creating a full circle around the fire pit. They made an effort to keep a fire stoked during the day. Kyle was working on building a larger bunkhouse in his spare time and had built the first three cabins.

Most SAR were fully portable but Kyle had worked with it for so long, he'd decided to make the base camp more stable with the agreement of the county, which gave permission to use the land as needed.

Once Zoey was settled in and had her wood stove stoked to warm up the cabin, she stepped over to the triage tent. Brandon was on shift, sitting at the desk, taking notes out of a textbook. He glanced up and smiled her way. He was in his mid-twenties and studying to be a nurse. He put his pen down, leaned back in his chair, and watched Zoey with his dark eyes. He ran his hair through his short, black, wavy hair.

"All settled? I have to admit, I like the idea of you being here when I'm on shift, as backup. I'll try not to bug you too much, though."

Zoey sat on the cot and propped her feet up on a chair. "Yeah, it's going to be weird always being around, but the experience will be priceless. I haven't worked the spring or summer, so it will be interesting to see how different those are."

Brandon nodded and glanced out the small plastic window by the desk. He tapped his fingers on the desk thoughtfully. "Me either. I plan to stay on during the summer but have already been offered a job with the hospital emergency room after Labor Day. Eventually, I want to work in Obstetrics."

Zoey could see it. Brandon had a kind face and gentle demeanor. Even when things got chaotic and stressful, he kept his cool and cracked jokes. He was engaged to his college sweetheart, and they'd already planned on children right after marriage. Zoey would miss him but understood him needing job stability. SAR was a great place to cut your teeth, but long term it took a certain type of person. She supposed she was that type

of person. The good thing was, the college always had a steady stream of nursing and paramedic students wanting to intern to get experience.

Kyle and Micah came in on snowmobiles, pulling a toboggan with a skier who'd fallen off a small cliff and broken their leg. Brandon jumped up and helped them get the guy inside. He checked his leg which was fractured but hadn't broken through the skin. Zoey helped him attach a splint and check the guy's vitals. Shortly after, an ambulance came and transported the guy to the hospital. Trek and Chef were laying on the warming side by the coffee maker and Micah sat down next to them on the couch. Megan and Jake were off, so it was just the four of them. Kyle leaned against the tent wall, surveying the triage area.

"Well, Zo, you are locked in now," he joked. "Do you need anything?"

"No, got the wood stove fired up. Probably need to make sure it still has coals going. Actually, about to head over to eat. I think Brandon is good."

Brandon waved in agreement. Micah stood up, signing he was heading home. He and Zoey walked over together, stopping between their cabins. They communicated about the day and weather, then they split off to their own places. Before he got to his door, Micah stopped and got her attention.

"Dinner at my place tomorrow?" he signed.

"Sure!" Zoey signed back.

He smiled and ducked into his cabin. She went into hers, now toasty from the stove. The fire gave a cozy cast over everything. She heated some beans and vegetables, putting them in a wrap. She could see a light glowing from Micah's cabin and

turned to see Kyle heading into his. It gave her a sense of being part of a tiny village, making her feel warm inside. She clicked on the radio, pulling in the local oldies station. Then she sat on her couch, eating and tapping her foot to Bill Withers.

The wood stove was burning steadily and she had a good stack of wood for the night. She threw a couple of logs in and peered out of the window. She could see Brandon in the triage tent, reading his nursing manuals. Kyle and Micah still both had lights shining in their cabins. She smiled and turned out her lights. She climbed into bed, listening to the crackling fire. For the first time since she was a child, in her room between her parents' room and her brother's room, she felt a sense of belonging and being in her own space.

The next day she was still off and drove into town for medical supplies and groceries, taking everyone's orders to make it simple. When she got back, Jake and Megan were in for their weekend shifts, doing maintenance on the equipment. She waved at them as she unloaded supplies into the tent. Brandon began sorting and recording the medical supplies immediately. Micah was out working with the dogs in the field and Kyle was focused on building the new bunkhouse. With all of them there, it reminded Zoey of growing up on the farm with her two brothers, sister, and parents. There had always been someone around, chatter, and laughter.

It was hard when her older brother, then her older sister moved away. She was glad her parents and Charlie were still around, but wished they could go back to the days when they all were together. As a child, she'd always imagined they'd all grow up, have families of their own, and live around each other. Not only had her brother and sister moved away, neither had shown any interest in having families of their own. Her sister, Matilda, had moved to Phoenix and was happily working as a senior administrator for an insurance company. Her brother, Alexander, had become a school teacher in Cheyenne, Wyoming and lived with his girlfriend, however, they hadn't talked about marriage or family. They were in their thirties but were not chasing the traditions of their parents. The American dream had changed.

Zoey couldn't say much because she was twenty-seven and had never been in a serious relationship, beyond dating for a few months here and there. She was so focused on becoming a paramedic the last couple years, she'd put off relationships as soon as they started requiring more of her time. Charlie was in school for Journalism, seeming more focused on dating a lot of girls, snowboarding, and hanging out with his friends.

Micah brought the dogs in, their tongues hanging out and tails wagging. He grabbed groceries out of Zoey's car and brought them into the warming tent to sort. The tent had a small cabinet, propane refrigerator, and stove, so they stocked the food for there and made three additional piles. One for Kyle, one for Micah, and one for Zoey. Each of them took their stuff to their tents as Micah reminded Zoey about dinner at his cabin at six.

Zoey wandered over a little early and brought chips and dip. She went to knock on the door, then stopped. Should she just walk in? She decided to knock anyway, and Micah came to the door. She was a little surprised, furrowing her brows.

Micah laughed, signing, "vibrations." He went on to explain how he could feel a lot of sound through vibrations and air movement. Like, if someone whispered behind him, he could

sometimes feel the change in airflow on his neck. Zoey asked if he'd always been deaf.

"From birth," he explained.

No one had known until he was about a year and a half old. When they realized they didn't have the resources to best help a deaf child, they put him up for adoption. Both the couple who adopted him had a deaf relative, so wanted to give him a stable, loving home. His older brother, Trent, their birth child was also hearing. He didn't seem too interested in having a baby brother and pretty much ignored Micah. His name had been Micah from birth, so they kept that. Their last name was Byrne. He'd tried to find his birth family but never could. His name was on file with the adoption agency in case they wanted to find him.

He handed Zoey a glass of wine and went to the stove. She opened the chips and dip and sat at the table. His shoulders were broad and muscular, his hips slender. He was just under six feet tall, a few inches taller than her. Like most redheads, his skin was lighter and he had freckles, but not an overabundance. In a lot of ways, they were complete opposites. She found him to be very pleasant to look at. As if he read her mind, he turned towards her and raised his eyebrows. Could he read minds better, too? She glanced down, focusing on her chip.

He brought over plates with sandwiches and pickles. He sat across from her and spelled out vegetarian and tempeh, explaining it was fermented soybeans. She took a bite tentatively and was pleasantly surprised. It didn't taste like anything specific but reminded her of a chicken salad sandwich. She smiled and took another bite. He was full of mysteries. They ate the chips and dip with the sandwiches.

"Do you like it?" he asked.

"It's different, but yes." She wasn't lying or being polite.

After they were finished, they moved to the couch and Micah stoked the stove, leaving it open so they could see the fire. They sipped on wine and conversed about their lives. Trek and Chef slept at their feet, moving only to readjust and fall back to sleep. They stopped chatting, mesmerized by the fire when Micah touched her arm.

"Can I ask you a question?" he inquired.

Zoey thought she understood what he was signing. "Sure?"

He turned towards her and blushed. "I like you."

Zoey stared wide-eyed. Guys had asked her out now and then, but no one had ever been so forward, so quickly. She cocked her head slightly, waiting for him to go on. When he didn't, she felt her cheeks get hot.

"That's not a question," she whispered.

He chuckled and shrugged, the tips of his ears turning pink. "No, it is not. Can I kiss you?"

Zoey met his eyes, considered it. She nodded. He put his hand on the back of her head and leaned in to kiss her. Not soft, but not forceful either. Zoey felt warmed by the kiss and responded in kind. When they drew back, they were both flushed and grinned at each other. They each took a sip of wine and leaned back on the couch.

"Now that is out of the way," Micah said, his hands carefully expressing what he was feeling. "I have wanted to do that since we first met."

"Really?" Zoey asked, surprised.

"Yes."

"Oh."

They observed the fire for a bit, letting that revelation sink in. Micah reached out and took her hand, holding it in his own as they rested back on the couch. He drained his glass and set it down carefully, facing her.

"You are the prettiest woman I have ever seen." His hands were moving quickly, but he'd pause and fingerspell any words he could tell her she didn't know. "I saw you the first day and you stopped me in my tracks. We are not kids and I wanted you to know that, instead of waiting."

He was so forward, she had a hard time wrapping her mind around what he was saying.

"Alright?" she said, not sure how to reply.

"I am going to want to kiss you a lot," he replied.

Her face flamed and she felt a little out of sorts. She glanced at him and his eyes were locked on hers. She couldn't deny she felt the same. They weren't kids, she was in her late twenties and he was in his early thirties. They didn't need to beat around the bush. They were both adults and knew what it was they wanted.

"Okay," she replied, this time as an affirmation.

He leaned in and kissed her again. This time they let it continue for a while. His mouth was warm and soft, he knew what he was doing. She moved towards him, letting her fingers drift through his hair. He took her breath away. She sat back and looked at him, her eyes hooded with desire.

"We'd better stop," she said softly.

"Alright, Z. For now." He smiled genuinely and held her hand again.

Zoey could honestly say she'd never felt this way with anyone. She didn't want to stop but knew if she didn't, they

wouldn't. She didn't want to rush things between them. She glanced at Micah as butterflies tickled her stomach. It was like she was a schoolgirl with her first crush. He caught her eye and winked. She shook her head, smiling. She needed to leave before it went too far.

"I have to go. Thank you for dinner." She stood up, feeling bashful.

He stood up, still holding her hand. He signed with one hand, "Thanks for coming over, Z. This was fun."

"It was, Micah. I will make you dinner next time."

He walked her to the door and kissed her on the cheek.

"I look forward to it."

5

 oey and Micah started spending much of their free time together, between him teaching her sign language and getting to know each other better. They decided to take things slow since their first kiss was so fast. They split cooking duties but always went back to their own cabins at the end of the evening. They held hands, kissed, and hugged each other but neither was ready for the next step, even though both of them were. As Easter approached, Zoey considered inviting Micah to her family's Easter dinner. She didn't know if he planned to go back to Colorado, but he hadn't mentioned needing any time off. He rarely mentioned his family as it was. Zoey's mother always went all out, cooking a huge spread. It sounded like this year it'd just be her parents, Charlie, and herself. Her other siblings declined to come home due to work responsibilities and not wanting to travel.

Micah was out repairing a cracked window on his cabin when Zoey came over to ask him. He was glazing a fresh pane

he'd cut to replace the cracked one. Zoey observed him silently, thinking he didn't know she was there.

"You know, I know you are there, right?" he asked, signing with one hand without looking up. He was like a ninja.

She laughed and came over next to him as he put the glass in place. "I did not. Do you need help?"

"Hold this." He gestured to the glass he was holding in place.

She put her hand on it and he shoved little pegs in to hold the pane still while the caulk dried. She took her hands away and it held in place. He wiped his hands on his jeans, smiling up at her.

"Thanks. How is it going?"

"Good. Hey, I was wondering. My mother does a whole thing for Easter dinner. Do you want to come?"

He considered it and chewed the inside of his lip. "Maybe. I do not have any plans. Should I bring something since I am vegetarian? Is that weird?"

She hadn't considered that and her mother traditionally cooked almost everything with some form of meat. "Oh, yeah. I am sure she'll have a couple of non-meat dishes, but we can make some to bring."

Zoey had been raised in a meat-eating home and never thought much about it, but now that she was spending most of her time with Micah, she'd been eating and cooking vegetarian out of respect for him. He never made an issue out of it but since they were cooking for each other, it'd been easier to just eat that way.

He nodded, then shrugged. "Sounds fun. Are you ready for me to meet your parents?"

"The real question is, are you ready to meet them?" She laughed and since she didn't know the sign, spelled out, "Scary."

He made a scared face and put his arm around her. They kissed and heard hooting from Jake, who was passing by the cabins. Everyone knew about the time they were spending together, and other than some good-natured ribbing, it hadn't been an issue. Kyle was divorced and seeing a woman in town, Brandon was engaged, and all of them suspected Megan and Jake were hooking up at the least. They spent a lot of time as their own little family and everyone was generally supportive of each other.

Kyle pulled her aside, and as her boss explained they needed to remain professional, no matter what happened. She agreed and assured him her job was of the utmost importance. She gathered Micah had been given the talk, too, as one day she saw Kyle and him in a serious discussion outside of the cabins. Kyle had learned to fingerspell, so while she couldn't totally see what they were communicating, she was able to make out her name and the word team. Micah glanced over at her during the talk and gave her a quick wink.

Before Easter, she called her mother to let her know she was bringing Micah to Easter dinner. That he was vegetarian and bringing his dogs. They already knew he was deaf just from her talking about her work team. Her mother made a clucking sound and sighed. Zoey let her know she didn't have to do anything special, but knowing her mother, she'd be digging out cookbooks for vegetarian dishes. Zoey let Charlie know Micah was coming to which he responded, "rad," then asked if they were seeing each other. Zoey said she thought so, to which Charlie chuckled at her, shaking his head.

When Easter came, Zoey woke up with a stomach of nerves. Maybe it was too soon. Her father was polite but standoffish. Her mother was stubborn and blunt. She was glad Charlie would be there because he at least made everyone laugh. He had no filter. She walked over to Micah's cabin and knocked. The door swung open and Trek and Chef were there to greet her. Micah said he wasn't worried about going over but had obviously cleaned up for the occasion, wearing a nice sweater and slacks. Zoey felt underdressed in her jeans and blouse. Micah offered to drive and the dogs were already at the cab of his truck before she agreed. She wrote down directions and handed them to him. He glanced over them and nodded, placing the paper in his pocket.

On the ride, the dogs crammed themselves between Micah and Zoey. Regardless, Micah put his hand over the dogs to hold her hand. She stared out the window and tried to quell the butterflies in her stomach. She hoped her parents were nice and didn't make it awkward. As they pulled into the drive, Trek stood up and stared out the front window, his tail wagging. The driveway was long to the quaint, white farmhouse she'd grown up in. They parked next to Charlie's car. Her father was on the front porch, rocking in a chair, and raised his hand in a wave.

The dogs bolted out the door and began sniffing everything. Zoey walked up and introduced Micah to her father, signing and saying it at the same time. She mentioned Micah could read lips. Her father nodded and observed Micah, sizing him up. Her father had been a military man and hid his feelings very well.

"Nice to meet you, Micah."

Micah signed as Zoey interpreted. "Thank you. Nice to meet you as well, sir."

They went inside to the tougher meet and greet, her mother. They walked into the kitchen and set down the rice pilaf and braised tofu they'd brought. Zoey's mother turned, eyeing the food. She watched Micah, who was motioning for the dogs to lay down in a corner of the kitchen. Micah met her eyes and smiled.

She gave a curt nod, then to Zoey's surprise she signed, "Welcome to our home."

Zoey thought she'd fall over and stared from Micah to her mother. Her mother shrugged.

"My grandmother was deaf, I know a little," she said matter-of-factly.

"Why didn't you tell me?" Zoey asked incredulously.

"You never asked." Her mother turned and went back to prepping food.

Zoey looked at Micah and put her hands in the air, mouthing the words, "I had no idea!"

Micah went over to her mother and offered to help. All of sudden, they were communicating back and forth, their hands moving so quickly Zoey couldn't keep up. Her mother was handing Micah things to cut and the two of them got busy prepping food. Zoey walked back out to the porch and sat next to her father.

"Did you know Mom knows sign language?"

"No, but doesn't surprise me. Your mother knows just about everything," he stated.

"Well, she and Micah are in there chatting up a storm. I got lost pretty quickly. I know some, but she's fluent."

Her father laughed and lit a cigar. "I love that woman. She never ceases to amaze me."

Zoey's parents had always been outwardly loving with each other and all the children. Her mother was the disciplinarian but her father backed up his wife always. Her mother was five-foot-two with black hair, almost black eyes, and dark caramel skin. Her father was six feet tall, ruddy, with light blue eyes. He'd been blond, but now was just salt and light pepper gray. Her mother's hair was still jet black and she'd hardly aged. They looked like opposites, but seeing them together it was hard to imagine them with anyone else. They laughed and teased each other mercilessly. Thinking of her mother, Zoey figured she should go in and make sure Micah was okay.

When she got back to the kitchen, Charlie had joined them and was jumping in, chatting with them as his mother interpreted what Micah was saying. Zoey paused at the door and smiled at the three of them. Of course, Micah would fit right in. He caught her eye and gave her a semi-dramatic wink. She laughed and went over to him. He put his arm over her shoulder.

"So, are you two like an item?" Charlie teased.

Micah didn't understand his terminology and glanced at Zoey for confirmation.

"He's asking if we're dating," Zoey explained.

Micah nodded, considering that, then signed, "Yes."

Zoey flushed a little at this. They'd certainly spent most of their time together and made out a lot, but neither had made it official. She met Micah's eyes and he appeared unsure for a second.

"Right?" he asked.

"Right," she replied.

So, it was official. He smiled, relief washing across his face.

Zoey's mother called her father in to eat and they carried the food to the table. Of course, she'd made multiple vegetarian dishes, so there was plenty to eat. They all tried the rice pilaf and braised tofu as well. If there was one thing Zoey could say about her family, they were welcoming. Her father stayed pretty quiet, but her mother and Charlie brought Micah into all conversations, getting to know him well. There were things Zoey hadn't even known about him, they managed to drag out. It was fascinating and Charlie seemed to catch on to a lot of signs quickly, attempting them unabashed. He'd never been a shy one. Micah sat to her right, holding her hand under the table, only letting go when he needed both hands to express himself.

After they ate, they all cleared the table and Zoey went to help her father wash the dishes. The deal was the cook didn't have to clean the kitchen after in their house.

Micah and Charlie went out to let the dogs run and seemed to be connecting over snowboarding. Micah was showing Charlie how to fingerspell and had a piece of paper and pencil if they got stuck. Zoey felt happy to see them communicating and laughing. Regardless of their differences, they were guys with common ground. She stacked up the dishes her father was rinsing and handing to her.

"So, you like this fella?" he asked, not looking over.

"Yeah, Dad. I do. Micah's really nice and funny. It's easy to be around him."

"Alright, then. He seems like he has a good head on his shoulders. Just be careful. Relationships take work." He stopped and met her eyes.

"I know, Dad. We're working on it. Getting to know each other first. It's been slow going with me trying to learn ASL. Maybe I should take Mom home with me."

They both laughed at this and the person mentioned walked into the kitchen.

"What are you two giggling at?" her mother asked.

This made them laugh even harder.

"Nothing, Mom. I was just saying, you're already talking more with Micah than I am."

Her mother nodded, looking serious. "He's got a temper. He told me it used to get him into trouble. He's obviously grown up a lot since then, but be aware."

Zoey felt admonished, even though she knew that wasn't her mother's intent. Micah told her as much, but her mother always had a sense about things. It wasn't directed at their relationship, rather at his dealings with the world. She tipped her head at her mother, understanding. She'd take heed.

Micah and Charlie came in, chuckling about something between them. Micah came over to Zoey and put his arms around her. He drew back, asking if she was ready to go. She was. They didn't like to be from base camp for too long and had already been gone a few hours. Her mother handed her food to take with them and kissed each of them on the cheek. Her father shook Micah's hand. He'd been accepted.

Charlie spelled out, "Monday?" to Micah, who responded, "Yes."

Zoey furrowed her brow, confused. Micah let her know he and Charlie were going snowboarding on Monday. She smiled her approval. It made her feel good to know they got on so well. They gathered the food and dogs, loading up in his truck. Her

parents walked them out and watched as they drove down the driveway. It'd gone better than Zoey expected and she sighed, relaxing her shoulders. Micah reached over, rubbing her neck. By the time they got back to base camp, it was getting dark and they were both worn out from all of the interaction.

Micah asked if she wanted to come in, which she did. He got the fire going and brought her a cup of hot tea. They sat on the couch, gazing at the fire while they drank their tea. Trek and Chef piled on top of each other by their feet. Zoey started to get sleepy and yawned. Micah touched her shoulder and she glanced over at him. He motioned to the bed. She bit her lip, unsure. That was a huge step.

"I just want to hold you, nothing else," he explained.

She nodded and they went to the bed. He lay with his back to the wall. She laid down next to him as he put his arm around her, her back to him. His breath was soft on her neck. He pulled covers over them and they fell asleep with their clothes on.

6

---

he following Monday, Charlie showed up at the camp to go snowboarding with Micah. Micah brought his radio and the dogs in case a call came in while they were out. They took a snowmobile, heading into the hills. Zoey was on shift and spent the day organizing and ordering medical supplies. They were restocking heavily as Spring Break was starting all over, and this meant more accidents and more injuries. Fortunately, it also meant more volunteers. Kyle had the basic bunkhouse built and was installing a wood stove. It could sleep up to eight volunteers, but they'd need to cook in the warming tent as the bunks and wood stove, plus seating around the stove, used up most of the space in the cabin. Jake and Megan had already claimed a bunk each for when they were on-site, instead of popping up cots in the warming tent. The area was beginning to come together as a small community.

They'd received a sizable grant, allowing Kyle to install solar panels to heat the bathhouse water and add in an additional

shower. Each cabin was given a composting toilet and a refillable sink. He put these in a corner and built walls around them with a door, leaving just enough room to turn around. This saved on having to run out to the bathhouse in the middle of winter, which everyone was thrilled about.

Volunteers were slated to begin arriving at the end of the week and they were already going to be running out of space to fit everyone. Kyle used the rest of the grant money to start building another small cabin, similar to Zoey's, but instead of a full-sized bed, it'd have bunks for four. He also began building permanent sides for the triage tent and was looking at roofing material to install. The land trust stated he could build whatever was needed, but the land would belong to the county in the event the SAR disbanded or moved. He was smart enough to know that wouldn't happen. Even in the summer, they were busy enough to justify having some full-time staff.

The budget allowed for one more full-time employee and one more part-timer. Since Brandon was leaving at the end of the summer, they needed someone who wasn't afraid to dive in. Megan didn't want to move to full-time as she was going to school, pursuing a forestry degree, but Jake had expressed an interest. Zoey hoped he got it because it'd be easier to have someone already trained and familiar slide into the slot. He had both first aid and wilderness training. He also helped her whenever he could in triage and didn't faint at the sight of blood, as far as she'd seen. The medical staff rarely left the triage area, but she'd gone out on calls when it was just Kyle and a handler on staff. More staff with basic medical knowledge was better.

She peered at the skies and could see a storm was moving in. This time of year was so unpredictable. It could be warm one

day, starting a thaw, then a snowstorm would bury them the next. They always had to be prepared for the worst. She saw Kyle outside, putting finishing touches on the bunkhouse, and went out to talk with him.

"Hey, Kyle. I see that storm rolling in, the weather says it's going to hit overnight. I'm going to make sure the cabins are stocked with wood and batten down the hatches. Anything else you need from me?"

"Shit. Yeah, how are we on food, propane, and gas for the generator? I have the solar panels in but can't hook them up until the end of the week at the earliest." He gazed up at the sky, which was getting dark off to the west.

"We're good on propane, both tanks are full. We have plenty of gas for the generator. Food is stocked, plenty of canned goods. I'm going to the woodshed and will put a stack in each cabin. I heard they put out warnings to stay off the mountains."

"Okay, I'm going to make a quick run into town. I need batteries and booze. Do you need anything?"

"No, I think I'm good. Micah is out snowboarding with my brother, but they should be back before dinner. The storm isn't supposed to hit until around eight. Jake and Megan are off today, so it'll be just the three of us... hopefully, the impending storm keeps people home."

"Your lips to God's ears," Kyle replied, grabbing his pack. He went to his truck and headed for town.

Zoey fetched a wheelbarrow and began hauling wood to each cabin. No one locked theirs, so she put stacks inside each one and a spare stack outside the porch door of each. Kyle's cabin was chaotic, like him. She could see he had his mind on multiple projects and had materials spread out everywhere. On

his fridge, he had a picture of his girlfriend and her two children. She'd never been up to camp, but he talked about her regularly. He'd been in SAR for almost twenty years and it had ended his first marriage. His child from that marriage was in his first year of college. She figured Kyle to be somewhere around early to mid-forties, but she'd never asked. It was hard telling because he was fit and only had a little gray in his light brown hair. He appeared like an actor who'd play someone in Search and Rescue on television. Rugged, piercing blue eyes. It was his passion and he fit the part.

Micah's cabin was neat as a pin. Everything in its place. She spent as much time here as she did in her own cabin and breathed in the familiarity. She stacked wood in her cabin as well and pulled out extra blankets. It was Micah's night to cook, though, so she'd only be back to sleep. She checked the coals in the wood stove and threw in a couple of logs to make sure they didn't burn out. It was easier to build a fire from coals than to start over.

Once she set all the cabins with wood, she checked the warming tent stove and stoked the fire. She added a stack there but didn't think anyone would be in there overnight. She checked her phone and radio, there were no calls. She turned on the weather radio for updates and it confirmed the storm would hit their area by eight at night. They should be set. It was going to be a heavy snowfall, they were going to get buried in. She double-checked each cabin had a shovel and peered outside the door to make sure the one for the triage area was still there. She heard Kyle's truck rumble over the hill. He drove in and started snagging bags out of the back of the truck. She went out to help him unload. They brought everything inside the tent and set it

on the table and cots. He had every type of battery she could think of, more gas, lots of beer, and a serious amount of snacks. He shopped like a teenage boy.

A little while later, Micah and Charlie came back, riding the snowmobile with Trek and Chef running alongside. It was getting close to five and the sky was getting extremely dark. She stepped out to greet them as Trek ran up and jumped on her. She rubbed his head and he darted off. Micah came up and kissed her, his face and lips cold from the ride. Charlie followed them into the tent and flopped down on the cot. His dark skin was ruddy and he was grinning ear to ear.

"Man, Micah has some moves! I barely kept up." He chuckled and laid back on the cot. "You see that storm brewing? It's looking pretty nasty out there."

"Yeah, it's going to be a bad one. We're stocked up here, but we're going to have to dig ourselves out once it's over," Zoey replied, picking up the weather radio.

The three of them headed to Micah's cabin to eat. Zoey had Charlie carry her table and chairs over to put next to Micah's, so they could fit everyone. She let Kyle know they were cooking and to come over when he wrapped up. He nodded and went to check the generator. They fired up the propane stove and Micah got chili going. It was enough to feed all of them. Zoey took out some premade biscuits and crackers. Kyle came in with beer as Micah opened a bottle of wine.

The storm rolled in earlier than expected, howling through the hills. Charlie checked and the college was closed the next day. Snow began coming in fast and heavy by seven. It was going to outdo the forecast. Zoey didn't want Charlie on the

roads now that it was snowing hard and asked Kyle if he could stay at base camp.

"Sure, the volunteer cabin is open, but I don't think the stove is going," Kyle said thoughtfully.

"Well, maybe he can stay in mine?" She had a full-size bed, however, didn't relish the idea of sharing it with Charlie. Still, she liked that idea more than him driving home now.

"He can stay here. Or you can?" Micah suggested to her.

Zoey blushed. She'd slept over a couple of times but they'd only slept. She didn't want anyone to get the wrong idea. No one seemed to even notice, or if they did, they didn't care. Charlie shoved a biscuit in his mouth and gave a thumbs up.

"I like that idea best of all. Cabin to myself!"

Zoey met Micah's eyes and he shrugged apologetically. He didn't mean to create any embarrassment. She sighed and nodded. "Okay, then. I guess I'll sleep here, Charlie can take my cabin. I already have the coals going, so you'll need to throw some logs in soon. You do need to let Mom and Dad know."

Charlie snapped his fingers and got up. He stepped out to call them and let them know he was safe, staying at base camp. Kyle was on his second beer and turned the radio on. He flipped around to a classic rock station, bopping his head along with it. Micah stepped over to check the chili and Zoey followed. He turned and met her eyes.

"Sorry."

"It is okay, you were trying to help. Not like I have not slept here before, anyway."

He nodded and stirred the food, then tasted it off the spoon. It was ready. They all grabbed bowlfuls and sat at the table. The wind started to blow louder outside, causing Zoey to

shiver. Micah got up to feed the fire and took extra blankets out. It was going to be a long night. Charlie and Kyle chatted about rescues and the most grisly recoveries Kyle had come across. Zoey shook her head, finishing her chili as fast as she could. She sipped on wine but decided to switch over to tea after a glass since she was staying over.

Kyle and Charlie started playing cards, putting beers back almost as quickly as they opened them. Zoey moved to the couch in front of the fire and stretched her legs out. Chef rested his head on her ankles and peered up at her with his droopy eyes. They'd become attached to each other over the last few months. Trek cleared out any spills from under the table and came to lay on Chef. Zoey smiled at them, leaning her head back against the couch. Her eye caught Micah watching her and the dogs. He brought a beer over and sat down with her, placing his hand on her thigh.

Kyle and Charlie drank until the beers were gone. They were pretty drunk when all was said and done. Without booze, the conversation fizzled and they stumbled off to their respective cabins. Zoey watched to make sure they each got in and Kyle paused at his cabin door and howled with his head tipped back. She shook her head, laughing to herself. Micah cocked his head at her in question and she waved her hand, pointing towards Kyle's cabin.

"Just Kyle, being Kyle."

It was close to midnight; the storm had already buried the fire pit outside and blocked the triage tent door. They doubted they'd have calls but brought radios and gear to the cabin in case. The snowmobiles were under the tin shelter Kyle made to keep them out of the weather and covered with tarps in

case of a quick exit. Zoey watched the snow for a bit but was tired and turned to face Micah. She'd slept over before, why was she so nervous? He put his hand out and she walked over to take it.

They climbed into bed in their long johns, facing each other. Micah brushed her long, dark hair off her shoulder and touched her face. She met his eyes and they watched each other for a moment. She leaned in and met his lips, chapped but warm. He tasted like toothpaste and a little like beer, making her chuckle. He smiled and ran his fingers across her cheek. He kissed her firmly, his hand sliding behind her to the small of her back. She instinctively moved close, pressing her body to his. They'd both been with other people and this was not new, so why did she feel so bashful? He sensed her inhibitions and drew back, meeting her eyes.

"This is enough, we do not have to do anything else," he signed, his eyes expressive in the firelight.

She felt silly about being so shy about it. Maybe it was because any time before she wasn't so invested, she didn't care as much. Micah was really important to her. He was part of her every day, she didn't want to ruin that.

"Micah, I love you." The words surprised her as much as they probably did him. She was going to say how important he was to her, how she cherished their time and didn't want anything to come between them. But she said *I love you* instead.

His eyes fixed on hers, his hands saying what she hoped to be reciprocated. "I love you, Z."

They let the moment hang like a butterfly in midair. From the beginning, this progressed at its own pace, both of them along for the ride. It had a mind of its own. Zoey breathed out, placing her hand on his cheek. They kissed for a while, finally removing their long johns and laying naked together. He was beautiful, muscular and lean. She ran her fingers down his chest, admiring the way his stomach met his hips. He ran his hands down her side.

"Like honey," he expressed.

She didn't know if he meant the color of her skin or the smoothness and met his eyes.

"Both," he replied without her asking.

He pulled her close and put his mouth on hers, their tongues touching, exciting her on a level she'd never felt before. She drew him to her openly. As they finally came together, she sighed, wondering why she'd been so afraid. Feeling him inside her felt natural. It felt like it was always supposed to be. Like they'd been searching for each other all along. He was gentle and strong, sensing her every need and meeting them with his movements. The wind screamed outside as they buried within each other, allowing their strength and vulnerability to become one. Zoey grasped onto Micah as he drew in and out of her with a steadiness of forever. Their eyes met and any doubt they had fell away. Zoey moved his mouth to hers as she shuddered in release, him following soon after.

She lay in his arms later and ran her finger along the freckles of his arm. Her arm against his was so different, yet they seemed to fit perfectly. Light against dark. She glanced up at him. His eyes were closed, his auburn eyelashes like feathers against his lower lids. She reached up and brushed them lightly. His eyes opened and he smiled at her.

"It was about time, Z."

7

---

he snowfall continued through the next morning, finally stopping around lunchtime. They'd brought their shovel in and had to chip away at the mound of snow blocking the door. Micah worked on removing that while Zoey built up the fire and made them brunch. When Micah finally broke through and started clearing a path out, it was early afternoon. He shoveled a path to Zoey's cabin and cleared the door. Kyle had already cleared a path from his cabin to the triage tent. Zoey went to her cabin to check on Charlie, who'd not brought a shovel in and wasn't able to get out if he'd tried before Micah cleared the path.

Charlie was still sleeping, passed out on the bed. He hadn't added to the fire, now almost completely out, and the cabin was freezing. Zoey threw some kindling in to get it fired back up and once it was going, added more logs. She shook Charlie awake; he groaned, covering his eyes with his hand.

"Too many beers," was all he said.

"Come on, Charlie, you gotta get up. We have food next door at Micah's cabin. Go eat something and soak up some of that alcohol."

He sat up and looked at her miserably, his black hair sticking up in spikes. "My first mistake was trying to match Kyle beer for beer."

Zoey laughed. Kyle was out there shoveling like he'd had a good night's rest. Charlie climbed out of bed and ran outside to throw up. Zoey changed her clothes and bundled up. They needed to get paths clear and make sure all equipment was in working order. Charlie came in and sat down on the couch, staring at the fire with his eyes glazed over. Then he got back up and went out to throw up over the rail again. Zoey waited until he was done, then assisted him to Micah's cabin. They needed to get liquids in him, and food, as soon as he could keep it down. Micah was sitting at the table, writing down notes when they came in. He took one look at Charlie, letting him know how hungover Charlie was.

Zoey met his eyes and shook her head. Micah guided Charlie to the table, then got him a cup of tea and some aspirin. Charlie took the aspirin and sipped on the tea, appearing like he might not be able to keep it down. After fifteen minutes he had, and he nibbled on some crackers from the night before. Before long, he was able to eat and drink without vomiting. He began to get some color back to his cheeks, so Zoey felt it was safe to leave him to go check out triage. Micah stepped out to fire up the snowmobiles with Kyle and clear any snow blocking them. The roads were still impassable, so the likelihood of anyone needing to go out was slim, but they still had to be prepared at all times. Charlie was definitely stuck up there for at least another day.

Zoey checked the tents and everything was in good order. The walls Kyle started to build around the tents gave them greater stability and insulation. She fed the wood stove in the warming tent and clicked on the radio for some music and updates. From the window, she watched Micah and Kyle quickly make the rounds in the camp, clearing areas and checking equipment. No one else would be able to make it up that day, so the four of them would have to make do. Really the three of them, since Charlie wasn't going to be any good to anyone for the rest of the day. She watched Micah shoveling, his strong arms tossing snow like it was nothing. Trek and Chef chased the snow as he threw it, catching clumps in their mouth.

Around dinner time, she headed back over to check on Charlie, who hadn't made an appearance. She found him lying on the couch with his legs over the arm. His head was resting back, his hands covering his stomach. A glass of half drank water was on the table by him. He looked a little less green and waved as she came in.

"Not drinking tonight, are you?" Zoey asked, not as a question.

"God no." Charlie shook his head vehemently, then held the top of his head like it wasn't attached. He sat up and sipped water. His shoulders slumped forward as he braced his head with a hand.

Zoey looked in the fridge for ingredients for dinner and decided on a hearty vegetable minestrone with rice. Charlie should be able to keep that down and it would warm all of them up. She chopped vegetables and added red kidney beans, getting them all boiling on the stove with some homemade stock. She cooked rice in another pot and once it was done, threw it in the

soup. Around this time Micah came in, breathing in deep, then smiled. He came over and put his arms around Zoey. He was cold from being outside and she shivered. He let her go and kissed her on the neck, stepping over to warm himself by the fire. There was a loaf of french bread, so she toasted that in the oven part of the propane stove, adding butter and garlic. Kyle decided to stay at his cabin this time around. He wanted to do some research on hooking up the solar panels as soon as he could.

The three of them sat and ate, focusing on their own food. Charlie was much less chatty and ate slowly, chewing each bite carefully. Micah asked him if he was feeling ok, to which Charlie shrugged and smiled sheepishly. His color was back, but he still had dark circles under his eyes.

"A little. It's been a rough day."

"Well, maybe you learned your lesson, huh?" Zoey asked in her best big sister's voice.

"Maybe," Charlie grumbled, looking up.

Probably not.

Micah snickered and patted Charlie on the back. "We have all been there."

Charlie bit his lip and laughed. He and Micah seemed to get on well, having formed a fast friendship. In some ways, they acted more like brothers. Zoey's other brother was the oldest and ten years older than Charlie, so they hadn't connected much growing up. Micah was also ten years older than Charlie, but they were both adults, making it easier. They also bonded over their love of snowboarding, so they had things to talk about.

After dinner, Charlie got up and motioned he was heading back over to Zoey's cabin. "If you two don't mind, I

really need to go sleep the rest of this off. Can I still use your cabin, Zoey?"

"Of course. Just keep the fire going this time, so you don't freeze."

"Thanks, Zo. See you in the morning." Charlie ducked out with a wave.

It was still early, so Micah and Zoey played cards until it got late. Zoey had the radio on the table and even though Micah couldn't hear the music, he tapped his fingers to the vibrations it created on the table. It was fascinating to watch because his fingers kept the exact rhythm. She yawned and set her cards down.

"Ready for bed?" he asked, his eyes hooded from sleepiness.

She nodded and made her way over. She brushed her teeth in the portable sink and stripped out of her clothes except for a t-shirt and long john bottoms. Micah let the dogs out for one last time and threw a couple of logs on. Once the dogs were settled, he brushed his teeth and climbed in next to her in his long john bottoms. They faced each other and wrapped their arms over one another. They kissed for a bit but both were exhausted from the day. He mouthed the words, "I love you," and she made the sign back. He met her eyes, his mossy stone to her rich earth. His eyes fluttered as sleep took hold and she moved in to rest her head on his chest as she fell asleep.

The next day, the sun was shining bright and she heard plows in the distance. Charlie joined them for breakfast, seeming much more like himself. Micah and Charlie went to snowboard for a bit before Charlie headed back to town. Zoey took the time to clean her cabin and take a shower. Kyle took their little plow out and cleared snow until he met the county plows on the main road. By the time Charlie and Micah got back, Charlie was able to head back to town. As soon as the plow cleared the roads, Jake and Brandon showed up. Kyle and Jake left to check mountain conditions and Brandon took over triage. Like clockwork, within a couple of hours of the road being plowed, calls started to roll in.

Zoey and Brandon treated at least six patients over the next twelve hours. Kyle, Jake, and Micah were in and out in a steady stream, bringing in injured people and helping guide lost people back to the main roads. There were no serious injuries, fortunately, though, and by the end of the day other than triage being a mess and needing supplies, Brandon was able to take back over.

The next morning was a Friday and volunteers began to arrive and get briefed. Spring Break was just around the corner; from this point forward it was going to be steady. Kyle called in his reports that conditions were stable but with the new snow over the old, there was a higher risk of avalanches. They'd need to keep a closer eye over the next couple of weeks. The month of April was back-to-back Spring Breaks, and the mountains were always full. Patrols would increase to three times a day, no one was allowed planned time off. All regional SARs worked with each other to ensure everyone was covered and had backup contingencies. It was exciting, but daunting at the same time.

Micah usually didn't trust anyone to work with his dogs, however, he showed Zoey commands and had her work with them, in case something were to happen to him. They'd already bonded with Zoey and listened to her almost as well as they heeded him. She made sure to only use hand motions to keep

continuity, pleased when she was able to get them to find the buried scent. Charlie volunteered some on the weekends as well, but she guessed it was more because of the friendship he was forming with Micah. He learned some commands, too, and began working with the dogs when he could.

The base camp quickly grew from just four to six of them, to about a rotating ten to fifteen. The bunkhouse was full most times and Zoey's cabin sat empty most nights as she and Micah pretty much bunked together since Charlie got stranded during the storm. Kyle approached her one afternoon while she was stocking supplies.

"Hey, uh, Zo? I was thinking. We have more volunteers than space some days and it's better when they stay overnight. I noticed you and Micah are pretty much staying in one cabin. Would you be willing to give up yours? For now? I could fit four people in there," he asked, his voice nice but firm.

Zoey bit her lip. That was a huge step and not one either she or Micah had even thought about. That would mean no turning back, at least during the busy times. If things didn't work between them, she'd be out, back sleeping on a cot until there weren't so many volunteers. Or she'd have to move to the volunteer cabin. But Kyle was right, there was no point in it sitting there empty the majority of the time.

"Can I talk to Micah about it? I don't want to presume-" her voice trailed off. That conversation might be tough at the least.

"For sure. I'm not pushing you out. But it would really help," Kyle answered.

She waited until she saw Micah coming in with the dogs and waved at him. He met her at the tent and they went in.

"Can we talk?" she signed, unsure of how to start.

He looked nervous and nodded.

"Kyle wants to know if we are willing to share your cabin. He needs mine for volunteer overflow."

The relief that washed over Micah's face was indescribable. He jumped up and grabbed her in his arms, hugging her tightly. He pulled back and grinned at her.

"Of course! I thought you were breaking up with me." His eyes locked on hers, she could tell she'd scared him.

She realized how it may have seemed at first and felt terrible. She kissed him, shaking her head apologetically. "I am sorry. I was nervous to bring it up and can see how that came across. You are okay with it?"

"Yes! Z, I love you. I want us to be together, and you are there most nights, anyway."

She'd spent her life waiting for roadblocks. Things that would prevent her from moving forward, yet every time she expected a roadblock with Micah, instead, he was there helping her over it. She smiled softly and blushed. He picked her up and spun her around, almost knocking over a tray next to the cot. He set her down and grinned like a kid opening a present. He motioned to the door.

"We can go get your things now."

They went to her cabin and gathered her belongings. It wasn't much, but still made his cabin feel more like hers, too. The dogs seemed to sense the change and sniffed everything, wagging their tails and coming over to lick her hand. Kyle let them keep both tables as a thank you. They cooked a meal in their cabin and sat down together to enjoy it.

Micah reached across the table and took her hand, squeezing it. He smiled the kindest smile she'd ever seen. Any concerns she had about them moving in together melted away. Micah let her hand go and waved his hand around the small cabin as he locked his eyes on hers.

"Welcome home, Zoey."

8

---

he trigger point of an avalanche is the point of origination. Environmental factors play a part, but the trigger is what causes the slide. It can be caused by snowmobiles, hikers, skiers, even animals. Contrary to popular myth, it isn't caused by loud noises such as yelling. High decibel sounds, however, such as explosions or gunshots, can trigger an already fragile slope, sending waves crashing down. Ski patrols often use explosives to trigger hills when no one is on them, to make it safer for when people are. They do this overnight or in closed areas to clear snowpack which is prone to avalanches. It is a tireless task and one that is not without fail.

Mid-April brought the largest crowds and most delicate conditions as the weather vacillated between warmer spring-like days and windy snowstorms. The team marked off areas at higher risk, leaving areas open the snow had time to pack. Visitors came from all over, some experienced, most less so. Snowboarders, hikers, snowmobilers, people with children and

dogs. Triage stayed busy, mostly with small injuries and weather-related damage such as hypothermia and frostbite. Smaller avalanches had been triggered, but no major injuries were reported and all victims were dug out quickly. It was steady and exhausting, but the team had been spared any major tragedies up to that point.

It was a sunny, warmer day. Triage was quiet and Micah was out working with a group of volunteers on training dogs for SAR. It was Spring Break at the college, so they had more volunteers than usual. Trek and Chef were enjoying the attention, and another SAR handler from a nearby team had her two dogs training with them. Zoey watched from the window, laughing as Trek ran circles around the group, kicking up snow and diving into the powdery mounds. Micah signaled to Trek and he ran over, sitting immediately at Micah's feet.

Jake appeared over the hill with a group coming back from ski patrol. Megan had stepped back to focus on school but joined them for the week and was in the group. Kyle motioned to Jake when he came over and they talked, heads bent together, jotting notes on a clipboard. Kyle looked up at the mountains and shook his head. The warmer weather they were getting was a risk, but they'd marked off where they thought the highest risk was. The news station ran a story on high avalanche danger, however, seeing the numbers of people on the slopes, the warning was being disregarded.

By afternoon, they began to breathe a little easier. Everything seemed to be holding. The temperature was supposed to drop overnight, which would help form the snowpack, making it safer all over. Just a couple more hours and people should be heading in for dinner, giving the snow a chance to set.

They just needed it to hold a little while longer. Kyle was in the tent chatting with Zoey when all hell broke loose. In the distance, motion caught their eyes. From the window they could see a huge slab avalanche starting from the top of one of the mountains, picking up speed and catching everyone in its wake. It seemed to come out of nowhere.

"Fuck!" Kyle yelled and grabbed the radio.

He began sending out alerts to all teams in the area. There had to be at least twenty-five to thirty people on that slope, and the avalanche was the largest they'd seen all year. He ran out the door and yelled to the team. Micah already saw it and was getting the dogs ready to go. He threw on his inflatable vest and ran to one of the snowmobiles, the dogs on his heels. The other handler did the same and they were off over the hill. The rest of the volunteers disbursed. Brandon joined them, hauling a toboggan on his snowmobile to transport the injured back. Kyle pulled another one and within minutes the camp was empty except for Zoey and two medical interns. The radios were going off constantly and she listened to the chatter to prep. They dragged out more cots, using the warming area as an extension for triage. The local hospital had already been alerted and was sending ambulances.

Zoey heard teams talking to each other arriving on the scene, assessing the damage. It was bad. Multiple people were completely buried, they didn't know how many. Some were up to their necks, but could be pulled out quickly. They were right, there were at a minimum twenty-five people up there, likely quite a bit more. At least fourteen couldn't be accounted for at all. Fear gripped her stomach. They'd been up there recently and while one could never be sure, they felt it would hold through

the day. What had triggered such a large slide? She couldn't think about it, she needed to be ready for the number of patients that were about to start pouring in.

Within minutes, the less injured and mobile began arriving, being dropped off so the team could get back up to help others. A snowboarder about her brother's age came in with a huge gash above his eye. She gave him a shot of novocaine and started stitching it up. He shook his head and mumbled, pointing to the mountain.

"Some fucking dude up there on a snowmobile was shooting off his gun and trying to do donuts. Asshole. A few of us snowboarding tried to get him to stop, but he laughed and pointed his gun at us. He was fucking hammered. A few seconds later, we heard the sound and tried to warn everyone. It was too late, we couldn't outrun it. I got pushed off the side by the impact and hit my head on a rock when I fell. My buddies... I don't know where they are. I tried to climb up but didn't see them. It looked like a war scene. People half-buried, people screaming and crying. People digging where they thought people were. The fucked up thing is, that dude somehow didn't get dragged down, he was above the slide. He rode off."

"I'm sorry. Are there a lot of teams up there?"

"Oh, yeah, they came riding over like the calvary from all directions. They snatched up those of us who could walk and got us here, this is the closest medical they said. You're going to have tons more."

On cue, the next wave came in. Broken limbs, gashes, concussions, shock. The three medical people couldn't move fast enough. There were a few children but luckily they'd be alright. As soon as they got people stabilized, ambulances were there to transport them out. Zoey knew the worst was yet to come. The buried. Brandon came over towing a toboggan, followed by Kyle. These were the ones who couldn't hold on to ride back. The more seriously injured, the unconscious. There was no sign of Micah, which meant they were still searching for those buried deep in the snow. She said a little prayer for him. For them.

After an hour, she knew hope was fading fast for any more survivors. One of the snowboarder's buddies came in, injured but alive. Some of the injured she didn't get hands-on. As soon as they came in, they were taken to the ambulances waiting because they were in such bad shape. Some possibly wouldn't survive. After another hour, she saw Micah come over the hill. Exhausted and defeated. They were now at the recovery stage, outside of a miracle. Miracles were rare. The rest of the team was digging out the bodies.

She checked the tent and everyone was currently taken care of. She stepped out to meet Micah. He saw her and came over, enfolding her in his arms. He stepped back and his eyes were dark.

"It is bad, they are about to start bringing bodies down. I think five or six," he explained to her.

Five or six? Zoey felt her stomach form in knots. That was the most they'd ever had at one time for as long as she could remember. She heard someone yelling over by the dog practice field and looked over. A very drunk guy on a snowmobile was demanding someone come look at his hand, which he said was injured. She took a step toward him but Micah grabbed her arm and held her back. The guy was waving a shotgun around. It must be the guy the snowboarder was talking about. The *trigger point*. Micah and Jake stepped toward the guy, as did a police

officer on the scene. At this point, every agency had someone there.

The guy was belligerent and stepped off his snowmobile, stumbling drunk. Trek and Chef picked up on the tenseness of the situation and were right at Micah's heels. Micah moved towards the guy and reached out for the gun, which the guy had dropped to his side. The guy drew back and took a swing at Micah. Chef, seeing this, came between Micah and the guy, barking. The guy jerked and kicked Chef as hard as he could, knocking him into the snow. Chef yelped in pain. Micah told Zoey he'd struggled with anger issues and now she witnessed it firsthand. In a flash, he grabbed the gun from the guy, flipped it around, and broke the guy's nose with the butt of the gun. The guy clutched his nose, screaming. Micah wasn't done with him yet and punched him as hard as he could in the cheekbone. The police were on Micah before the guy hit the ground. If they hadn't stopped him, Zoey was sure Micah could've killed the guy. She watched in utter shock.

As the police dragged Micah away, Kyle came over the hill pulling a toboggan. He gestured to the ambulance driver, who nodded knowingly. The bodies. Zoey stepped out to help but Brandon stopped her. Kyle met her eyes for a second and then Brandon's. He walked over to the police officer, took him aside, and said something quietly to him, gesturing to the toboggan. Micah understood what he said and tried to pull away from them.

Both the police and Micah looked in her direction. What the hell was going on? Kyle continued talking to the police, who'd now let Micah go. The ambulance crew was at the toboggan, moving the person to the ambulance.

Micah made it to Zoey seconds before the police and Kyle. She saw his eyes and panic took over. He put his arm around her just as Kyle said the words.

"Zo, it's Charlie."

Her knees buckled as she realized the body on the toboggan was her little brother. She tried to get to him, but Micah held her tight. The police officer was saying something but she couldn't hear it. The ambulance crew loaded Charlie's body in and drove away. She pushed against Micah, attempting to get away. He let her go and she ran after the ambulance, screaming. Tears streamed down her cheeks. She spun and was face to face with Kyle.

"What happened Kyle? What-," her voice trailed off as sobs overtook her.

Kyle wrapped his arms around her. "He was too deep. He must've been closer to the top and gotten carried down. He was buried so far down, by the time we got to him..."

He didn't have to finish. Charlie must've been one of the snowboarder's friends. She didn't even know he was out there. He was on Spring Break but hadn't said anything about coming out to snowboard. She wanted to kill the snowmobile guy, however, when she glared around looking for him, he was gone. Micah was watching her, waiting.

"I'm going to have Micah drive you to the hospital. They're notifying your parents and you need to be there. We'll take care of things here. Zo, I'm so sorry. I wish I had more to say," Kyle said softly.

Zoey was numb. Her parents. This couldn't be happening. She walked over to Micah and cried on his shoulder. He held her as long as she needed. She met his eyes, then nodded.

She needed to be there for her parents. They took Micah's truck into town, as she pressed herself against the door for something to hold on to, her head against the cold glass. They parked outside the emergency department.

She stared in for a minute, not able to move, feeling out of her body. Finally, she sighed and unbuckled her seatbelt. Micah came in with her without having to be asked. They went to the front desk, getting the attention of a nurse who was on the phone. Zoey didn't know exactly what to say.

"Uh, my brother Charlie Sanders was brought in?"

The nurse looked at her with an expression of shock and sadness. He got up and led them back to a room where a police officer was waiting. Her parents came in a few minutes later, confused and scared. A doctor who didn't look older than Zoey joined them. He cleared his throat and made eye contact with them.

"Hello, Mr. and Mrs. Sanders, I'm Dr. Jenks. I'm really sorry to have to tell you this. Unfortunately, your son, Charles was brought in but he didn't survive. He suffered severe hypothermia and suffocation. We were unable to resuscitate him. I'm very sorry."

He'd barely gotten the words out when Zoey's, and Charlie's, mother hit the floor in a heap. She was sobbing uncontrollably, calling out for her baby no longer there. Zoey's father kneeled next to her, holding her. He waved the doctor and police officer away. They apologized again and told them to use the room as long as they needed to. Zoey met her father's eyes and had never seen him cry. Tears streamed down his face as he bent to try and comfort her mother.

Zoey stepped out of the room and crouched down against the wall, attempting to catch her breath. The hallway swayed around her and she felt like she was going to vomit. Doctors and nurses passed by her but didn't say anything. She could hear them talking about the other victims as well. It was one of the biggest tragedies they'd seen. Five deceased in all, including Charlie. A twelve-year-old girl, too.

All because of one person's selfish decision.

Micah sat down next to her and took her hand. She couldn't even look up, the weight was dragging her down inside of herself, farther and farther from the surface. She could hear her mother wailing in the room behind her, saying Charlie's name and "why" over and over again. Her father was silent.

Her family was destroyed.

9

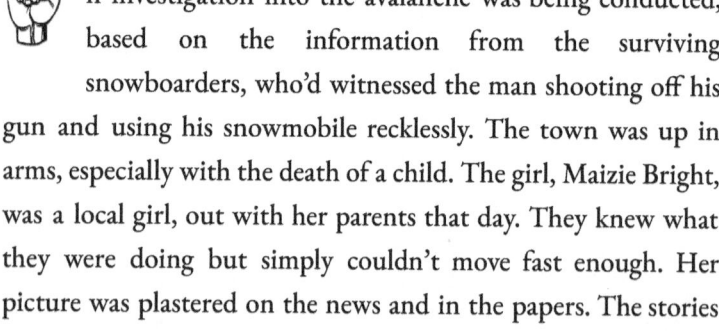

n investigation into the avalanche was being conducted, based on the information from the surviving snowboarders, who'd witnessed the man shooting off his gun and using his snowmobile recklessly. The town was up in arms, especially with the death of a child. The girl, Maizie Bright, was a local girl, out with her parents that day. They knew what they were doing but simply couldn't move fast enough. Her picture was plastered on the news and in the papers. The stories mentioned Charlie and the other victims as well, but the news stations knew how to get viewers.

Dead children got viewers.

Kyle gave Zoey a six-month leave of absence and told her if she needed more, he'd always make sure she had a job with SAR. She thanked him, packed her few belongings, and moved back into the farmhouse with her parents. Her last conversation with Micah was painful because she didn't know if she could ever feel anything again. Her heart died with Charlie that day.

Micah helped her put her things in a box and sat down at the table, meeting her eyes.

"I am here for you, Z."

She sighed and nodded. "I know, Micah. I just need to go be with my parents. They have no one out there now."

"I understand. I cared about Charlie, I want you to know that. I love you, Zoey."

"I love you, too."

With that, she picked up the box and took it out to her car. She felt so empty inside. The only emotion she could feel was grief. Micah stood outside his cabin door, watching her leave. She couldn't even feel anything for him right now. She hated herself for it, but she didn't know how to make it any different. He waved as she drove out. She raised her hand and let it drop. Everything was gone.

The farmhouse was quiet when she arrived. Her mother locked herself away, not wanting to talk to anyone. Alexander and Matilda had come for the memorial service but left shortly after. They'd walked away long before all of this. Charlie was so much younger than them, they didn't have those connections. He'd been the baby. He and Zoey had been close simply because they were the two youngest. When he came along, she'd felt like she had her own little baby. He followed her around everywhere. While they fought when they were older, it was just squabbling; they still told each other everything. They'd both planned to stay in the area and she'd liked the idea that one day they'd raise their kids around each other.

Now, it was just her.

Her father was sitting on the porch smoking when she came up. He looked older, smaller. She sat down next to him and

stared out over the fields. As kids, they'd played hide and seek out there. The farm had been his parents before he took it over. It was supposed to get handed down through generations. Charlie had helped him run things and keep them up. Her father breathed out and looked over at her.

"You sure about this, Zoey?"

"Yeah, Dad. I can't be out there now and I'm worried about Mom."

"She's hurting. A mother's love is like nothing else. What about your friend? Micah?"

"I don't know. It's unfair for me to be around him right now. I have nothing to give anyone. I feel like I'd suck everything out of whatever we had. I'm just a shell. I need to be alone and work all of this out, you know?"

"I know. But none of us is actually alone."

She didn't know what he meant by that and didn't have the energy to ask. She shifted her focus to what happened that day. "So, the guy who shot off the gun? Are they charging him?"

"Yeah, they charged him, but I don't know if it will stick," her father replied.

"Why wouldn't it? He did it, there are witnesses," Zoey said, gritting her teeth.

"Well, yeah, there are, but you know how it is, Zo. Can they charge him with being reckless? Sure. Can they charge him with killing five people? That's a lot harder to prove."

She knew he was right but hoped the District Attorney would push the issue. They sat in silence and watched the sun go down over the field. Neither wanting to go into the empty, dark house. Finally, her father stood up and rubbed his head.

"I need to check on your mother. You alright?"

Zoey nodded, both of them knew it wasn't true. He stepped inside, leaving her alone on the porch. This had been such a happy place all her life. Like her father, she felt the call of the land, a desire to stay and make something of it. Even after moving out, she loved to come home. Seeing her mother out in the garden, Charlie joking around in the kitchen, her father fixing this and that. It had been her sanctuary. Now, it was like a photo negative of her memories. She stayed on the porch until her eyes were heavy, then climbed the stairs to her childhood bedroom. She could hear her parents talking softly, her mother's voice sounding distressed. She paused at Charlie's room and flipped the light on.

Due to their mother's wishes, he'd stayed home while going to college. His room was a mixture of when he'd been a small boy, teenager, then a college student. Little toy figures, posters of bands, and his snowboards. He had a few of those because he liked the different designs and what to use them for. Above his dresser, there were pictures of his friends. One with the two snowboarders who survived. One photo caught her breath. It was of him and Micah out snowboarding; she wasn't sure who would've taken it. Maybe one of the other guys. They were smiling on their boards, Micah's red hair blazing against the snowy background, a contrast to Charlie's black hair and tan skin. She took the photo and put it in her pocket.

She knew she was making this hard on Micah, but she didn't know any other way. She couldn't conjure emotions and felt dead inside. She was sure she still loved him, but love seemed like a foreign concept. It was a story she could tell, but couldn't bring to life. It wasn't fair and she still needed him. It was like

standing on either side of an abyss, trying to reach each other. It just wasn't possible right now.

She went to her room which was part of her past since she'd moved out right after high school. The floral wallpaper and purple bedspread, untouched. All of her childhood books were still there and apparently dusted by her mother's fastidious hand. As a girl, she'd loved reading adventure stories and tales with heroes and heroines. She'd play rescue with her cat's kittens, pretending they were caught in a fire and she needed to get them out. Sometimes she'd make Charlie hide in the treehouse and she'd climb the ladder to save him. He'd giggle and run from her. Charlie was always such a happy child, his dark brown, almond-shaped eyes twinkling under his black eyebrows.

Tears slipped down her cheeks. She needed to stop this ride. Torturing herself with memories wasn't bringing him back or making it hurt any less. Charlie had been her best friend most of her life. She couldn't imagine never seeing his big grin and mischievous eyes again. She climbed into bed and pulled a blanket over her. Her parents' room had gone silent. The old house creaked and pipes made strange sounds. Charlie had always had his radio playing; Zoey couldn't remember ever hearing it so quiet. She clicked on the radio and willed herself to go to sleep.

The next morning, she slipped down the stairs and saw her mother standing in the kitchen. She wasn't doing anything, just standing in the middle of the kitchen, staring off. Zoey came in quietly and sat down. She cleared her throat.

"Hey, Mom. Do you need something?"

Her mother turned towards her, her eyes red from crying. She was still in her nightgown and her hair was

disheveled. She stared at Zoey blankly, then shook her head. "No. I guess no matter what, the sun is going to rise. The world will still go on."

"Mom, I'm sorry. I wish I could do something."

Her mother gave her a weak smile, then shrugged. "There's nothing to be done. This is it. Until I die."

She shook her head again and walked out of the room, back up the stairs to her room, shutting the door. Zoey sat in silence, unsure of what to do about anything. She'd come home, thinking her presence might help, but instead she was getting dragged farther under. She wandered outside, the air was warm and she could see areas where the snow was beginning to melt. Something that could just disappear so easily, literally took the life from her brother.

Her mind went back to that day. What happened? She could picture Charlie snowboarding with his friends, cutting up and pushing limits. Then what? Some drunk guy came up on a snowmobile and started shooting off his gun, driving crazy. Had Charlie confronted him, asked him to stop? His friends said the guy pointed his gun at them. Then they heard the sound of the snow separating. Charlie would've known immediately and searched for a way out. They'd tried to warn the other people on the slope. Had they heard? Had they managed to save some people?

But Charlie couldn't get away. It caught him, tossing and tumbling, burying him as it took him with it down the mountain. Had he tried to claw his way out? Was he disoriented? Did he understand what was going to happen to him as he ran out of air and froze to death? And the guy, he just drove off. He didn't try to save anyone. He came down the mountain and

demanded to be treated, all while her brother was dead in the cold ground.

Zoey couldn't contain the rage overtaking her and ran out into the field as far as she could. She hit her knees, screaming at the top of her lungs. A flock of birds was startled and took off into the air, screeching back at her. She rested her head forward on the ground and bawled. She'd dedicated her life to helping people, to saving people. But she couldn't save Charlie. Her baby brother. It was all a waste. There was no point in anything anymore.

Later, when she walked back to the house, she saw her father standing on the porch, looking out at her. She walked up and hugged him as hard as she could. He hugged her back and put his hand on her head like he did when she was little.

"I know, Zoey. Sometimes you just have to let it out."

Her mother was in the kitchen when they came in. She was cooking something on the stove and had put on regular clothes. She was still zombie-like moving around the kitchen, but she was trying. Zoey placed her hand on her mother's shoulder gently and grabbed a few plates out of the cabinet. They served the food and sat at the small kitchen table, eating in silence. After lunch, her mother walked out and up the long driveway. Zoey glanced at her dad for reassurance.

"It's okay, Zoey, she needs to find her footing again. Just let her be."

Zoey understood but still felt so helpless. She cleaned up the dishes and went out to help her father fix a tractor. They spent the rest of the day doing chores around the farm, attempting to stay busy. At dinner, the three of them sat together again and ate wordlessly. Once dinner was done, they cleaned up. Zoey's mother went to bed and Zoey and her father sat on the porch again. It was all they could do. Her father dealt with his grief by telling stories about Charlie when he was little, how he helped fix that fence or got that tiller working again. Everyone had their own way to try and keep Charlie from slipping farther and farther away.

This went on for weeks. As summer approached and the days became warmer, Zoey's mother would go out to the garden and spend her days there. Zoey continued to help her father with the farm. It wasn't progress. It was just survival. One evening, after they ate and went to bed, Zoey swore she heard her mother laugh. Not a big laugh, just a soft laugh between couples, a brief release. She wasn't sure she even heard it, but it gave her hope. Charlie had been gone two months and no one had so much as cracked a smile since then.

The town moved on from the tragedy and the investigation shifted behind closed doors. The girl's family moved away, unable to deal with the loss of their daughter and the guilt they had from bringing her out to the mountain that day. As Zoey's father had expected, the man was only charged with reckless endangerment, operating a vehicle while impaired, and reckless discharge of a weapon. The five people he caused to die would never get justice.

They reasoned the avalanche may have happened anyway, but Zoey knew better. She knew the team had checked conditions that morning. Avalanches were always a risk, but this one was triggered by a specific person. Her hatred of that man grew inside of her, and for once she could understand the rage Micah said he battled with. She replayed him grabbing the guy's gun and smashing him in the face with it. It gave her some source

of satisfaction. In her mind, she liked to create an alternate ending where the guy never got back up.

As summer came to a peak, she felt the uncontrollable anger eating her up inside. Her father could see it, but nothing he said seemed to matter. It began to consume her waking moments and she became afraid she was going to lose it on someone one day. Or if she didn't, she'd lose her mind completely.

10

 t was late July when things came to a head for Zoey. Her parents began to form a new reality, accepting they couldn't change what happened and needing to move forward, carrying their grief with them. Her mother was quieter, more withdrawn, but stayed busy. Her father kept the farm running with Zoey's help. Zoey had less than three months before her leave of absence was up, and she wasn't sure what she was going to do about it. She and Micah hadn't spoken since the day she left, and she knew he was being respectful about her grief. It was like they were all planets circling the sun together, but never connecting.

That was why she was surprised one day when she and her father were coming in from the field and saw Micah, leaning against his truck in the driveway. He watched them approach, his face unreadable. Trek and Chef spied her and began wagging their tails, dancing around Micah's legs. Zoey's father motioned for her to go and talk to him. As she walked up, he stood up,

seeming embarrassed. Trek and Chef came over, sniffed her, and licked her hand.

"Hey, Zoey. I do not want to intrude, but I wanted to see you. To talk."

His hair was to his shoulders and lighter from being in the sun. He had a little more color to him and his eyes stood out against his skin. Zoey came and stood a little closer to him, feeling a mixture of fear and relief. Neither of them knew what to do. He went on.

"I know things have been tough and I wanted to be here as a friend."

"Thank you." It was all she could think to respond.

Part of her wanted to embrace him, but the other part felt like she might shatter if she did.

"Do you want to take a walk?" he asked, his hands moving slowly like he was unsure. He pointed down the driveway.

"Okay."

She knew she wasn't giving much back, but she didn't even know where to start. She'd shut herself off from the world and any opening might cause her to fall apart, or worse. They headed down the drive, neither making an effort to communicate, walking within feet of each other but worlds apart. The dogs bounded in front of them, excited to be back at the farm, unaware of the changes in their people. Finally, about halfway down, Micah put his hand on her arm and stopped her. She turned to face him. She met his eyes, then glanced away.

"Zoey, please talk to me." His eyes were pleading.

"I don't know what to say." She didn't try to sign, just said the words flatly.

"I know losing Charlie hurts. He was just my friend and I have struggled with that. I cannot imagine how you all must feel." Micah was trying to get through her wall.

"No, you can't. He was our family. We lost part of ourselves that day," she said coldly.

It wasn't his fault, why was she treating him like it was?

"I am sorry. I honestly am. I am not trying to say what I felt was the same. I want you to know I cared about Charlie. I care about you. I am just trying to be here for you. You matter to me. Your family matters to me. I have missed you every day since you left." His hands were moving rapidly in an effort to explain, but she understood what he was saying.

She just couldn't feel it.

All of a sudden, all of the rage she felt about losing Charlie bubbled up, the anger about no one paying for his death. The frustration, the isolation. It was like she stepped outside herself and couldn't control it. In her mind, she was directing it at the man who'd caused the avalanche, even though she could see Micah standing in front of her. She knew she was wrong as soon as it happened, but she couldn't stop herself. The gates opened and Micah was in the way. He'd no way of knowing to save himself.

"You don't understand! You'll move on and forget Charlie. Losing him almost killed my mother. I have to go past his room every day and see him not there, hear her cry at night. He was my best friend! You can just go on with your life. Mine is over. I don't truly matter to you, Micah! We can't even understand each other. We speak two different languages! I need someone I can actually talk to, not someone I struggle to understand!"

Micah winced and took a step back as if she'd struck him. She might as well have. The color drained from his face, and for a moment she could see the rejection he felt growing up wash over his face. Zoey wished she could take the words back but they hung out there, a thick cloud between them. He stood frozen, crushed by her words. She hadn't meant what she'd said and hadn't meant to direct the anger towards him. She'd let rage fester inside of herself for too long and took it out on the first person who'd tried to get through to her. The one person who'd always been loving and open to her. She went to open her mouth, however, nothing came out. She wanted to reach out but let her hand drop.

Micah didn't respond. His eyes lowered and he moved past her back towards the house. She said his name but he never turned back, even if he was aware. Chef and Trek looked back at her confused, then followed him up the drive. She watched as he got into his truck and backed out. She wanted to stand in the way, to stop his truck and apologize, to beg his forgiveness. But as he drove by, she just stepped aside and hung her head. Shame washed over her and the tears she'd been holding back began to flow. What she'd said was horrible and unforgivable. She took the one thing about him that was vulnerable and threw it in his face. It wasn't true. He'd understood her better than anyone, they'd connected on a deeper level than she even knew existed.

Her father was sitting on the porch when she got back to the house. He patted the seat next to him and she sat down. "Zoey, it's alright to be angry, it's not okay to be cruel."

She was too ashamed to say anything. He was right. It was too late now, though. She'd driven Micah away and had no right to ask his forgiveness. She wasn't even mad at him. She was

mad at herself. She was mad at the town. She was mad at the man who took her brother from them. Nowhere in there was she angry at Micah. However, she'd taken all of that rage and spat it in his face.

She skipped dinner and went straight to bed, wearing her shame like a shawl. She couldn't face her mother, or her father's knowing eyes. Lying in bed, she thought about the expression on Micah's face when she'd said such terrible things. He wasn't expecting it. He'd driven all the way out there, not knowing if she wanted to see him. He did anyway as a friend and she'd turned on him. He'd put himself out there, bared his soul, and she'd used it against him. She could almost hear Charlie's voice in her head.

"You need to make this right, Zo. Micah is a good guy."

Micah was a good guy and the man she loved. Maybe if she went to him, he'd let her apologize. Beg his forgiveness. Yes, she'd go tomorrow and ask him to forgive her, to give her another chance. This resolve settled her mind enough to sleep.

She didn't go the next day or the next. She worked the farm. She helped cook dinners and tended the garden. One day turned into weeks and weeks into months. Before she knew it, it was mid-October and she was due back to base camp. The night before she was heading back, she lay in bed and turned everything over in her mind. It was too late. Too much time had passed. Hopefully, she and Micah could be civil to each other. Maybe they could find a way to be friends again. She pushed down the anxiety in her stomach and hoped for the best.

The next morning, she loaded up her things and went in to say goodbye to her parents. They were sitting at the table discussing something serious and looked up when she came in.

Her mother glanced at her, then at Zoey's father. Her father leaned back and smiled at her, his face tired and aged.

"You all set?" he asked.

"I think so, but if not, I know where you live," she joked.

A look passed between her parents and her father motioned for her to join them at the table. She sat down, staring at them, confused. Her father cleared his throat uncomfortably.

"So, Zoey, we've been talking and need to let you know what is going on. What we're planning to do," he said softly

"Planning to do? What do you mean?" Butterflies formed in her stomach.

"Well, with Charlie gone," her mother began and then stopped, fighting back tears. Her father put his hand over hers.

"With Charlie gone, and you heading back to camp, we've decided it's time to sell the farm," her dad continued.

"Sell the farm? You're kidding, right? You can't do that! This is part of our family!" Zoey could feel the heat rising in her cheeks. This was all they had left.

Zoey's mother spoke up, "I know this is hard, but we're getting older. Alex and Mattie are never planning on coming back and now that Charlie is gone, we can't do this on our own anymore."

"I can stay. I can help," Zoey bargained.

"No. You need to go live your life. Even with your help, it's getting to be too much. Farms are a lot of work and don't make much money. We can sell the land and retire," her dad reasoned.

Zoey knew what they were saying made sense but after losing Charlie, she couldn't bear to see the farm get sold off. It was their whole childhood, it was their family. If they sold it,

94

they'd be erasing part of their history. Part of Charlie. Everything was falling apart. She stood up and shoved her chair in.

"So, now we are nothing!"

She walked out, slamming the door behind her as hard as she could. A year ago, she'd started with SAR as an intern with all of these hopes and dreams. She'd met Micah, fallen in love, and began to bring them all together. Now, Charlie was dead, Micah probably wouldn't speak to her, the farm was being sold, and she had nothing. She grabbed an ax and went out to the fenceline, swinging it over and over against the post until her arms were too tired to move. Bits of chipped wood flew in the air with each swing. She felt her father come up behind her. She dropped the ax and turned to bury her face in his shirt, sobbing into his chest. Finally, he put her back and looked down at her firmly.

"Zoey, life doesn't always turn out as you expect it to. You have to appreciate the good and accept the bad. Most of all, you need to not be the reason things around you fall apart. It's hard enough to hold things together you can control, much less the ones you can't. You have to stop being part of the problem."

Zoey knew what he was saying, even if she wasn't ready to hear it quite yet. She was trying so hard to hold onto the past, she was destroying the future. The farm was a memory she didn't want to let go of, but it was causing her parents stress and holding all of them back. Charlie was gone and she couldn't bring him back no matter how hard she tried. Her anger over losing Charlie had driven Micah away. She was her own worst enemy. She met her father's eyes and rubbed her nose.

"Thanks, Dad. I think I needed a swift reality kick," she said apologetically.

"We do sometimes, Zo. We all do."

As she drove out towards camp, she knew it was time to stop living in the past and figure out what she was going to do about the present.

Only then, would she be able to have a future.

11

 ase camp was almost unrecognizable when Zoey drove in. The triage and warming tents were now enclosed with walls and a roof. Another single cabin had been built on the other side of Micah's, making a total of four smaller cabins and the bunkhouse. The bathhouse was bigger with additional showers and changing areas. Everything was powered primarily with solar panels, using the generator as a backup. The snowmobile covering had been turned into a completely enclosed garage, allowing them to be maintained inside. The fire pit between the cabins was extended and was now concreted in, with benches all the way around. Another storage shed had been built outside of the warming tent. When she first arrived, camp was a small and largely portable area, now it looked like a little town. She suddenly felt like a newcomer all over again, left behind and left out.

Kyle met her outside and gave her a big bear hug. "You don't know how much I've missed you!" he said, setting her back

down. "It's good to have you back. Come on, let me show you your cabin. Jake took over your old one."

They headed to the newly completed cabin, a little larger than her old one. They walked in and she stopped in surprise. Instead of being just one big room, Kyle had built out dividers, giving the bed its own space. There was also a small bathroom with an actual shower. Just a corner with a curtain, tile floor, and walls. But an actual shower! The kitchen had a small fridge, counter, and stove. A bit more space than her previous place. The same table as the others but with four chairs. By the wood stove were a couch and coffee table. Her mouth hung open as she peered around.

Kyle laughed. "I know, right? Getting fancy now."

"Nobody else wanted this?"

"Well, probably, but we took a vote and decided we wanted you back more and thought you might like the space."

Zoey felt humbled by their kindness, especially since she'd made no effort to contact or see anyone. She wandered over to the kitchen and stared out the window. It faced Micah's cabin, looking into the window by his living room space. She nodded and turned around to Kyle.

"I don't even know what to say. So, other than you, Micah, and Jake, who's here?"

"Well, honestly, that's pretty much it. After the big avalanche in April, we lost at least half our volunteers. Megan decided to switch her major to teaching and gave her notice. I think she and Jake split up, if they were even together. Brandon started his nursing job last month but said he'd come back once he was settled to volunteer every now and then. Once school was

back in, we dropped to just one or two volunteers, if that. It's mostly call-ups now."

"And medical? Who's been handling that since Brandon left?" Zoey asked, furrowing her brow.

"No one, really. I mean, we all do first aid and can do basic things but mostly just hold the person off until an ambulance arrives. As I said, we're glad you are back. Zoey, I'm truly sorry about Charlie. I'm here to listen whenever you need to talk. When you're ready, I want to show you a memorial we made for him here. We've really missed you."

He said we, but she knew he meant himself and maybe Jake. She doubted Micah wanted to see her. She was touched they'd made a memorial for Charlie but wasn't ready to see it yet. She just needed to get in and get situated. Bury herself in work. She dropped her shoulders, putting her head down. Kyle came over and hugged her.

"No rush. Besides, I have a ton of work for you to do." He chuckled. "Inventory, supply order, triage is a nightmare. You'll see. Hey, just a word of warning. I suspected things came apart between you and Micah after Charlie died. Well, he's been getting in a lot of fights in town. I know it's not your problem but thought you ought to know. That you might want to know. He's pretty banged up most of the time nowadays. Bruises, cuts, things like that. Anyhow, I'm glad to have you back, part of the family."

She met his eyes and nodded, thinking about what he said about Micah. Kyle was a rock. Without him, there would be no team, no community. He cared about all of them and was always looking out for everyone.

"Thanks, Kyle. I missed you, too. Let me get settled and check out triage. Try to get my bearings. Can we meet up in a bit, so you can walk me through everything?"

"Sure thing, Zo." He walked to the door and paused. "Welcome home."

He left and she went around the cabin, taking everything in. It felt more like a little home instead of a place to crash at the end of the day. She pulled the photo of Charlie and Micah snowboarding she'd framed and put it on a shelf on the wall by the couch. She unpacked the rest of her things, including personal items she'd brought from the farmhouse. With her parents selling the farm, she wanted a piece of it with her here. Her mother had given her a box of dishes and some knickknacks. She went to the car to grab out the last of her things and paused to glance around. The last time she'd been there was when she'd grabbed her things from Micah's cabin. She hadn't seen him or Jake yet and guessed they were out doing tasks.

She walked towards her cabin slowly, carrying her box. Just as she got to the small porch, Trek came up behind her, brushing against her as he jumped around. She set the box down and kneeled down to him. He licked her face as she petted him on his face and sides. He was warm and tried climbing in her arms, almost knocking her over. Chef came up and rubbed against her. She was happy to see them and glad they were welcoming her back. Knowing what it meant, she stood up and turned around to see Micah coming over the hill towards camp. He saw her and paused. Her heart ached and she wanted to go to him, but it wasn't her move. She'd burned that bridge.

He clapped his hands and signaled to the dogs, who ran back over to him. He made his way carefully in her direction, also

the direction of his cabin and the rest of camp. He was dragging a wagon of wood he'd been chopping for the woodshed. He hesitated when he was between her and the woodshed. His face was impossible to read.

"Hello," she signed to him.

He stared at her, then signed, "Welcome back."

He turned his back to her and headed for the woodshed, without looking back. Her heart fell, she'd ruined any chance of their friendship... at best all she could hope to be was teammates. He was professional and wouldn't make anything personal they needed to do together. But she wanted it to be personal. She wanted his friendship. She wanted to feel his arms around her and his lips on hers. She couldn't expect that, and knew even him being civil was more than she deserved. She took her box in and set it on the table. It was time to check out triage and see what she had to work with.

Triage was worse than she could've imagined. It was a mess with open packages and supplies scattered everywhere. What supplies there were left. Cabinets were bare and opened supplies were no longer sanitary. Everything would need to be taken out, sanitized, and most supplies left would need to be thrown away. She started dragging all the cots and moveable equipment outside to air out. Once she'd cleared those, she hauled in a trash can and began throwing away anything which was not safe to use. By the time she was done, the triage area was an empty shell. She made up a sanitizing solution and went outside to wipe everything down before she brought it back in.

Jake was outside and came over when he saw her, giving her a huge hug. "Zoey! I heard you were back. Sorry about triage, we did the best we could. Do you want some help?"

Jake joined the team the summer before she had, as a kid fresh out of college. Now, he looked like a mature man. His light brown hair was shorter, not the shaggy in his eyes hair he'd had before. His face looked leaner and his brown eyes had small lines around them. He still had a boyish grin though, making her think of Charlie.

"Sure! I'm wiping everything down with this solution and bringing them back in after. You want to carry them in once I wipe them down?"

"I'd love to." He chuckled and picked up a tool table she'd already wiped down.

They spent the rest of the afternoon cleaning everything and bringing it back in. He filled her in on the summer and the rescues which happened since she'd been gone. He told her he and Megan had tried dating but in the end, it just wasn't there. She'd met a guy at college and left not long after the big avalanche, as they all referred to it now. He was fine with it as he wasn't ready to settle down any time soon. He told her Kyle and his lady in town had split as well, she was wanting a commitment he couldn't make. Just a bunch of single guys up here now, he told her, laughing. When he saw her flinch at that, he reached out.

"Sorry, Zo. I forgot. I gather you and Micah split sometime around when you left?"

She nodded and sighed. She wasn't ready to go there yet. "Yeah. I needed to be there for my family, you know?"

"I know. I'm sorry. If you ever need to talk, you know I'm here," he said, his voice tight with emotion.

She'd underestimated the bond they all shared. "Thanks, Jake."

The one thing she'd never taken into consideration was that she had a family here, too. Kyle, Jake, even Micah were her family. She'd shut everyone out when she left, but they'd left their hearts open to her. Micah had come to her wearing his heart on his sleeve, and she'd crushed it. Fresh shame washed over her. She was so wrapped up in being there for her mother and licking her own wounds, she hadn't seen the team waiting for her, to welcome her back into their strong arms. Arms she truly needed around her right now.

Once they got the triage area put back in order, they sat on the couch in the warming area. A real couch, not the makeshift cot they'd been using. Jake took out a couple of sodas and handed her one. He sat down next to her and leaned back.

"Can I tell you something?" he asked, sipping his drink.

She nodded and met his eyes.

"Micah's not been the same since Charlie died and you left. He's drawn inside himself. He doesn't try to communicate outside of work. He used to joke around and you know, be here. Now he works his ass off, but just isn't here."

"I messed up, Jake. I pushed him away and not in a kind way," Zoey admitted.

"You had a lot going on."

"I did. But I was cruel about it."

"Have you tried to apologize?"

That was the worst part, she hadn't. She shook her head.

"Well, Zo. Start there. Micah's a nice guy. He may understand." Jake got up and smiled down at her. "I'm glad you're back. We need you here. Clearly, from the state of things."

She stood up and hugged him as hard as she could. She needed to hear that. He chuckled, hugging her back. After he

left, she made a list of all needed supplies to be ordered. Being back in the triage area felt like home, she was glad to have purpose again. Even though she'd been helping her father on the farm, she felt like he was doing it more for her, than her actually making a difference. Here she felt like she was important. That she made a difference.

By dinner time, everything was in place and ordered. She closed up the triage tent and headed to her cabin to eat. Micah had the dogs out in the field and glanced over at her, watching as she crossed. She met his eyes for a second, then looked down, her cheeks hot with shame. She quickly let herself into her cabin and took a deep breath. Jake was right, she needed to apologize, but she was afraid to. She was afraid he would shun her... like she'd done to him. A little while later, she saw a light flick on in his cabin. She imagined him in there, thinking about her, and wondered how she could bridge the gap.

The next morning, she went out with Kyle to check the area. They'd only had light snows which melted off but come November, steady snows would start. They needed to check paths and trails for weak areas and stock up as much wood as they could. Everyone was doing wood runs multiple times a day, she was no exception. The woodshed was about half full and needed to be full by the end of the month. They hauled wood most of the morning and took stock of all supplies needed for the upcoming weeks.

Zoey laughed at how they'd been shopping. A lot of snack foods, things that didn't go together, and too many perishables. She created a complete pantry list, then sent Kyle and Jake into town to get all the items. The second storage shed was going to come in handy for canned and dry goods. They'd

swing by and pick up the medical supplies as well. By the end of the day, the camp was completely stocked and ready for the first real snow to hit.

Zoey sat down in triage, taking out the sign language books she'd been studying since her fallout with Micah. If he was willing to communicate with her again, she was committed to only using sign language, not depending on him to read her lips. It was her way of proving what she said wasn't true. She needed to get him willing to talk to her. She glanced out the triage window and saw him stacking wood outside each cabin. He was beautiful, the muscles in his arms cut from constant work. He had his hair tied back, now well past his shoulders. He stopped and stood up, stretching his back. He reached his arms out in front of him and rotated at the waist. Zoey was mesmerized. At one point, she'd had the right to touch that body, to hold him next to her. To feel him inside her. That thought made her blush and she stared down at the book in front of her. What had once been so natural, was now a pain point.

When she looked back up, he wasn't there. Probably gone into his cabin for the night. She took this chance to pick up her book and head to her cabin. She paused at the porch and peered out at the mountains. It was getting dark but she could see the outline of them in the rising moon. It took her breath away. Regardless of what this year had brought in pain and loss, the mountains were still her home. She sighed and let herself into her cabin.

What she hadn't noticed was Micah watching her from his cabin window. He could see the pain in her and felt it, too. His heart was broken. He was stuck on the other side of the abyss, not knowing how to reach her.

12

O ver the next couple of weeks, the focus was on preparing supplies and equipment for the impending snow. The woodshed was nearly full but it wouldn't even last a season, running four to five wood stoves almost constantly. They needed to chop wood and have it outside the shed covered by tarps as well. The calls coming in were minor, mostly lost people. Occasionally, a person was found dead, either from a health condition or by their own hand. For the most part, however, the days were quiet. Kyle kept the camp running year-round through grants and donating his own labor.

Micah and Zoey figured out ways to work around each other without creating issues. Both were focused and professional, and the dogs diffused any awkward moments with their presence. Before long, they were communicating about tasks and issues without feeling such fragility between them. The team came first and there was always plenty of work to do. This kept their minds busy, even if at times one would watch the

other longingly, quick to avert their eyes when needed. It was what it had to be.

One evening, as day turned to night, Zoey was sitting studying her medical and ASL books when she heard a commotion outside the triage tent. She didn't have a chance to get up before Jake burst through the door, with Micah following reluctantly behind.

"Zoey! He's being ridiculous. Please make him show you his hand. I was chopping wood and lost my grip, hitting him with the ax in the hand as he was stacking wood. He was reaching down to pick up a piece and I wasn't paying attention when the ax slipped, hitting him between the fingers. He won't let me look at it, but he's bled through two handkerchiefs already." Jake was speed talking and Micah stood behind him, holding his hand against his chest.

Zoey got up and came around Jake to see how bad it was. Micah drew away initially, but she sighed as she grasped his hand and pulled it towards her, unwrapping the makeshift bandage. He opened his hand and blood, which had been pooling in his palm, poured out onto the ground. Zoey gasped. It was much worse than he was acting. The two fingers on either side of the gash hung oddly, the skin and tissue between them having been severed. She didn't know if she could handle this.

She guided him over and sat him on the cot, checking for extensive damage. It didn't feel like any bones were broken, however, his hand almost looked split down the middle of the top half. Jake took one glance and went outside to vomit. Zoey needed to determine if there was nerve damage or served tendons. She grabbed a scalpel and pressed it into the tips of his fingers. He winced each time, which was good. She turned his

hand over in hers, pressing the scalpel in different spots, noting pain response each time. Somehow the ax hand managed to miss his nerves and bones, cutting through only soft tissue, muscle, and skin.

She still felt he needed to be assessed for surgery. Especially since he used his hands for everything, including communication. She asked him if he could wiggle his fingers; he could but not without pain and weakness. As she peered closer, she could see the wound stopped about two inches from the start of the skin between his fingers. There was extensive damage to the tissue.

"I think you need to go to the hospital. I can stitch this up but it would be two layers of stitches and you may lose partial use of your hand. I do not think so because it somehow managed to miss your nerves and you can still move your fingers. But I do not want to risk it."

She met his eyes, which were clouded with pain and he shook his head roughly. He stuck his hand back out to her, using his other hand to sign.

"Stitch it. I am fine."

"Micah, if I stitch it and it heals wrong, you may not have full motion. You need that."

"Zoey, just stitch it. I will not go to the hospital. If it does not heal right, then I will go. I trust you."

"I do not trust myself on this," Zoey replied. She didn't. The damage was deep and if she did it wrong, she'd never forgive herself. His hands were his voice.

"Please. You either do it, or I wrap it back up and hope it heals on its own."

He was serious.

If she didn't do it, he was just going to go to his cabin and risk completely losing the use of his hand, or worse... infection could make him lose his hand altogether. She took a deep breath and checked it again. She could numb it some, but there was no way she'd be able to get it completely numb in the deeper tissue. He was going to feel a lot of what she did. She washed her hands and slipped on gloves. She squirted antiseptic deep into the wound, causing him to flinch and sweat to break out on his brow. She made him look at her.

"This is going to hurt. A lot. I can put some novocaine in there but you are still going to feel it. I cannot get the solution all the way in there. Do you understand, Micah?"

He nodded, appearing a little green. Jake came back in, but she waved him away. This was going to be a long tedious process and someone watching her would only make it worse. Jake gratefully left, leaving just Micah and Zoey hunched over the steel table she'd need to work at. She laid his hand out and stuck a needle in the wound to numb what she could. He wavered and she thought he might fall over, but he stayed steady. She let the novocaine take effect while she gathered the supplies she'd need. The inner layer would need dissolvable stitches, which she had because most people didn't want to, or wouldn't, come back to have stitches removed. On the outer layer, she'd use non-dissolving stitches since they were always getting their hands wet and this would require he'd come back in to have her check it regularly.

She came over and placed her hand firmly on his shoulder. "You ready?"

He bobbed his head but didn't look ready. He took a deep breath and stuck his hand back on the table. She changed

her gloves and shined the light on the exposed tissue. She bent close and began drawing the inner tissue together with the needle and thread. Each stitch had to be perfect, aligning the tissue together so it would heal with as little scar tissue as possible. She got so far into the zone that when Micah shifted in his seat, it startled her. She glanced up and his eyes were closed, his brows furrowed in pain. A newly formed scar lined his brow which hadn't been there prior to her leaving camp after Charlie's death. She wondered what it was from and thought about Kyle saying how Micah was getting into fights. She paused and touched him on the arm to get his attention. He opened his eyes and gazed at her, his eyes a darker gray.

"Do you need a break?" she asked, realizing she was pushing through so hard, it was probably causing him a great deal of pain.

He shook his head and closed his eyes. He was like her in that he wanted to get things over with, no matter how much it hurt. She bent back down and continued to bring the tissue together. Once the inner stitches were done, she put more shots of novocaine in to make sure the area was numb. The ax had made a fairly clear-cut line, which was easier to bring together than torn flesh. She was able to rapidly sew together the inside of his hand, then rotated his hand over to stitch the top, noticing scabs on his knuckles. She peered at the clock; they'd been at it for over an hour. He still had his eyes closed but his face was more relaxed. The novocaine was working on the outer skin. She lined the skin up and stitched it on top, meeting the line in between his fingers. She rinsed it with more antiseptic. She'd need to check for infection the next day but it looked pretty clean.

Micah opened his eyes and stared at his hand. He flipped it over, admiring the stitches. He tried to move his fingers, then winced in pain. She put gauze over the stitches and bandaged his hand.

"Just for tonight, then we can switch to a light gauze covering on the wound. I will need to check for infection in the morning," she signed everything she said. "Keep the dogs away from it, elevate it if you can for swelling. If I say so in the morning, you go to the hospital, okay?"

He smiled and nodded, color returning to his cheeks. "If you say so. When did you learn so much ASL?"

She met his eyes. It was time. "Micah, I need to apologize to you for what I said at the farm. I did not mean it. I was angry and upset about Charlie's death, how no one was having to pay for it. I was full of rage and wanted to lash out. You did not deserve it. You showed up when I was at my most angry and feeling fractured. What I wanted that day was to hold you. But instead, I said the most horrible things I could ever say. You need to know none of it was true. You were the person I felt knew me best. I never saw how we communicated as lacking. You made me laugh, let me vent, share my secrets. I loved you. I love you. I began studying ASL every day after that to prove to you that you are everything to me. At this point, I just want us to be friends again. I do not expect anything else, and I certainly do not deserve your consideration. But I want you to know, I never meant to hurt you like I did."

He watched and took in what she was saying. He sat motionless when she was done. He dropped his eyes to look at his hand. Zoey reached out and touched his arm.

"I am not asking anything from you, Micah. I just needed you to know."

He stood up and walked to the door. He paused, glancing back at her. "Thanks, Z."

He turned and left. Zoey watched the empty doorway for a moment and let out a deep breath. It was about what she'd expected. She got up and began cleaning up the triage area. Bloody rags were on the floor and the table. She scooped up everything and threw it away. They didn't have access to cleaning up blood properly, so losing a few rags was fine. She sanitized the surfaces and put all of the surgical tools she'd used in the autoclave to sterilize them. She did a last check of the area and closed the door. She was exhausted, physically and mentally. She walked to her cabin and paused outside the door, peering over at Micah's cabin.

She couldn't read his response to what she'd told him, but she'd said it. She'd put herself on the line and come clean. Everything else would just have to be what it was. She couldn't go back to change what happened, however, she'd sincerely apologized from the heart. The ball was in his court. Regardless, she felt lighter and more at peace. She slept hard that night.

The next morning as requested, Micah came to the triage tent and let her look at his hand. It was swollen but no discharge. It didn't feel abnormally hot to the touch. She dug around in the medical supply closet and found some antibiotic samples she'd snagged from the hospital. She wrote down how to take them and gave them to him. She reminded him not to use the hand for at least a week until she could assess if it was healing without excessive scar tissue. It was hard to tell this early. He needed to come every day to have her change the bandage and

check healing. He tried to brush her off, so she grabbed him by the shoulder.

"I am serious, Micah. This is the deal. You come every single day or I *will* make Kyle knock you out and take you to the hospital. This is no joke."

He stared at her wide-eyed, then nodded. "Okay, okay. I will. I promise."

He did. Every morning before the day got rolling, he came in and let her change the bandage. By the end of the week, she could see the tissue was healing appropriately. He was able to move his fingers and felt a pain response when she poked him in the hand. He told her he thought she was doing it sadistically.

"Trust me, if I was, you would know," she responded and covered the wound.

He laughed and got off the cot. He went to the warming tent and poured two cups of coffee, bringing one to her. It was a small olive branch, and one she should be offering, but she took it. They drank their coffee and communicated about the upcoming snow. The ground was now covered, however, they were due a heavy snow in the next few days. The season was about to kick into full gear. The team was ready and a few more volunteers had trickled in.

A week later, Micah came to the tent to have the stitches removed. Zoey slowly snipped them to make sure as each one was removed, the skin held. The internal stitches would take longer but would dissolve on their own. Once all the stitches were out, Micah held up his hand and wiggled his fingers without pain.

He fingerspelled the alphabet, then turned to her and signed. "Thank you, Zoey, for saving my hand and not making me go to the hospital."

She laughed and threw gauze at him. "You did *not* give me a choice."

He caught the gauze and met her eyes. For a second their old heat was there and they both looked away, breaking the trance. Zoey pulled herself together.

"Remember the skin still needs to heal, toughen up. You do not want to rip this back open and go through all of that again," she reminded him.

"I will be careful, do not want to undo all of your hard work."

"Please. You will have a nice scar to tell stories about. You should show Jake since this was his handiwork."

Micah chuckled and stood up. He grabbed his coat and slipped it on, thanking her again. Jake was outside hauling wood, so Micah went out and showed him his hand. Jake stared at the wound which was scarring over and shook his head in astonishment. Micah patted him on the shoulder. Zoey stepped out to get some air and Jake raised his hand to her.

"Nice work, Zo! I break them, you put them back together," he joked.

Micah looked over and winked at her, as he and Jake brought the rest of the wood to the shed.

13

ovember brought in heavier snow and increased calls. The team barely had time to get back from one before another came in. This is where they shined. Kyle came alive and proved why their team was so solid. Zoey got another nursing intern on weekends and some evenings. A small, mouse of a girl with curly, dirty blond hair and hazel eyes, named Callie. She stayed focused on her work and kept her head down. She couldn't have been bigger than five feet tall or weighed more than ninety pounds, but as soon as they needed to move someone off the toboggan, she showed strength that almost seemed impossible. Jake was smitten. Suddenly, he always found a reason to be in the triage or warming areas. Callie was very focused on her job and paid him little mind.

Zoey and Micah found common ground and were able to start forming a work friendship. They shared lunch sometimes and chatted easily. Now that she was fairly fluent in ASL, they naturally fell into daily conversations about work and life. She

noticed he often had scabs on his knuckles and a black eye or busted lip every now and then but didn't know how to bring it up. He was obviously getting into regular fights and she didn't know why. They weren't close enough to discuss it, so she let it slide. But a niggling feeling ate at her about it.

Late one evening, Zoey was wrapping up her work in triage, as Callie was keeping an eye on things overnight. Along with Jake, who was hanging out on the couch in the warming area. Having Callie around had given Zoey a chance to let her guard down and take much-needed breaks. Zoey put away her things and told them goodnight, giving Jake a quick wink. He grinned sheepishly. Eventually, he'd make his move, until then he'd hang around like a forlorn schoolboy. She gestured her head towards Callie and he nodded. He got up and went over to make small talk. Callie glanced up and smiled. Zoey read a flicker of interest in her eyes as Jake joked with her.

Her work there was done.

She meandered towards her cabin and peered up at the sky. It was super clear and the moon was full. She loved nights like these. The weather was still and not very cold, even though the ground was covered with a thick layer of snow. She took a deep breath in, liking the way the cool air felt in her lungs. She went inside and ate leftovers at the table. She stoked the stove and sat on the couch. Though she was always around people during the day, the nights sometimes did get lonely. She put her feet up and picked up a book to read when she heard a soft knock at the door. She set the book down and looked at the time. It was after nine. She got up and opened the door, surprised when she saw who was standing there.

Micah was holding his hiking poles and snowshoes. He had a backpack slung across his shoulders and handed her the snowshoes. He had snowshoes on his own feet.

"You want to go for a hike?"

Zoey took the snowshoes, staring at him. A hike at night? She couldn't deny she did. She nodded and grabbed her hiking poles, coat, and gloves. She slipped on the snowshoes on the porch and they headed out. They hiked for some time, with only the crunching sound of snow beneath their feet. The moon lit their path as Micah led the way. Zoey loved the way the moon made the snow sparkle, a mass sheet of glittering white around them. The air smelled clean with a tinge of pine to it. She watched Micah move in front of her, deftly traversing the snow. The stars twinkled above them, so crisp and clear it almost didn't look real. Micah had his hair tied back and with the way he was moving, his hiking poles stabbing powerfully into the ground with each step, it made her a little breathless. No matter what had transpired between them, he still was the most beautiful man she'd ever seen.

As they crested a hill, he changed direction and began heading down to a grove of pine trees. When they got there, Zoey could see there was a fire ring and a few stacks of wood. The logs around the ring had been brushed clean to sit on and she realized he'd planned this. He set the pack down and bent to ignite the fire which had been prepped. Within a couple of minutes, the fire was blazing and Zoey took off the snowshoes to step closer to it. It was warm and made the area glow, the flames creating dancing shadows on the trees around them. Micah pulled a thermos out of the backpack, filled a mug of hot tea, then handed it to her. She met his eyes, which looked like gray tree bark in the light. He poured himself a mug of tea and smiled at her. The fire was getting hot, so she sat down on a log near it. Micah sat down across from her, the flames flickering over his face. He was just so damn attractive.

"I wanted to bring you out here because we need to talk," he signed to her. "There is too much between us unsaid and we need to clear the air. Start over."

"Okay. I agree." She waited for him to continue as she felt this was his lead.

"Zoey, we moved so fast last time, I do not think we let each other know who we were. At least I did not. I was so drawn to you, I just wanted to be with you. The moment I saw you, I was head over heels." He blushed and shook his head. "That dark hair, those deep, dark soulful eyes. You had me. But I did not truly let you know who I was. I mean, I told you my history in basic terms, but I did not let you know what I had been through." He paused and looked at her. He glanced up at the trees thoughtfully, then went on.

"I told you I was adopted. My adoptive parents were good to me. Loving, and it helped with being deaf since they were familiar with that world. They used ASL with me at home. My brother, Trent, was their birth child, four years older than me, and was hearing. He was raised with sign language, so that wasn't an issue. He used ASL with me at home, but spoke verbally at school and with his parents. I guess we just did not connect. He had been an only child for five years until I was adopted. He did not want a sibling. I wanted him to be my big brother, but to him, I was a nuisance. My parents and Trent still spoke verbally to each other at home, which made me feel left out, so I learned to read lips to know what they were saying.

Anyway, I did not fit in at school either. At first, they put me in special education but I tested off the charts, so they moved me to regular classes. Sometimes they had someone who would come in and interpret, but because ASL is not taught in schools, it was only when they had someone who could volunteer to do it. There was not a school for the deaf nearby, so I had to adapt. Learning to read lips helped, but I felt shut out. Alone."

He paused and got up to refill his mug and motioned to see if she needed more. She nodded, holding her mug out. He smiled and refilled it. She wanted to get up and wrap her arms around him to comfort him, but that is what got them stuck in the first place.

"Thank you," she said.

He stood by the fire and took a sip from his mug. "By seventh grade, I had a lot of pent-up frustration. Kids that age are cruel and I began getting teased a lot. I remember this one day in the cafeteria, I was sitting eating when a teacher came by and asked me how I was doing. I was always this charity case to the adults around. Like being deaf made me stupid. Anyway, I told them I was fine and this kid behind the teacher began mocking me. I do not know what happened, but I snapped. I waited for the teacher to leave, then walked over to the kid and punched him in the head. He hit the ground and I dove on him and started wailing on him. It was like everything up to that point came to a head. They dragged me off him and sent me home. I think they hoped it was isolated, but to be honest, it felt good. I began to look for any chance to fight. A wrong look, mocking, anything. By the time I was in high school, I was getting into fights weekly. Eventually, I got suspended so many times, my being deaf was no longer a valid excuse for my

behavior... their words not mine. I was expelled and my parents homeschooled me the rest of the time. I knew college was out of the question because of my anger issues, so I took wilderness survival training and trained rescue dogs. Part of me wanted to connect with other deaf people, but by then I had isolated myself so much with my anger, I was afraid they would shun me, too. By the time I was twenty, I was working Search and Rescue. It is all I have wanted to do. I do not have to interact with people and dogs do not have hang-ups. Did Kyle tell you why I came here?"

Zoey shook her head, Kyle hadn't. They needed a handler and Micah showed up. She'd never given it any thought. He breathed out, staring off, then continued.

"So, in Colorado, I was a handler for about ten years. On a mission, I had the dogs and we were looking for this missing girl. The dogs were having a hard time finding her scent because so many people were on the scene. I was trying to get them back on scent and this guy, I guess a family member of hers, got in my face and started doing mocking sign language, yelling at my dogs. I lost it and punched him in the face. Long story short, we found the girl, I was charged with assault, and lost my job. I was out of work for a while when a person I knew from SAR told me about the opening here. I contacted Kyle, who hired me on the spot. He knew I was deaf, and about my history, but did not care."

That sounded like Kyle. He loved SAR more than anything and as long as someone had a passion for it, he wanted them around. Zoey thought about the day Micah broke the guy's nose with the butt of the shotgun. It was so fast, almost expert-like. He'd been fighting by that point for twenty years or so, she figured. Gentle Micah who had touched her so delicately. Who treated his dogs like they were his children. She stood up to stand by the fire next to him. He glanced over at her, attempting to read her face. To see if there was disapproval. She reached up and traced the scar above his brow. He let her, then cocked his head.

"I guess you figured out I have been fighting again. Bar fights mostly. The day Charlie died, the day I broke that guy's nose, it all kind of bubbled up again. Then the day at the farm when you lashed out at me. Zoey, you broke my heart. I let my guard down for you. I trusted you. Then you took all of that and threw it in my face. I was shocked... then I was crushed," he paused and met her eyes hard.

Zoey felt so ashamed but she needed to know it, to understand the damage her words had done. This was her doing, she was the bad guy in this scenario. She bit her lip as tears welled up in her eyes. He turned his eyes away. She wasn't owed forgiveness on this.

"I drove home feeling devastated. It was like if your mother told you she did not love you anymore. That you were worthless. You made me feel worthless. Do you understand that?"

It wasn't a real question. It was an accusation. Zoey nodded and wiped away a tear that had escaped. She looked up at him and saw he had tears on his cheeks. She felt like such a piece of shit for this. She went to wipe away his tears and he grabbed her hand, pushing it away. She persisted and put her hand on his cheek again to wipe away the tears. She turned his face to her firmly.

"I am sorry. If I could cut out my heart and give it to you to prove it, I would," she insisted. "Please just let me tell you this."

He kept his eyes on her, waiting.

"Micah, there is no excuse for what I did. I know that. I cannot go back and fix it, but every single moment since that day, I have hated myself for it. I am not perfect. I was dealing with Charlie's death and the change in my mother. I said terrible things to you and I did not mean any of them. You mean the most to me. That day, I said we could not understand each other, but you are the only one who took the time to get to know me. I said I needed to talk to someone other than you, but you were the only one I wanted to communicate with. I have cried and ached for you. I lost Charlie, then drove you away and put myself in my own hell for it. I love you. That will never change. I am glad you told me about yourself and what happened to bring you to this place. That means a lot to me. At this point, I would be honored just to have your friendship. But I want you to stop fighting. I worry it will take you away. Or worse, put you in jail. We need you at camp, Trek and Chef need you. Damnit, Micah, I need you as my friend."

Micah watched her, his face emotionless, but he flinched slightly at her last words. She could tell he was afraid to let her in again. She took his hand and put it over her heart.

"I swear on my life, I will not ever do that again. I would hurt myself before I would hurt you. Please believe me," she pleaded.

His face relaxed, his shoulders dropped and much to her relief, he reached out and hugged her. She nestled into his warmth and sighed. Right now, this was all she needed. Just to know he didn't hate her, that they could be friends. Not just coworkers, but true friends. He'd been her closest friend and she wanted that back. He pulled back and stared at her, the face of

the Micah she remembered. He brushed a strand of hair out of her face.

"I am holding you to that," he told her.

"Cross my heart," she swore.

They packed up and hiked back towards camp. This time they walked side by side and pointed out stars. A deer ran in front of them as they neared camp and disappeared into the woods, making them both stop in their tracks. Zoey glanced at Micah, who grinned back at her. It was magical. He put his hand out to her and she took it, not letting go until they got to their cabins. As they parted to go into their own places, they stopped and paused, staring at each other. They each smiled as the abyss between them finally closed.

14

 yle came into triage late one afternoon and asked Zoey to join him to chop some wood. Callie was there, making a supply order, and waved her away. Zoey found it odd, but Kyle was just that way sometimes. They headed out from camp up a trail towards the mountains, not their usual place to find deadfall. Kyle was quiet and led the way, his strong legs cutting through the snow like it was powder. Finally, they came to a clearing, and up ahead Zoey could make out a shape made out of granite. As they got close, she realized what it was and tears sprang to her eyes.

Charlie's memorial. She'd forgotten Kyle told her they'd made one and she hadn't seen it. It was a large stone with a snowboard carved into the face of it. Below were the words, "Live life to the fullest," something Charlie always said. Below that were Charlie's full name, birth, and death dates. At the bottom of the stone was a small fire holder. Zoey ran her hand across the face of the marker and noticed there were pennies in

the fire holder. She looked at Kyle, confused. She scooped a couple of pennies and held them tightly in her fist.

"We leave a penny whenever we come here," he explained.

"We?"

"Me, Micah, Jake. One of us comes every day. I knew you jumped right back in and wanted to give you time to adjust to being back, but I needed you to know this was here. We all chipped in to have this made and brought up here. We wanted you to know you weren't alone... that we cared."

She met his eyes and saw deep sincerity. She nodded and brushed snow off the top. She noticed a small bench off to the side made out of a log. Kyle's handiwork. She went and sat down on it, noticing how it gave a perfect view of the memorial and the mountains in the background. Tears fell unabashed down her cheek. She glanced at Kyle, who was teary as well.

"You don't know what this means to me. Since Charlie died, I haven't had a way to be with him, you know? He was cremated and my parents are selling the farm, so I haven't had anything tangible. No place to go. This is perfect."

Kyle smiled and cocked his head. "I'm glad you like it. I was nervous I was being too bold in putting this here. But Charlie meant so much to a lot of people, to all of us. He was our family in a way. You're our family, Zo. I hope you know that. I'd do anything for you."

Hearing that made Zoey feel something she'd never felt before. To her family had always been flesh and blood, but now it meant so much more. Without thinking, she signed, "thank you," to Kyle. She laughed at her mistake, which wasn't one, when he signed, "you are welcome," back.

He let her know he was going to head back to camp but to stay as long as she wished. He waved and went back down.

The mountains shifted in their majesty as the sun moved in the sky, exposing nooks and crannies at different times. It was like watching a living painting. Zoey stayed until the sun started to dip into the sky, then decided it was best to go back before it got dark. When she stood up and turned around, she saw Micah in the distance, leaning against a tree, observing her. She lifted her hand towards him and he came over.

"I did not want to disturb you, but did not want you walking back alone once it got dark," he explained.

They stood and stared at Charlie's rock for a few minutes. Zoey turned to Micah.

"This means a lot to me, and that you have been coming here every day. That would have meant so much to Charlie."

Micah nodded. "You are not alone, Z. We all have been watching out for you, whether you wanted it or not."

Zoey reached out and took his hand. "Thank you."

They headed back to camp as the sun dipped behind the mountains. Kyle was cooking in the warming area, so they all ate dinner together. Zoey incorporated ASL whenever she communicated with anyone on the team and was pleasantly surprised to see all of them had a basic grasp of ASL. Callie was even trying to learn but was still struggling with the alphabet. It was a mishmash of spoken word, ASL, writing, and spelling out words, but they could all communicate this way. Zoey sat back in her chair and looked around the table at her new family. Kyle met her eyes and winked. She smiled back at him. He'd been the anchor of all of this, building the camp, bringing in the right people, and putting himself out there. It was hard with her parents selling the farm, but at least now she had a home.

"So, Kyle, can you explain how this all works? Like, I know you built everything here, but how do you know one day the county will not come in and tell you to remove it all, to get out?" Zoey asked.

Kyle rubbed his chin, thinking of how to explain. "We worked out a contract for the land. The county retains ownership, however, we have the rights to build and stay here as long as our services for SAR are needed. We don't own the land, so can't buy or sell it, but we're pretty much leasing it through our service. So, I can build and add water, electricity, that kind of stuff as long as it's used in conjunction with our service to the county. Now, that's not to say that one day they won't sell the land out from under us. But while they own it, we're contracted to stay here."

"Other SARs don't have this though, right?" Jake chimed in.

"Nope. I went to them and pointed out the benefits of having staff on hand full-time versus just calling up volunteers. Statistically, we're saving the county money because we're here, save people faster, and our presence reduces incidents because people know they're being watched. Besides, I basically am only paid through grants, so the money they save on my salary covers land costs."

"What happens if you leave?" Callie asked.

"Where am I going?" Kyle chuckled. "I plan to die here."

They laughed, knowing he wasn't joking. This was Kyle's kingdom. He'd be an old man running the mountain long after they were all gone. For those of them that would leave.

"My plan is to build a lodge this spring with a full kitchen, tables, and entertainment area. Maybe a couple of actual houses. We'll see."

Zoey liked the idea of that. Maybe one day families could live up there. She glanced over at Micah, who was deep in thought. He was like Kyle, he'd no reason to leave. She wasn't sure she did either. One day she did want a family of her own, but she'd cross that bridge when she got to it. Micah caught her eye and smiled softly. She blushed and looked away, knowing she still wanted it to be with him. They weren't there yet. Still working on their friendship and rebuilding trust.

It was Callie's night to watch triage, so Zoey got up and washed her dishes. Jake joined her, not wanting to be far from Callie's side. They washed in silence for a bit then Jake whispered to her.

"Hey, Zo? Can you give me some advice?"

Zoey glanced at him and raised a brow.

"So, I like Callie. Like *really* like her. Thinking maybe she is the one."

"The one? Jake, really?"

"I know, it's not been long but there is just something there. Something I've never felt before."

"Okay, so what are you asking?"

Jake blushed, then shook his head, laughing. "I'm not sure, but I don't want to scare her away. We're talking and flirting, but I want to make it real. Like, ask her to be my girlfriend."

"Have you done that yet?"

"What like just asked her? No."

"Start with that. If you're waiting for a perfect moment, it won't happen. But be honest about who you are and what you want. Don't pretend to be something you aren't."

Jake considered this, then nodded. "Yeah, you're right. Okay, I'm going in."

"Wait! Right now?"

Jake grinned at her, his boyish charm showing through. Callie would be missing out if she didn't see that. He went to the triage side and started talking to Callie quietly. She was about a foot shorter than him and was peering up into his face intently. He paused, waiting for her to respond. She watched him and a small smile twitched at the sides of her mouth as she tipped her head, her eyes sparkling. Jake leaned in to kiss her and she stood on her tiptoes to meet him. Zoey cast her eyes back to the dishes and smiled to herself. She turned to put the dishes in the cabinet, catching Micah's eyes. He'd seen what transpired as well and it reminded both of them of their first kiss. They looked at each other for a moment and Zoey raised her hand in the *I love you* sign, which he signed back. Her cheeks flushed and she turned back to the dishpan. When she glanced back, he was gone, out with Kyle doing the nightly rounds.

She wrapped up and headed for her cabin. When she got to the door, she looked down and saw a daisy on the doormat. She peered over and saw Micah talking with Kyle. He glanced over, then shrugged.

"How?" Zoey asked.

"Magic," he responded and went back to talking with Kyle.

She picked up the flower and sniffed it. It smelled fresh and clean. She rubbed it against her cheek and smiled. Once

inside, she stuck it in a cup of water. A little while later, she saw a light click on in Micah's cabin. He always had a light on even at night, which she found comforting. She'd asked him once why he left a light on and he told her because it made him feel more secure if he woke up in the night and could see if something was going on he couldn't hear. Waking in pitch black being deaf was disconcerting at a minimum and terrifying at times. If he could see everything was alright, then he could go back to sleep. He felt more connected to the outside world with it on. It'd never bothered her as she grew up with nightlights, but she'd never thought of it that way.

Her father called the next day. They had an offer on the farm and were accepting it. Did she want to come out for one last dinner and help pack? Zoey was sad about the farm but knew she needed closure. She wondered if Micah would want to go with her. Her parents weren't going far, just moving to town into a small two-bedroom place. The sale of the farm would pay for that place and leave them a nest egg to live off of. Likely, her father would find work anyway, because he could never sit still. Even so, she didn't want to go out by herself, for fear it'd be too overwhelming. Plus, her mother liked Micah and might enjoy chatting with him again. She let her father know she'd be there and hung up the phone. So, this was it. The end of an era. She sighed and sat down to process it all.

She was born and raised in that farmhouse. Her parents had met when her father was stationed in Guam. They fell in love and got married quickly. He did his four years and wanted to move home to take care of his aging parents and the farm. Zoey's mother was sad to leave her home but wanted to be with him and have a family. They'd moved back and lived in a

one-bedroom apartment until she found out she was pregnant with their first child, Alexander. Then they moved to a little house closer to the farm. Zoey's grandfather fell ill and passed away shortly after Alex was born. Mattie came a couple years later and Zoey's grandmother could no longer keep up with the farm, so Zoey's parents moved out to the farm with their two small children and took over daily operations.

Zoey came along a few years after Mattie and just two years before her grandmother passed. She didn't remember her. Charlie had been a surprise five years later. By then Alex was almost eleven. No one expected it, and Charlie turned their world upside down. He was an energetic baby, walking by the time he was eight months old. He clung to Zoey and became her shadow. She didn't mind as she was a quiet, shy child, usually buried in books. Charlie got her to explore the outside world and kept her on her toes. He cried when she left for school and would be waiting for the bus when she came home. Her older siblings joked she was his second mother, and her mother was relieved to not have him underfoot all the time.

Zoey smiled, thinking about his beaming, little face gazing up at her. She guessed their being so close was the reason they both had planned to stay in the area. She wanted to go out to help pack and see if her mother would part with some photos of them as kids. She wanted history, something to share with her own children one day. Maybe some of Charlie's things. Even though the farm was being sold, they could carry their family into their own homes.

Hearing snowmobiles pull in, she looked out and saw Jake and Micah coming in from a call. She slipped on her coat and walked out, waving at Micah. They eased into camp on the

snowmobiles. Micah climbed off the snowmobile, grabbed his gear, and came over to her.

"Hey, Micah. My parents sold the farm. I need to go for dinner and to help them pack my next day off. Do you want to go? I know my mother would like to see you," Zoey asked, trying to not seem obligatory. She hoped he would, but didn't want to put pressure on the delicate bonds they'd begun to reform with each other.

Micah met her eyes, sensing her sadness. "Of course. Your family is my family."

Zoey was surprised he said that. "You still feel that way?"

"I will always feel that way, Z. I will be there. For them, and for you."

15

 he drive to the farm was painful and passed too quickly. They took Micah's truck in case they brought more than a little back with them. Zoey was anxious and didn't want to face the inevitable. As they pulled into the drive, the home already looked different. Her father had sold off most of the equipment, except what the new owners purchased with the farm. All of her mother's wind chimes and flower pots were gone. The house seemed less familiar, which should've made Zoey feel better but didn't. Micah, sensing her tension, reached out and took her hand, giving it a squeeze. She smiled appreciatively and stared out at the fields.

Her mother and father were waiting outside when they drove up. The plan was to pack as much as they could in the afternoon, then grill out for dinner since it was a sunny, clear day. Micah brought some veggie burgers and corn to throw on the grill. Zoey got out and hugged both of her parents, trying not to cry. Micah came around and shook her father's hand and

her mother embraced him for a long time. She placed her hand on his face with tears in her eyes. A connection to the son she'd lost. Micah signed his condolences about Charlie and she smiled through her tears. It would never not hurt.

The dogs ran off to a field with Micah's blessing. The rest of them went into the house with boxes. Much of the house was packed, leaving mainly the bedrooms. Her parents went to pack their room and anything left in Alex's room. This left Zoey's room, one she'd shared with Mattie until Mattie left for college... and Charlie's. Micah and Zoey started with hers, Micah teasing her about all the teenage girl stuff in there. Most of it would be donated to charity, but she packed up special books and mementos she wanted to keep. Her parents were moving to a tiny home with no storage, so everything needed to go elsewhere. Once they sorted her room, they moved to Charlie's.

Zoey knew she wanted to keep the snowboards and any pictures. She also wanted to pack a box of toys and things to give to her children one day. Most of the clothes they donated. She pulled all of his pictures down and put them in a book for safekeeping. Micah was eyeing one of the snowboards.

"You can have it, you know? Charlie would want you to," she offered.

He held it to his chest. "Thank you. I will hang it on my wall, maybe use it now and then."

She nodded, Charlie would love that. He was always so open and giving. Her parents had already taken anything from his room they wanted, so anything not going with Zoey was going to charity. They boxed up everything going to charity and set their boxes aside. The furniture was going to charity as well, which was just a bed, end table, and dresser. They pulled the

dresser out to check behind it and Zoey saw a glow-in-the-dark, plastic, ghost necklace she'd thought she'd lost when they were kids. She laughed. Charlie had obviously snagged it from her, then hid it, so he didn't get caught. He must've forgotten about it. She slipped it over her head and ran her fingers over the smooth, cartoony ghost. Micah cocked his head towards her, glancing at the necklace.

"Charlie stole this from me, like fifteen or sixteen years ago. I looked all over for it but thought I had lost it. Little shit," Zoey explained.

Micah laughed and came closer to look at it. "Nice. Very Charlie."

It was very Charlie and she'd treasure it. Finally, the room was sorted and they carried the boxes they were keeping down to his truck. Zoey walked through the house and picked a few more sentimental items, but in the end, most of it was just stuff. Her memories were untarnished. The thrift store was sending a truck out the next day to pick up all of the donated items, and her parents had hired movers to transport the heavy stuff to their new home. It was a cute home in town. A small yard, two bedrooms, and a basement that could be renovated if they needed more space. They were ready to spend more time with each other and less time working.

It was getting close to dinner time, so they all gathered outside at a picnic table. Zoey's mother had a variety of food items she wanted to use up and had made a quick potato salad, baked beans, chopped vegetables, and a cake. She insisted everyone had to eat it all, so they didn't have to move it. Her father threw their burgers and Micah's burgers on the grill, making sure they didn't touch. He cracked a beer and handed it to Micah. He offered one to Zoey, but she decided she was already going to be weepy and didn't need alcohol to amplify it, so she declined. He opened a beer for himself and sighed, looking around his parent's farm. Zoey's heart ached for him. He'd also been born and raised there, then raised his own children in the home as well. She went over and gave him a hug. He put his arm around her and smiled down at her.

"It's alright, Zoey. As long as I have your mother, and you kids, that's all I need."

"It's okay to be sad, Dad."

He gazed at her knowingly. "True, and I am. But it's time."

She squeezed him hard. Her parents had always been there whenever she needed them, sometimes it was easy to forget they were humans with their own hopes and dreams, too. Not just her parents. She let him go and went to sit down at the table. Micah and her mother were chatting through sign about the farm and the new house. Micah glanced at her and gave her a quick check with his eyes. Was she okay? She shook her head. She wasn't. He nodded and wrapped up the conversation with her mother.

Once they were done, he came over and put his hand out to Zoey. She took it and they walked down the long driveway. The same driveway she'd told him she didn't need him. When they got to the spot where she'd said those things, she stopped and pulled him to her, winding her arms around his waist. They held each other tightly, not wanting to let go. When she let go, she met his eyes.

"I am sorry."

"Water under the bridge," he assured her.

They walked back towards the house as the wind was starting to pick up. The dogs had run back towards the house, sensing the shift. Her mother was grabbing the food and bringing it into the house. They'd have to eat in there. Zoey and Micah gathered the remaining items and brought them in, her father following with burgers. In Montana, the weather could change on a dime. It'd been fairly balmy for November but the wind turned bitter in minutes. They ate around the table, trying to finish everything, however, it was too much. They ended up with a box of leftovers to take back to camp as well. Kyle would be thrilled. There was never a leftover he didn't like.

The following week was Thanksgiving, but both Micah and Zoey had to be at camp, holidays were usually busy. Her parents waved it off. They were fine moving into their new home and getting settled. Cooking a big meal was not in the plans and was a relief to not have to worry about. Zoey felt a weight off her conscience about that. She didn't want to abandon them on the first Thanksgiving without Charlie, but they'd never rebounded with volunteers from the big avalanche, so she couldn't leave the team high and dry, either. Her parents assured her it'd been years since they'd wanted to cook for Thanksgiving, they'd been doing it for the children. They agreed to make some new traditions.

Micah's family was about the same. They were getting older and didn't expect him to come back for the holidays. They'd been older when they adopted him and now were almost seventy. They'd talked about moving to Florida where Trent, his wife, and kids lived. Zoey could tell even though they loved him, Micah felt slighted by them having a birth son they tended to favor. They loved him and sent him letters and care packages, but once Trent had children of his own, they focused more in that

direction. If they moved to Florida, it'd be a nail in the coffin, so to say. He acted like it didn't bother him, but she could see it did at times when they spoke about them.

The evening drew to a close and Zoey knew it was time to go. Her parents had trucks coming in the morning and needed their rest. She wandered through the home by herself one last time, taking mental pictures to store away. No matter what, those times had happened, they'd always exist. She stopped in Charlie's room and put her hand on the ghost necklace. He was here, he existed. Nothing could change that. She came down the stairs and watched Micah conversing with her parents out by his truck. They were laughing and she thought she hadn't seen her mother this happy since before Charlie died. Her hands were flying as she interpreted to Zoey's father, Micah responding in kind. Zoey took one last mental picture and stored it with the others. She opened the door and the wind hit her. She drew her coat around her tightly. It must've dropped at least fifteen degrees over the last couple of hours.

Micah asked if she was ready to go and she nodded, coming out to the truck. She hugged each of her parents, trying not to let tears out. They had enough to deal with, without trying to make her feel better. Which they *would* do. She kissed each of them, then climbed into the truck. Chef and Trek jumped in, settling at her feet and on her lap. Micah got in and cranked up the heat. They backed out, waving at her parents. Once they got to the end of the driveway, she asked Micah to stop. She got out and gazed back at the house. Where she'd lived most of her life. She tried to take a mental picture but the tears began to fall, blurring her vision. It was so hard to let go. In her mind, her own children were going to run those fields one day.

Now, it'd just be stories she'd nostalgically tell them as they rolled their eyes.

She climbed back into the truck and continued to let the tears fall. She'd been strong for her parents, now she needed to allow herself to feel it. She fished a napkin out of the glove box and blew her nose. Her eyes stung as she cried. Micah reached out and brushed her hair off her shoulder. She glanced over through her hot tears.

"I am sorry Z. I know this is hard. You okay?"

She shook her head, then hung it down. He pulled her over towards him and slipped his arm around her. He kept it there on the ride home. When they got back to camp, they sat, letting the truck idle. He let the dogs out, then slid his arms around her. She laid her head against his shoulder and sighed a shaky breath. Now, this was her home completely. She loved all of her team and felt this was her place. She sat up and brushed off strands of her hair stuck to her face by her tears. Micah reached out, placing his fingers on her chin. She looked over at him, imagining how wretched she must look. He leaned forward and kissed her lightly. He drew back, meeting her eyes.

"You are not alone. We are family," he said sincerely.

She nodded and they climbed out. The wind was starting to whip, so they covered everything in the bed of the truck with a tarp to bring in in the morning. Except for the box of food which they barely got to the warming area before Kyle was already digging in it, eating with both hands. Jake and Callie were on the triage side and made their way over to see what the goods were. Zoey was glad they'd taken the food at her mother's insistence because within minutes it was pretty much gone. Kyle

snagged a few items, stashing them to take back to his cabin. He peered at her and could see she'd been crying.

"You alright, Zo?" he asked, concerned.

"Yeah, I think I will be," she replied and meant it. The reality had set in and her mind was beginning to accept it as the way things needed to be.

She was exhausted and excused herself to go to her cabin. Micah talked to Kyle for a second, then caught up to her outside her porch. She was brushing her boots off and glanced up. His eyes were intent as he watched her, biting his lip before asking.

"Hey, can I come in?"

His cheeks were ruddy and she couldn't tell if it was from the weather or feeling bashful.

She bobbed her head; she was tired but not ready to go to sleep yet. "Sure, I can make us tea."

They went in and he immediately went to get the fire going while she made tea. Chef and Trek crashed out in front of the fire like it was their home. Once the fire was blazing, Micah wandered around, admiring the bigger cabin. His eye caught the picture of Charlie and him on the shelf. He picked it up, grinning.

"I remember this day. It was the two of us and a couple of his other snowboard buddies. It was perfect out, clear, and the snow was so smooth and crisp. We were flying, you know? Charlie asked me about my intentions with you that day. He was serious, too. You were the most important person to him and he wanted to make sure I was on the up and up. I have to admit, he made me a little nervous, like if I answered wrong, he might try to beat my ass."

Zoey laughed at this. That sounded like Charlie, though she doubted Charlie would've been able to get an upper hand on Micah. She poured them each tea and came to the couch. Micah put the picture back and sat down next to her. They sipped tea, watching the fire. The wind was howling now. Zoey thought about what he'd said about Charlie demanding what his intentions were. That was back when they were living together. She didn't know for sure what his intentions were then, but she'd thought they'd be together forever. It'd all seemed so natural.

She turned to face Micah. "What did you say?"

He wrinkled his face in confusion. "I do not understand. Say about what?"

"When Charlie asked you what your intentions were, what did you say? I mean back then?"

He peered at her thoughtfully before responding. "My intentions have always been the same."

"Which means?"

"Which is this right here. You, me, the dogs. I told him I intended to grow old with you."

Zoey stared at him. She wasn't sure how to respond. Did he mean this now? They were coming back to each other, however, there was still so much they were repairing.

"Z, nothing has changed. My intentions are the same. If yours are."

She leaned in against him, then nodded. She made the "I love you" sign against his chest. Then she made the letter M against her heart. He made the letter Z against his. Their intentions were the same.

16

 oey's father surprised her mother with a trip to Guam for the winter holidays, in the hopes it'd take her mind off their first Christmas without Charlie. They left in mid-December, without plans to come back until the new year. Zoey knew she'd be busy anyway, but was still sad about not having the family together. Everything had changed and she kept her chin up, however, her heart hurt. Kyle put a string of solar lights on each cabin and around a nearby pine tree, giving the camp a sense of holiday magic. Zoey appreciated his efforts. He was alone as well, though his son, Christian, was supposed to come up for Christmas Eve. Christian was around the year before, but Zoey had been new then and didn't interact with him. He was nineteen and in college. He was a younger cookie-cutter version of Kyle. Tall, light brown hair, with piercing blue eyes.

Micah's parents made the official move to Florida to be near their son, Trent, and his family, putting their house in

Colorado on the market. Jake and Callie decided to visit both sets of parents the week before Christmas, and since she had duty on Christmas Eve, they'd stay at camp that night. Her family was Jewish, so she volunteered to cover Christmas Eve and morning, visiting her family during Chanukah. Zoey didn't have plans but appreciated the gesture. She thought she'd pack breakfast and hike to spend time at Charlie's rock.

She was out shoveling snow off the path from her cabin to triage when Jake ran over to her.

"Hey, Zo, you have a minute?" he asked breathlessly.

She leaned against her shovel, taking the moment to catch her breath. "Sure, what's up?"

"I need some woman advice, I guess. I know Callie and I've only been seeing each other for like six weeks but I just know she's the one. Like, I was with Megan before, however, it wasn't serious. We hooked up and hung out, but I never felt this way. With Callie, it's different. So, anyway, I'm thinking about asking her, you know?"

Zoey eyed him. "What, like to move in together?"

"No," he replied, redness creeping up his neck. "The other big thing."

Zoey's mouth hung open. To get married?

Jake's face turned bright red. "I know it's fast, but I just know. I mean, we don't need to get married right away and all, but I want to know she feels the same. I've always beat around the bush with girls, but this time is different."

"So, what are you asking me?"

"Well, as a woman, would this freak you out?"

Zoey thought about it. Her parents had met and married quickly, but that was a different time. None of her siblings had married and while she loved Micah, she didn't see marriage as a pressing necessity for love. Callie came from a strong family she was very close to, with a few siblings. Jake was also close to his parents and had a younger sister. It seemed fast, however, not necessarily rushed.

"You know, Jake, I'm not sure I'm the expert on this. I think you need to go with your gut. But give her an out. Like, if she says no, maybe it's just not right now, and don't feel like it's over. Maybe instead of a lot of pomp and circumstance, simply discuss it with her. If you want a ring, then have one, but maybe not the whole down on one knee, putting her on the spot type of situation."

Jake thought this over and broke out in a mischievous grin. "So, no horse-drawn carriage, or Christmas Eve proposal?"

Zoey laughed. "Well, no horse-drawn carriage, but she's Jewish, so I don't think Christmas Eve holds any special significance either way."

"True, true. Maybe now it will." He winked and gave her a big hug. "You're like the all-knowing sister of this place."

Zoey flushed at the compliment. Since Charlie died, she hadn't felt like anyone's sister, but Jake had given her that back. Kyle was like their father but in a fun way. Maybe more like an uncle or much older brother. The rest of them formed a ragtag family of sorts. She didn't know if she would've been able to get through Charlie's death without them. Jake gave her a tip of his imaginary hat and practically skipped off. Zoey was nervous about him taking such a big leap. Hopefully, Callie was at least kind in whatever she decided.

In making the supply list, Zoey threw in some holiday food items to be picked up. They were going to do a spread in the warming area on Christmas Eve. She made sure to have vegetarian options for Micah and a couple of treats for Chef and Trek. She tacked the list up for Kyle and Jake to take into town later that day. She double-checked medical supplies and walked the camp to check wood stacks. Micah was out working with the dogs and waved at her. She waved back and watched them for a few minutes. Chef was starting to slow down, the cold affecting his joints. Trek had become a strong lead, allowing Chef to take it easier. Trek lost his puppiness, filling out to mostly muscle. Micah talked about possibly adding another young rescue to the pack, so he could let Chef skip some calls. Chef still really loved the chase, though, and would want to go regardless until he just couldn't. His back right leg dragged a bit now and then, but as soon as they were called up, he was up and running.

That afternoon, Kyle and Jake headed out for hopefully the last supply run before the holidays. Micah brought the dogs in and was feeding them when a call came in. Zoey was in the triage area with Callie when the alert went off. She grabbed the radio and listened. A family had been fishing and the bank they were standing on collapsed, dumping them into the river. A couple of them made it out, but one person was stuck in the middle of the river, holding onto a mostly submerged rock. Zoey knew it'd be too long for Jake and Kyle to make it back and ran as fast as she could to Micah's cabin.

"Family in the river."

It was all she got out before they were running out the door with the dogs. She knew she needed to go and snagged a pack with carabiners and ropes. She grabbed blankets and hooked up the toboggan to the snowmobile. Micah was already on and she climbed in behind him. They sped over the hills

towards the river. The 911 call was able to give them coordinates and she let Micah know which way to go. By the time they were in visibility of the river, she could see a couple of people on the banks, shivering. They were waving and pointing to the river.

When they got closer, they could see the person on the rock was a child about nine or ten years old. The child was soaked and crying, clinging onto about a foot of exposed rock. Zoey jumped off the snowmobile and tossed blankets to the two, what seemed like older siblings, on the river's edge. Micah was hooking the rope with a carabiner to a tree on the bank. Zoey threw on a life vest and grabbed the end of the rope. They couldn't risk the child not being able to hold on to the rope and getting washed down the river. She needed Micah's strength on the bank to pull them back in. He appeared worried. Chef and Trek were running back and forth on the bank anxiously.

She wrapped the rope around her waist and clipped it with a carabiner. She eased herself into the freezing water which took her breath away. She met Micah's eyes, then nodded. The water was shoulder deep, so her feet were swept out from under her almost immediately. She'd need to swim. The water kept trying to take her downstream. Micah only gave her enough rope at a time to keep her as close as possible while she forced herself through the water to the rock. She was running out of steam but once she got to the rock and secured the child, Micah and the other people could drag them back. She began to feel her legs go numb and kicked as hard as she could. Her arms were rubbery. She reached the rock, then realized it would be safer to attach the child with the rope and hold onto them, so she unhooked herself and slid the rope with the carabiner around the child's waist. She pulled off her life vest and secured it over the child. She could see

they were slipping into shock and knew they needed to get the child warm as soon as possible.

Once the child was hooked securely, she waved her arm at Micah. He and the other family started pulling as hard as they could, fighting against their weight and the pressure of the water. Despite the vest, the child began to slip under, so Zoey held their head above the water. About ten feet from the riverbank a large branch came toward them and Zoey knew they couldn't get out of the way. It hit them hard, making her lose her grip. She felt the child slip away from her but knew they were safe since they were attached to the rope. She tried to break free of the branch but it was heavy and carried her downstream. She saw Micah's eyes grow big when he realized what was happening.

The child was towed to shore just as she was whisked away out of the line of sight. She was smashed against rocks and tried to get her bearings. Her temperature was dropping too low and she could feel herself slipping under. Trek and Chef were running down the bank after her, barking and trying to get to her. Chef jumped in and was at her side. She tried to reach him but her arms wouldn't move. She started to lose consciousness, not sure where she was anymore. Just as things went dark, she thought she felt hands grabbing her and dragging her out.

Charlie was sitting in front of her in a dark empty cabin. Zoey peered around, wondering how she got there and why Charlie was there with her. He was shaking his head. "That was stupid, Zo. You know rescuers need to keep themselves safe first. You can't put Mom through this. It will kill her."

All of a sudden, she was back in triage with Kyle staring down at her. She was stripped and covered in warm blankets. She

was going in and out and his eyes were scared. He shook her and moved his face down close to hers. His voice was desperate.

"Zoey, come on. Don't do this to us. Fuck, I should've been here. I got the call and we turned around, but it was too late. You were gone when I pulled you out. Please come back."

Zoey tried to get to the surface but kept getting dragged back down. She heard sirens in the distance and gave up trying. Charlie's face flashed in front of hers and she just wanted to hug him. He kept shaking his head. He stared hard at her and said the one word which opened the door back.

"Micah."

She gasped, attempting to catch her breath. Lights were around her and she didn't know where she was. Her head was pounding and she was shaking uncontrollably. Voices were yelling over her and she felt a hand grab her own. She tried to focus but everything was a blur and disorienting. The hand squeezed hers and she tried to squeeze it back but wasn't sure she did. She slipped back under, feeling closer to the surface this time.

She swam towards the surface and broke through. She could breathe but her lungs were on fire. She pried her eyes open and glanced around. She was in the hospital, hooked up to machines. She ached everywhere and wasn't sure what happened. She remembered being hit by the branch, then nothing else. A nurse peeked in. Seeing Zoey awake, she came in and smiled.

"You gave us a scare," she said, checking Zoey's vitals. "You have someone waiting to see you."

Was it Micah? Kyle peered in and saw her eyes open. He rushed over, hugging her as hard as he could. She was too weak to hug him back but placed her hand on his back. Her voice

sounded foreign when she spoke, weak and crackled. "What happened?"

"You broke the first rule of rescue. You can't save people by placing yourself in danger."

"It was a child, they were too weak... I wanted to make sure they got rescued. Did they?"

Kyle nodded but was fighting back tears. "They did. They're all okay. It was a little boy and his brothers. They shouldn't have been out there. Their parents didn't even know they were."

"A boy? I couldn't tell. They were so wet and frail. Who pulled me out?"

"I did. Jake and I heard the call and rushed back. We got there right after the kid had been hauled in. Micah let us know as he was getting the kid onto the shore. We took our snowmobile along the bank until we saw you. You were slipping under, Chef was keeping you up as best as he could. I was able to get off the snowmobile and into the water to get you out. We didn't think you'd make it, Zo."

She waved her hand weakly, dismissing the thought. He shook his head.

"It's not funny. What you did was stupid. You could have died. Imagine what that would've done to your parents."

Zoey flashed back to when she was under. "That's what Charlie told me."

Kyle stared at her, confused, when it dawned on him. He leaned back in his chair with the realization of what she was saying. If she saw Charlie when she was under... "Jesus, Zo."

"Where's Micah?" she asked, disappointed he wasn't there.

"He needed to go take care of the dogs. He'll be back. He's been here the whole time."

She was relieved to hear that. She was afraid he was angry at her for unhooking herself and taking off her life vest.

"Oh, he's pissed at you for sure," Kyle said, reading her mind. "But it was a kid and none of us can say we wouldn't have done the same thing to save him."

Kyle stayed with her for a bit until she dozed back off. It was evening when she woke up, and she was disoriented as she looked around. She felt arms around her and glanced up to see Micah laying in the bed with her. He peered down at her and brushed the hair out of her face, his eyes worried but relieved.

"Do not ever fucking do that again," he signed with one hand as he drew her in tight with his other.

17

---

he doctors agreed to discharge Zoey by Christmas Eve day if she promised to take it easy. It was a simple promise to keep since she was still too tired to do much. Micah was there to get her on the dot at her release time and had Trek and Chef with him. The hospital staff made her take a wheelchair to the exit, from there Micah was by her side. Chef watched concerned, while Trek was beside himself with joy. Micah helped her get up into the truck and Chef took his station by her side. Trek licked her face over and over until Micah pulled him away, laughing. Zoey was grateful for the attention, as she'd felt poked and prodded constantly in the hospital, but never quite like herself.

The sun was shining and the snow on the mountains was a glorious sight. The trip up the mountains was quiet and Zoey rested her head against the glass. She was healing and just needed to get her strength up. Micah reached over, touching her hand. She glanced at him and smiled. She'd asked all of them to

not tell her parents what happened. She wanted her mother to have a nice trip to Guam and not be worried about yet another child. She'd clean it up and let them know a gentler version once they were back home. The newspaper had done a blip about it but didn't get into the scary details. The boys, ages nine, thirteen, and fifteen were all good, lucky to have survived. They'd been standing on what looked like the bank of the river but was actually a snow shelf that collapsed under their weight, knocking them into the river and carrying the youngest down until he grabbed ahold of the rock.

Once they got to camp, Zoey dreaded facing everyone. She'd seen Kyle in the hospital but asked no one else to come by, so she could deal with everything. The camp was decorated with red bows and garland, along with the lights Kyle strung up. It was still daytime, so those weren't visible yet. They'd planned a big dinner that night and Zoey decided she needed until then to prepare herself mentally. Micah helped her to her cabin and she noticed a cot set up in the living room. She looked at him, raising her brows.

"I wanted to be here for you," he explained. "I do not want you to be alone."

"Oh. Well, you will not need a cot. I want you next to me," Zoey insisted.

He smiled. "I did not want to presume."

He folded up the cot and slid it under the bed. She sat on the couch, noticing someone had already fed the fire. It was raging. Chef refused to leave her side, moving wherever she did. She wanted a hot shower since she hadn't been able to take one during her stay at the hospital. She stood up and eased her way

to the bathroom, feeling Chef right behind her. She laughed and patted his head.

"I think I will definitely need to get another dog to train," Micah joked. "Chef is yours now."

Zoey looked down at Chef, who focused his sad eyes up at her. She was okay with that. She climbed into the shower and let it beat down on her. Kyle had set up power through the solar panels to heat the water and it was glorious. She stepped out and wrapped a towel around her, staring at Micah stoking the fire. His long, red hair was down and fell almost to his shoulder blades. It was wavy and a deep hue of auburn with golden strands. His shoulders were moving as he shifted logs around to keep them going. She admired the lines of his back and the strength of his hands. It stirred something in her, and she was reminded of what the doctor had said. Take it easy. She chuckled to herself and went to put on warm clothes. She found one of Micah's button-down flannel shirts, slipping it on over her long johns.

Micah made sandwiches while she was in the shower and hopped up to heat up some soup. He smiled at her in his shirt. They sat and ate, home-cooked food tasting so much better than the hospital's. She felt Chef lay on her feet and rubbed him with her feet, his fur tickling her toes. After they ate, she realized how tired she still was and went to lie in bed. Micah came and lay next to her as she dozed off, falling into a deeper sleep than she'd had in the hospital.

While she slept, she dreamed she was standing on the bank of the river. Instead of the child she saved on the rock, it was Charlie as a child. She screamed his name and peered around for a way to get to him, but she was standing barefoot in her

nightgown. She looked back at him and he climbed on the rock, turning from his child self to his adult self. He stretched his arms out, transforming into a blue heron, then flew away.

Zoey jolted awake and caught her breath. The sky was dark and she was alone. She sat up in bed, gazing around but no one was in the cabin. Panic gripped her stomach and she put her feet on the ground. Was she even awake now? Afraid to get out of bed, she held onto the edge, digging her fingers in. She took deep breaths to calm her nerves. All of a sudden, the door swung open and Chef and Trek came bounding in, Micah behind them with a bundle of wood. He saw her face and dropped the wood to come over to her.

"Are you okay? You were sleeping when I left."

"I just had a weird dream. About Charlie. Not bad necessarily, but it made me feel strange."

She told him about the dream and he watched intently. After she was finished, he put his arm around her and kissed her head.

"Sounds like Charlie is letting you know he is free. I mean, I do not want to make it seem like I am telling you what to believe, but that is what I understood."

Zoey thought about that. The dream wasn't scary. Intense, but not scary. She'd saved a child, so another mother wouldn't have to grieve. She couldn't save Charlie, but he was free now. Somewhere out there, a mother was looking at her child and counting her blessings, even though her own mother was facing a holiday without hers. The world didn't make sense, yet sometimes did at the same time. Zoey nodded and slipped on pants over her long johns and her boots. She'd have to think

more about all of it, but right now she was famished and there was a huge holiday meal waiting for her with her camp family.

Micah made sure she was good on her own and gave the dogs food to eat. Chef didn't want to leave her, but Micah insisted. They walked over to the tent and Zoey took a deep breath. They stepped into the warming area, which was transformed into a holiday wonderland. Lights twinkled all around them, and the long folding table they'd erected was covered end to end with food. Kyle saw her and made his way over, giving her a signature Kyle bear hug.

"I *can* say you look a lot better than the last time I saw you," he joked.

"That isn't saying much," Zoey responded.

Jake and Callie came over together and gave her a cup of very spiked punch. Jake gave her a playful shove on the shoulder.

"Taking on nature all by yourself, huh?" he teased, winking.

"Apparently." She sipped the punch and winced. It was almost pure alcohol.

Callie laughed and brought over some apple cider to water it down. "Bet you can guess who made the punch?"

They glanced at Kyle and snickered. He caught their eyes and raised his brows in question, which made them laugh more. The guys were already digging in, so Zoey picked up a plate and wandered around the table, selecting food she thought she could stomach. She sat on the couch and Micah joined her. Kyle sat on a decrepit recliner they'd added to the break area and Jake and Callie sat on a cot together. The food was warm and delicious, even if it lacked her mother's touch. Holiday classics played from the radio and the lights strung across the original tent walls gave

it a holiday wartime feel. They all ate multiple plates of food, then divided up the leftovers. Zoey was sleepy and stuffed, so she rested her head against Micah's shoulder. He laid his hand on her leg and leaned his head against hers. Kyle, a few sheets to the wind, started singing along with carols... terribly.

"Be glad you cannot hear this. Painful," Zoey signed to Micah, who laughed.

"Yeah, but I can still see it," he replied.

It was quite a sight to see. Kyle had stood up, holding one hand in the air with his drink in it, and was belting out pretty much the wrong words the whole time. Zoey started signing what Kyle was actually singing, making Micah laugh even harder. Jake and Callie watched in amusement, then Jake bent his head down and said something in Callie's ear. She bobbed her head and got up to put her coat on. Jake caught Zoey's eye, giving a little nod. He was going to do it. She crossed her fingers at him and smiled. Jake held the door open for Callie as they stepped out into the night. Kyle was really going for it, so Zoey decided it was time to head back to her cabin. She got up and kissed Kyle on the cheek. He winked and kept singing. Micah grabbed their leftovers and they headed back over.

Chef was at the door waiting for them.

Zoey turned on the radio and curled up on the couch with a blanket over her. Micah made them hot tea and joined her. She sang along quietly to the music and noticed him observing her. She took his hand and put it against her throat while she sang. He watched, mesmerized. He blushed, then bit his lip.

"Say your name," he requested.

"Zoey."

He softly said her name back. Almost a whisper. It was beautiful and tears sprung to her eyes. He said it again. Micah never spoke out loud, which Zoey respected, so this was a surprise.

"Say my name," he signed.

"Micah."

He nodded, so she said it again. A huge smile broke out across his face. He wrapped his arms around her and hugged her tightly. She reciprocated. This was a delicate moment between them, something just theirs.

He drew back, his eyes twinkling. "Beautiful."

A little while later, Micah ran the dogs out for the night and Zoey climbed into bed. He joined her and they lay intertwined, not needing anything else. She could see him in the cast of the light they left on at night. It was in the kitchen but gave a soft glow to the cabin. He was lying with his eyes closed, his free hand on his chest, breathing easy. It reminded her of when she was little, how when Charlie would get scared, he'd climb into her bed and snuggle under her covers with her. Except now it was Micah giving her comfort.

The next morning, they were up early with the dogs and watched the sunrise. Zoey wanted to go out to Charlie's rock but didn't have the strength. They drank coffee and let the dogs play in the snow. Her parents sent her a gift basket from Guam with fruit and local delicacies. She had a few gifts to give out but wasn't in a rush. It was nice to just hang out with the dogs and Micah. They went back in and ate some of the fruit with toast.

Micah went to his cabin and came back with a present for Zoey. It was a silver pawprint-shaped necklace. Inscribed on the back was Z, I love you, M. She put it on and handed him his present. It was a metal, hammered bracelet inscribed with the date he started with the team, the day they met. With it, she'd made a copy of the picture of Charlie and Micah in wallet size, so he could keep it with him. He slipped it into his wallet and smiled. She had Charlie's extra snowboards to give Jake and Kyle since Micah had one already. She kept her favorite for herself. She had an engraved stethoscope for Callie with her initials. Kyle, as usual, was out and about early, so she went out to meet him.

"Hey, I have something for you." She handed him the snowboard. "It was Charlie's."

Kyle turned it over and grinned. "That's awesome!"

He disappeared to his cabin and came back with something behind his back. He pulled it out and Zoey caught her breath. It was a hand-carved blue heron, standing with its wings folded behind its back. She stared at it and racked her brain, trying to figure out how he could've known. She didn't remember ever telling him about her dream and knew Micah wouldn't have without her permission.

"I've been carving this for weeks for you. I don't know why, but something told me you'd appreciate it."

Zoey was floored. He didn't know. Not directly. She clutched it to her chest and beamed. "Thank you, Kyle!"

"Now, don't go telling Micah and Jake. I only got them new folding shovels," he said, laughing.

Zoey couldn't wait to show Micah her gift. He was in the shower when she came in and she set it on the table. She heard the shower turn off and he came out with a towel wrapped around his waist. Their eyes met and she blushed. Damn. She focused on the dogs as he got dressed. He came out and poured a

cup of coffee. She glanced up, biting her lip. He chuckled knowingly.

"I know. This is not easy for me either," he told her.

They'd laid together and kissed but after what happened last time, they were trying to take it slower and truly be there for each other.

"Oh, look what Kyle made me!" she exclaimed as she got up and held up the blue heron.

His eyebrows raised, with the same thought she had. How? He came over and ran his hands across the smooth wood. Kyle was a true artist with his hands. Micah nodded with appreciation and set it back down.

"Impressive. He thinks the world of you, Z. He was beside himself when you were in the hospital."

This warmed Zoey's heart. She felt the same. Kyle would do anything for any of them, but they had a special bond. Zoey dug around in the cabinet and found a hammer and nails. She hung the bird on the wall by the front door. It made her think of Charlie and felt like he was watching over them.

Part of him always would be.

18

ake and Callie announced their engagement a few days after the holidays. No rush on the date but possibly the following fall. Neither was ready to think about leaving the team, but Callie was still an intern and needed to find paying work once her internship was up. The funding was there, just not for another medical person. Jake was full-time and didn't necessarily want to leave camp quite yet either. For now, they were engaged, which seemed to be enough for the two of them at the moment.

Calls were steady over the holidays, due to people taking their winter vacations and getting all kinds of new equipment as gifts they didn't know how to use. Lots of stitches, broken bones, and the like. While they had smaller avalanches, nothing had taken a life, thankfully. People seemed more cautious on that front since the big avalanche. But people eventually forget or think they're above it. Late winter and early spring typically brought the most risk when thaws started.

New Year's came and went without much thought, as the day before had been busy and everyone was spent. Zoey watched triage to give Callie a chance to be with Jake, and Micah kept her company. At midnight they did imaginary cheers and went back to what they were doing.

A few weeks later, Zoey realized it was coming up around the anniversary of when Micah joined the team. She thought back to the day she saw him get out of his truck and how struck she was by his beauty. That hadn't changed. He still stopped her in her tracks every day. Now, he looked more like a mountain man with his long hair and scruffy, thick beard. She teased him that one day he'd just disappear into the hills, never to be seen again. She liked his long hair but thought to herself, she'd never actually seen him without a beard. She was staring at him one morning over coffee, attempting to picture it when he caught her eye.

"What?"

"Oh, sorry. I was wondering what you looked like without a beard," she explained bashfully.

He rubbed his beard and shrugged. They finished coffee and he disappeared with the dogs for a while. She cleaned the cabin, listening to the forecast on the radio. They had a storm rolling in at the end of the week. She'd need to do a supply run before then and check wood stocks. Kyle was adding a couple more solar panels and was seeing if there was a way to install a washer and dryer. It was needed for triage and would save them having to drive to town to do laundry each week. Little by little, the camp was becoming more permanent, more self-sufficient. Kyle now had a battery house the panels fed into, and off that each cabin had power for lights and to heat the water. A washer

and dryer would take a lot of energy, however, he thought he could swing it.

About an hour later, she heard the door open and the dogs ran in. She glanced up and gasped. It was Micah, but he was clean-shaven and almost unrecognizable. He looked years younger and was absolutely stunning. He wasn't hiding a weak jaw or scars under the beard. He had a defined, strong jaw and without the beard, his eyes were like beacons. She stepped over, closing her open mouth before something flew in it. He blushed, which made him even more beautiful. She reached up and ran her hand along his now smooth face and shook her head in disbelief.

"Why were you hiding this under that beard? My god."

He laughed and leaned in to kiss her. It sent shivers down her spine. His lips were soft and accessible. She had to break away before she lost herself. She mouthed the word, "wow," staring at him. He was rugged and handsome with a beard, and a chiseled statue without. His eyes met hers and she found herself swimming in a sea of glass and stone. She tried to stop staring but couldn't.

"Okay, Z, you are making me feel vulnerable. Kyle let me borrow his razor. I suppose now I have to get one?"

"I mean, I like you both ways, but yeah." Zoey didn't try to hide her admiration.

"Now you know how I felt the first time I saw you," he replied.

She flushed at this. "So, now we are equal. You realize how hard it is going to be able to resist you now?"

"Then do not resist me," he said, meeting her eyes.

Damnit, if they didn't have a way to stop this speeding train, they'd end up somewhere they weren't trying to go to yet. She bit her lip and smiled. He nodded, chuckling.

"I know. Okay, well, I am going to go do something to keep my mind off this." He grabbed his pack and motioned to the dogs. Chef seemed torn, wanting to stay with Zoey.

"He can chill with me if it is okay," Zoey assured.

"Maybe I will take a ride into town to the animal shelter. I think Chef is ready to take a step back, and I want at least two dogs trained at all times."

"Do you want me to go?" Zoey asked.

"No, it is best if I go alone, so I can see how they respond to me. Dogs like you way too much and will be vying for your attention." He winked and kissed her, his lips supple and warm.

Damn.

"Seriously, you need to go before I rip your clothes off," Zoey teased.

He grinned, then headed towards the door. He stopped at the door, giving her one last look before he slipped out. Zoey went to triage with Chef in tow. She liked having him around because being older, he just laid down wherever they stopped. Ever since he jumped into the river to save her, he was happiest by her side. No one was either in triage or the warming area, so she sat and studied medical books while it was quiet. She saw Jake and Kyle pass the window, going out on patrol with a volunteer. Callie was at school, so this left Zoey alone at camp.

At that moment, fear gripped her and she felt a panic attack coming on. She'd never dealt with them before the day at the river, but now they were a regular occurrence. The room seemed to close in on her and she couldn't catch her breath. Her chest began to hurt, she felt like she was dying. Reminding herself she wasn't only helped a small amount because her brain liked to trick her into not trusting herself. She tried to take tiny breaths, but the more she thought about it, the worse it got. Chef came over whimpering and pawed her leg. She heard him but couldn't breathe. He did it again and again until she focused on him. She wrapped her arms around his neck and leaned into his fur. His presence was helping to redirect her brain and she felt the grip loosening. After what seemed like an hour, she was able to take a deep breath and leaned back. Chef watched her, concerned, and didn't move from her side. Once he saw she was okay, he laid at her feet,

"Thanks, Chef," she whispered. She hadn't told anyone about the attacks, feeling ashamed of herself.

She heard a truck rumble up the hill and peered out. Micah was back. He got out and let Trek out, who ran in circles around him. He reached into the truck and took out a young, raggedy-looking dog on a leash and set him down. The dog was freaked out by the new situation and trembled at his feet. Trek got low to the ground to play. The dog eyed him but didn't react. Zoey opened the door and walked out with Chef. Chef went over and sniffed the dog for a moment, then came back to Zoey.

"You found one!" She came over and let the dog smell her hand.

It looked like a mix of a small shepherd-type dog and a coyote. It sniffed her and peered up, its tail wagging slightly, unsure where it was or who they were.

"Yeah, he is about seven months old. Cannot see it now, but he is really bright and super energetic. He caught on quickly to hand motions and treats."

"Does he have a name?"

"I call him Spin, you will see why later."

They walked around camp letting Spin get used to the smells. They took him into triage where he promptly went to lift his leg and Micah scooted him out, giving the hand signal for outside. Spin finished his business and Micah rewarded him with a treat. Zoey's stomach grumbled and she asked Micah if he wanted lunch.

"In a bit. I am going to work with him for a little while and will meet you over there in about thirty minutes?"

"Sure, let me whip something up."

She knew he needed to set leadership with Spin, so the dog would know who was in charge and who to listen to. She'd limit interacting with him until Micah has established the pack. It was imperative in a high-stress situation, Spin knew who to follow and focus on.

She made tacos and was putting everything on the table when Micah came in. He guided Spin to the bed and placed him on it with the signal for bed. Spin laid down and didn't move, whether from being worn out from the excitement or because he was that good. Micah told him to stay and came to sit down. Chef sniffed Spin again, then laid down next to him. Trek was still amped and couldn't settle.

Zoey eyed Micah again as they ate. He caught her eye and shook his head.

"Stop!" He laughed. "Keep this up and I will have to cover my face."

"Sorry. You are just so handsome."

He grinned and stuffed a taco in his mouth, shaking his head and trying not to laugh.

The rest of the day, he worked with the dogs and made Chef join them. Until Spin was consistent, Chef would still need to lead the group with his expertise. Trek was strong but Chef still had the calmness they needed. Kyle and Jake came back and met Spin. Micah was right, he was focused. He wagged his tail at them but kept his eyes on Micah. He was a good pick and Micah was a good teacher.

Within a couple of weeks, Spin was already to the point Trek had been when Micah first came. He was smaller than Chef and Trek but was faster than both of them. He was easy to spot in the snow, too, his reddish-brown coat visible anywhere he was. Now that the pack was established, Micah had Zoey work with Spin on commands, so if ever needed, she could guide him. Not that she'd need to since they were really Micah's dogs. Well, except Chef, who was choosing her now.

She did get to see why he was called Spin. Whenever he would complete a task and get rewarded, he would spin around rapidly in circles with his hind legs tucked in, moving him around. It was hilarious. He was a funny, intelligent, little dog.

One night as they lay in bed, Zoey had an idea and clicked on the light next to the bed.

"You should train dogs. I mean, not just your own, but also teach people how to train rescue dogs."

Micah looked at her, considering it. "I guess I never thought about it because of my general dislike of people and anger issues. Well, and being deaf. Most people don't know ASL and I need to train them as much as the dogs. Maybe even more."

"You would be so good at it! I could help. Maybe talk to Kyle about setting up a training area here, that other rescuers can come to. Design a guide with universal hand signals?"

"Well, I mostly use ASL, but I see what you mean. Let me think about that. You would need to interpret and be my buffer with people, though," he replied, chuckling.

He was actually great with most people, but she knew certain people rubbed him the wrong way and he didn't have the tolerance for them. He preferred the company of dogs and a select few humans.

"Of course," she leaned up and kissed him.

The next day, she saw Micah talking to Kyle. They were out in the training field, pointing to different areas. Kyle was nodding and patted Micah on the back with a big grin. Micah headed over to the triage tent and practically burst through the door. He grabbed Zoey, giving her a huge hug.

"I talked to Kyle, he thinks we could get a grant if he turned this into a regional, or even national, dog training facility. The county had mentioned possibly selling the land to him and if he could get up the funding, we could expand. He wants to build another bunkhouse for dog trainers and add kennels. I think he was more excited about this than I was."

Zoey beamed. This was the most amped about anything she'd ever seen Micah. He sat down and started sketching out a design for the facility. He peered up at her, his eyes lit up.

"We could rescue more dogs, too. Have a whole team up here!" His excitement was contagious and Zoey found herself grinning stupidly.

"Hey, can I tell you something?" she asked, sitting down next to him.

"Of course," he directed his attention to her.

"Okay, so since I was rescued from the river, I have been having anxiety, um, panic attacks. I did not want to tell anyone

but they got bad. I had one a few weeks ago and Chef helped me get through it. Now, once they start, he immediately comes over and they are not lasting as long or getting as bad. I wanted you to know because I think these dogs can do more than find buried or missing people. They are so in tune with humans, they know when we are emotionally suffering."

He watched her for a minute, then reached out, placing his hand over hers. He looked at her sadly. "I wish you told me sooner. I am here for you, Z. I am glad Chef knew to help, but I am upset you were going through that alone. You know you can let me in."

"I did not tell you because I was embarrassed and scared. I am telling you now."

He nodded and glanced down at Chef, who was as always at her feet. He rubbed him on the head and looked back at Zoey. "He did what I could not at the river and now. From here on out, we are all a team. You, me, and the dogs. We need to stick together."

Zoey bit her lip, loving the man she was sitting next to and his compassionate heart. They both stared out at the training field and imagined a time when people and dogs worked together to save lives. To create lifelines.

Knowing Kyle, it would happen sooner than later.

19

 month later, Kyle had the framework for the bunkhouse and kennel combo. Each area would be able to house up to two people and their dogs. It was four units side by side. Word had already spread and the summer was filling up with training slots from all over the country. Experienced handlers that wanted to incorporate sign language into their training program. Plus, other non-SAR interested in incorporating hand signs into teaching their dogs. The program would pay for itself even though Kyle was working his grant writing magic. Micah's salary would be covered by the program, leaving more funds to add more staff for the rest of SAR. Kyle incorporated an office and additional kennels on one end for rescue dogs. It was just the basic frame but he and Micah took time to work on it every day they could.

With all of the work, Micah and Zoey weren't seeing each other as much and tried to get in time together on the fly. They always made time for breakfast, even if it meant getting up

early to do it before one of them was out the door. They tried to bring each other dinner as well, and the nights they were together, they happily wrapped up in each other. Spin rapidly caught on and Micah was already considering adding another dog. The cabin was getting too small for that, so he was holding off until he and Kyle at least got the office done at the training center.

Micah and Zoey continued to resist getting intimate while they took time to define and develop their relationship. They'd pretty much moved back in together. Jake and Callie moved in together into Zoey's original cabin, even though Callie still officially lived in town. Workload and exhaustion made it easier to stay focused on taking it a day at a time. There was very little downtime and everyone was on edge. Brandon started coming back a weekend a month, bringing the team back together. He and his fiancé had gotten married and were expecting a baby in the summer. They'd bought a home in town, not too far from Zoey's parents.

A storm rolled in one weekend Brandon was covering and Zoey was glad for the relief. It'd been going nonstop and she relished the idea of sitting in the cabin with her feet up and watching a bit of television. Kyle got the additional solar panels going and they were all able to add a few amenities to the cabins. She was hoping to find a good documentary to curl up with. Brandon was reading with his feet propped up and waved to her as she left. She paused and smiled back at him, she'd missed him being around.

Micah was at the table when she came in, much to her surprise. She guessed the storm must have halted work on the training center and secretly was glad it hit. They didn't get much

awake time together. She went over and brushed the hair away from his neck to kiss him. He seemed distracted and she noticed he had a letter folded under his hands. She came around to sit next to him.

"Hey." She tried to read his face, but it was like stone.

He glanced at her and sighed, his face relaxing and showing lines of stress around his mouth. He slid the letter towards her. Her stomach knotted.

"What is it?"

"Read it. It is from my birth mother."

Zoey raised her brows. She didn't know they were in contact.

"I had written the adoption agency and asked them to help me find my birth family after my adoptive parents moved to Florida. I did not think much would come from it, but I got this back today."

Zoey unfolded the letter and began reading.

Micah,

I received your letter a couple of weeks ago. I didn't know how to respond and honestly didn't think I would. It's a chapter of my life I'd closed a long time ago. I was young, twenty, when I found out I was pregnant with you. I was dating your father, we worked together. We talked about getting married but neither of us was ready for that at the time. I had you, really because my mother insisted I did. I wasn't ready to be a mother. My mother pretty much raised you the first year and a half. Around that time, she noticed you just weren't responding to sounds and were using your hands and grunting a lot to try and communicate.

We had you tested and found out you were completely deaf. My mother's health was declining, so I talked to your father and we agreed since we didn't have insurance and couldn't afford things, we'd put you up for adoption. A nice family adopted you and sent me letters and pictures for a while until I asked them to stop. A couple of years later, my mother passed away. Your father and I never could make it work and split around that time. He married a few years later and I think maybe had a child, or maybe she already had one. I don't know. His name was Chris Anglin. He passed a year or so ago, heart attack. We weren't in contact, but it's not a big town.

I wish I had better things to tell you. You were a sweet baby. I guess, you really lived more with my mother. My father was absent, so I can't tell you much about him. His last name was Burroughs, mine and my mother's Dallow. In case you want to know that information. I was their only child. I never had other children. I was never meant to be a mother.

I hope your life has been a good one and you find happiness. I'm not including a return address because all of this is something I left in the past. I put a picture in of your father and me. I guess before I was pregnant with you. Also, a picture of my mother holding you when you were eight months old from the note on the back. She loved you and was devastated when you left. This was if you were wanting some family history, now you have it. I wish you the best in your life.

I won't write again.

Best,

Abigail Dallow

Zoey closed the letter and stared at Micah. It was written as a factual account, with no love or emotion to it. That had to hurt. He met her eyes and put on his expressionless face.

"Micah, it is okay to be hurt by this. It was so cold."

He bobbed his head, then slid the pictures over to her. The first was of a young couple. A strapping, young guy with brown hair and gray eyes, leaning against a car with his arm around a slim, young girl with long red hair. They were laughing at someone off-camera. They appeared to be late teens without a care in the world. The next picture was a lady holding a redheaded baby, who was staring up at her, his eyes bright and focused. She didn't seem that old, but as Zoey thought about it, she might've been just in her mid to late forties. Not like her own grandma, who'd seemed ancient from pictures. So, his grandmother and father died young. Probably something to note for health history.

She smiled at the cute baby, then at Micah. "You were so adorable!"

"Yeah, surprise no one wanted me, right?" he responded, his face lined with bitterness.

Zoey met his eyes and could see decades of hurt and rejection in his eyes. She didn't know what that felt like but could read it all over his face. She reached out and took his hand. "You remember how after Charlie died, you told me you were my family? Well, that goes both ways. You are my family, too. I am sorry about your adoptive parents and your birth mother. They are missing out on the most amazing person I have ever met. It is their loss, however, I know it still hurts. Besides, I want you."

Micah tried to push away the sadness, but it was still present on his face. This would take some time. Zoey knew she needed to let him work through it no matter how long it took. Like he did for her when Charlie died. Sometimes things just couldn't be changed no matter how hard they tried. His birth mother didn't want a relationship. His adoptive parents loved him, but Trent and his children took precedence. They were blood. Zoey's heart ached for Micah and she came around behind him, wrapping her arms around his neck.

She kissed his ear and whispered, "I want you."

Whether he sensed what she said or just felt her breath on his ear, he leaned back against her shoulder. She straightened up, tapping him on the shoulder. He turned around and peered at her. She put her arms out wide to him. He smiled and got up to hug her. They embraced for a moment and when Zoey drew back to see if he was okay, she knew. Their lips met and the warmth flooded over both of them. She moved towards the bedroom, not wanting to break their lips apart.

As they separated to take their clothes off, they paused and admired each other. Micah ran his hand down the side of her breast. She stepped in and placed her hand on his back where it met his buttocks. There was no turning back now. They took time to touch each other and when it became too much to bear, Zoey pulled him into bed on top of her. He met her eyes as they came together and she swore she'd never let them be apart ever again. As she felt him join her, she knew it was worth fighting for. They moved together gently, honoring their connection. Zoey pressed herself to Micah, their skin becoming one. Micah placed his hand against her cheek as she tangled her fingers in his hair, wanting him as close as possible. They took their time, letting the sensations take over until both were spent and laid on each other breathless.

The wind howled outside and snow was coming in hard. Micah got up to check outside, sliding his long johns on. Zoey watched him dress, resisting the urge to reach out and touch him. She slipped on one of his shirts and her long john bottoms to go to the kitchen. Micah grabbed the snow shovel and brought it in along with any wood they'd stacked outside. He let the dogs run out for the last time before they were snowed in, then fed the fire. Zoey sautéed veggies and seared some marinated tofu. She took out pita, cheese, and homemade avocado dressing, setting them on the table.

By the time the food was ready, the dogs were back in front of the fire like they'd never moved. Zoey put the pictures and letter from the table on the shelf next to the picture of Micah and Charlie. Micah could decide if he wanted those out or tucked away somewhere to be dealt with when he was ready. Micah joined her and they took the food to the table. She made them each a lemonade, lit a candle at the table, and sat down to eat. He reached across the table at one point and squeezed her hand.

"Thank you."

She squeezed his hand back and met his eyes. "You are mine."

He blushed, his face transforming for a moment to that baby, so trusting. He did the sign he had for her, the Z over his heart. No more needed to be said. The rest of the evening, they sat on the couch by the fire and chatted about the training facility, excited about the possibilities. By summer, it'd be up and running, and they were already booked through fall. To their surprise, they had equal interest outside of SAR, from therapy dogs to training ADA service dogs. Micah was researching all of

it to see what they could take on. It allowed for more grants the more they did, and the hope was to buy the land from the county, so they could do whatever they needed to.

Micah put Zoey's feet in his lap and rubbed them as they talked. He let his hand wander up her calf mindlessly but it was very distracting. Zoey placed her hand over his as his hand moved up her leg. She bit her lip, grinning.

"Do not do that, unless you are going to put out," she teased.

His eyes lit up and he was up in a flash. "You do not have to ask me twice."

They barely made it back to the bedroom before they'd taken their clothes off. Zoey giggled as they fell into bed and tangled into each other.

A little while later, Micah had fallen asleep and she murmured, "You are the love of my life."

He didn't move, his chest rising and falling in deep sleep. She rested her head against his chest and listened to him breathing. She thought of the little baby who adored his grandma, who one day woke up with a different family and in the end, lost them all. She traced her finger through the soft red hair on his chest and sighed. People could be so unforgiving. So thoughtless.

She pushed down the guilt she felt for the day in the driveway. They'd worked through that. But her mind wandered to what it must've been like for him standing there with his heart on his sleeve, taking her vicious attack. His eyes had appeared like they had after he read the letter from his birth mother. Distant and hurt. Micah had learned at a young age to take people's abuse until he snapped.

He never snapped on Zoey. Even when she'd spit vitriol at the thing he couldn't change about himself. The one thing that had broken him time and time again, even though it was what made him strong. The thing he didn't know made him the most beautiful of all. In him, he held a different world. One he'd learn to cherish once he realized people's perceptions were their own and their weakness. Being deaf didn't make him any less than anyone else, even though at times the world told him otherwise. His anger was his shield, yet he put it down to take her abuse that day in the driveway. Zoey glanced up at his face while he slept peacefully.

Now it was her turn to fight for and protect him. No matter the cost.

20

A t the one year anniversary of Charlie's death, the team was hit with a tragedy of a different kind. The family of Maizie Bright, the girl killed in the avalanche, sued just about every agency on the mountain that day... including the Mountaintop SAR. Technically, they were being sued as part of the county since they fell under that umbrella. A sheriff came out to deliver the court papers and she and Kyle talked for a long time. The sheriff's department, the county, and anyone else connected had been served. The charges were neglect and delay of services, even though the team was on their way before the slide even hit the bottom. For Zoey, the lawsuit hit too close to home. Charlie had also lost his life that day, but none of her family would even think to sue the people who'd tried to save him.

The family included the guy on the snowmobile in the lawsuit, however, it was pretty clear they were going after those agencies involved in the rescue. Kyle showed Zoey the papers as

he sat down at the table in the warming area. She glanced over the legal jargon, attempting to understand what the bottom line was. She saw the snowmobile guy's name, Michael Andrews, and skimmed past. The family was suing for a total of over a million dollars. Her mouth fell open and she sat down next to Kyle.

"What does this mean for us?"

"I'm no lawyer, but I'm guessing it's not good. The sheriff thought the county would likely settle for a lot less. Regardless, it's a stain on us. We didn't do anything wrong, but it won't matter. Fucking hell." He ran his hand through his hair and shook his head in frustration.

Zoey had never seen Kyle so destitute. All this could affect both county funding and grants for the team. They were using county land, which the county now was hinting at wanting to sell in the long term because of what happened. This would likely push them to do so, in the hopes of recouping some of the losses. Kyle put his head in his hands, trying to read the document but got discouraged and threw them across the table just as Micah came in. Micah stared from Kyle to Zoey, reading the room.

"We are being sued by Maizie Bright's family," Zoey explained.

Micah walked over and picked up the papers and read through them. He shook his head in disbelief. "Why us?"

"It is not personal," Kyle answered. "They lost their kid, they want someone to pay."

It was probably true. No one had been prosecuted and this was the only way for them to get justice for their daughter. They were just taking it out on the wrong people. Kyle sighed, then stood up.

"I suppose I need to make some calls. Figure out what we need to do next."

He picked up the papers and headed out, leaving Micah and Zoey alone. They looked at each other, worried. Could this shut them down? Could they lose everything and have to stop moving forward with the training center? Zoey chewed her nails and considered their options. She could always get a job at the hospital. What about Micah? Would he have to leave to find work? The idea scared her, so she shook it away. They just needed to get more information. She glanced at the clock and remembered she was having dinner with her parents that evening. A sort of memorial for Charlie. Micah needed to stay on the mountain because it was their high call season; he couldn't be spared that night. They agreed to go into town for lunch the next day while they were in for a supply run.

Zoey went and changed clothes to meet her parents. She grabbed her bag and went to let Micah know she was leaving. He was in a deep discussion with Kyle, who now was almost as fluent in ASL as she was. They paused when she walked up, watching her approach. They knew this day was tough on her, and dragging her into the lawsuit wasn't something she needed to deal with. Kyle gave her a card to give to her parents, then hugged her.

"I'm sorry, Zo, I shouldn't have told you yet. You have enough on your mind."

"No, this affects all of us and I need to know. It sucks, but I'm glad you told me."

"Give your parents my love," Kyle said as he left to fill Jake in on everything.

Micah gave her a half-smile. "I wish I could go with you. Please let your parents know I am thinking of them."

"I will. You need to be here. We cannot both be gone in the evening. We will have a nice lunch tomorrow, okay?"

He nodded, then kissed her gently. "You know, I am thinking about Charlie. Was going to take the dogs over to his rock here in a bit. I know today is shit."

"Thanks, Micah."

Zoey went to her car and peered out at the mountains. At this time last year.... no, she wouldn't go there. It was too painful. She looked back at Micah and gave him the *I love you* sign. He made it back and watched as she drove away. The drive into town was quiet, giving her time to reflect. She didn't blame Maizie's family. They needed to feel like someone paid for their daughter's death. She wanted someone to pay for Charlie's but knew the one person who could, never would. Instead, she packed it into a box in her heart and pushed it into a corner.

Her parents' cozy house was lit up and the inner door was open, just the storm door between them and the outside world. Zoey walked right in and found her parents in the living room. It wasn't the farmhouse, but they'd made it feel like home. Pictures of their four children were hung above the mantle. All were school pictures, so they looked the same age in them. Alex always appeared almost professional in his school pictures. Mattie was the fashionista. Charlie went out of his way to look like he was cracking a joke in his, his eyes twinkling with mischief. Zoey just seemed like she'd never had a picture taken before in her life, her expression a cross between confusion and impatience.

Zoey handed her mother the card from Kyle and sat down. "Micah wanted to be here but needs to be there for any calls. Have you heard about the lawsuit?"

Her father raised his brows and shook his head slowly.

"Maizie Bright's family is suing SAR. Well, really the county, but because of us."

Her parents sat motionless. Their child had been buried that day, too. Her father cleared his throat. "I can't judge them, or their reasons, however, I hope the courts see you weren't at fault. I'm sorry, Zo, I'm sure you didn't need this on today of all days."

"It won't bring her back," her mother said softly, setting down the card from Kyle.

Ultimately, that's what it came down to. Maizie's parents were hurting and they couldn't bring her back, so they were trying to do something. Anything. Zoey's heart hurt for them. They'd give up everything to have her back like her family would for Charlie. She nodded at her mother and bit her lip. Time didn't make it better, it just made it farther away, like a boat unmanned and unanchored, slipping away from shore.

They moved into the kitchen and ate Charlie's favorite meal. Spaghetti and meatballs. Zoey skipped the meatballs and loaded up on garlic bread. When they were done, her father poured them each a glass of port and they made a toast to Charlie. He'd always be part of them, part of their lives. Death could not take that away. They retired to the living room and listened to jazz records her father collected. As it got late, Zoey knew she needed to head back to the mountain. She didn't like driving up the mountain too late as the roads would begin to ice over. She kissed each of her parents and headed out, taking a

plate of food for Micah her mother packed, which she knew he'd appreciate.

The roads were beginning to get slick, so she took her time going up the mountain. It was eerie and she felt like the only person on earth out there. She was relieved to see the lights from camp ahead, feeling the tension release from her shoulders. Camp was still but she saw lights shining in three of the cabins, a comforting draw. She drove in and treaded carefully to her cabin door. She pushed open the door to three brown noses and wagging tails. Micah was reading on the couch and jumped up.

"I was getting worried. It is getting icy out there," he said, giving her a hug.

"My mother sent you food," she replied, pushing the plate into his hands.

He grinned and peeled off the foil. Good, they'd remembered not to add the meatballs. He sat at the table and dug in. The dogs looked on hopefully, so Zoey gave them each a dog biscuit from the cabinet. She poured Micah and herself each a glass of wine to settle her nerves and clicked on the radio. She turned it up when she realized it was Big Band music. Her father always had all types of music playing when she was a child, but her favorite was Big Band. She bobbed her head and tapped her foot along to the upbeat song. Micah finished eating and sat back, watching her. He stood up and put his hand out.

"What?" Zoey asked, confused.

"Dance," he responded.

She took his hand and stood up. He drew her close and they moved in time to the music. His moves were impeccable and he never lost the timing of the music. It made her breathless and she smiled at him.

"You are full of surprises." She knew he felt the vibrations of music but had no idea he could dance like that.

A slower song came on and they leaned against each other, swaying gently. His muscular body both supported and carried hers. She let her hips move in sync with his and pressed her face to his neck, which smelled like cedar and snow. As the song ended, she glanced at him. Now she didn't know what she'd do without him. He was her other part. He met her eyes and smiled slightly. He knew.

The next day, the full team was there, so they were able to slip away for an extra long supply run. They left the dogs in the cabin and drove to town. They hadn't had much time alone and stopped for lunch after picking up supplies. They went into an Indian restaurant downtown and ate. After they finished, Micah needed to run to a pet supply store across the street and Zoey wanted to pop into the pharmacy for higher-quality bandages than they were getting in their orders.

She was checking out at the register when the sight of someone familiar made her stomach drop. She couldn't be sure, so she waited until she was outside to get a better look. On the sidewalk, a store down, stood Michael Andrews, the guy who'd started the avalanche. He was obviously drunk and acting belligerent. Zoey didn't know what came over her, but she walked over to him.

"Didn't you learn anything? You killed a bunch of people last year because you were drunk and triggered an avalanche. Or do you even remember?" Her voice was hard, even though she thought she might cry.

He stared at her blankly, then shrugged. "Who the fuck are you?"

"I'm the sister of one of the people you killed." She didn't know what she expected him to say or do with that information, however, she didn't expect what came next.

He shoved her to the ground and laughed as he spit the words, "Shut up, you stupid bitch."

He hovered over her like he might hit her when Micah came like a flash out of nowhere and threw him against the concrete wall. The guy's face didn't even register what happened before Micah was punching him repeatedly in the face. Micah was going to kill him! Zoey jumped up and grabbed Micah by the shoulder. He turned to her but it wasn't the Micah she knew. He was being driven by blind rage. His eyes had a veil over them as he spun back to keep hitting the guy. A couple of bystanders dragged him off and were holding him back when the police pulled up. Michael Andrews was lying unconscious on the ground in a pool of his own blood.

The police were trying to talk to Micah as an ambulance drove up. Zoey realized the police weren't aware he was deaf... and Micah wasn't trying to let them know, his eyes still locked on Michael Andrews. He was staring with murder in his eyes. Zoey ran over to the police, who put their hands up to block her.

"He's deaf!" she yelled at them.

One police officer faced her, attempting to understand what she was saying. "The guy on the ground?" he asked, staring from her to Michael Andrews.

"No, Micah. The guy you're holding."

The police officer peered at Micah and shook his head. "This guy is deaf? Shit. We need to read him his rights."

Zoey felt faint. If they were reading him his rights, they were arresting him. In all fairness, they probably would, seeing as

Michael Andrews was unresponsive, saturated in blood. The police officer went to his car and withdrew a copy of the Miranda Rights from the glovebox, handing them to Micah, who barely noticed. Zoey asked if she could interpret for him, saying she was his co-worker. The police officer nodded, then told her what Micah was facing.

Zoey walked over to Micah and made him look at her. "They are arresting you. Those are your rights on the card. They are taking you to jail, for charges of assault and battery, most likely." She glanced over and saw the EMTs loading Michael Andrews onto the gurney. He was not responding to their tests. She turned back to Micah, who was sitting completely still. "Micah, do you understand?"

He met her eyes hard, then cocked his head defiantly. "Yes. I understand."

The police took this as him understanding his rights and went to handcuff Micah, his hands behind his back. Zoey put her hand out to stop them.

"If you handcuff him, he can't communicate. Do you have an interpreter?" She was winging it, not knowing what the law allowed for. She kept her voice even and confident, hoping that was enough.

The police officer stood frozen, considering his options. He shook his head.

"I can interpret. Is that okay?" she asked, hoping they let her. If not, Micah was screwed. He'd be surrounded by people deciding his fate, with no way to communicate anything.

"Okay, but you have to follow in your car back to the station. I'm required to handcuff him for the ride, it's policy. I can unhandcuff him once we get to the station."

Zoey nodded and relayed this all to Micah, who simply stuck his hands out to be cuffed. They cuffed his hands in front of him, so he could still use them to gesture. He met her eyes for a second and she briefly saw behind the veil. He was worried. Angry, but worried. They put him in the back of the car and left. Zoey watched as they drove off, her mind racing with how to save Micah.

The ambulance with Michael Andrews inside was driving off in the other direction towards the hospital, sirens blaring. Zoey ran to Micah's truck, grateful he had a spare key in the wheel well. She drove to the station and realized she needed backup. This was bigger than her or Micah. She dialed Kyle's number, her hands shaking with panic. She was relieved when he picked up on the first ring.

"Hey, Zo, what's up?"

Zoey took a deep breath, thinking how to explain what happened on their run into town. "Kyle, I need you now. Something happened. Micah's been arrested and is being taken to the police station."

"Fuck. On my way."

21

he police station was crowded and loud, causing Zoey to jump at every turn. She went to the front desk and let them know she was a deaf interpreter, figuring it would get her to where she needed to go quicker than saying she was Micah's girlfriend. A fact she hoped to keep under wraps, so they took her seriously. She was led back to a room with about four desks and the name placards were all detectives. This seemed odd, but she didn't know exactly how this would be handled. She sat in a chair against the wall, closed her eyes, and waited for guidance.

A little while later, she could hear Kyle's voice and went to see where he was. He was trying to explain who he was to the officer at the front, but she just stared at him dead-eyed. Zoey didn't want to risk getting sent away, so she stayed back. When Kyle turned, he caught her eye. He nodded, he was aware they'd serve Micah best if they came at this from different angles, separately.

A plainclothes police officer led Micah into the four desk room and sat him down at a chair in front of one of the desks. The officer saw her sitting on the wall and motioned to her.

"Are you the interpreter?"

"Yes. Well, no. I mean, I *can* interpret. I'm Micah's co-worker. I was there when..." She didn't want to give too much information, but didn't want to risk jeopardizing the situation either.

"Oh?" He looked at the papers he'd placed on his desk, flipping through them. "I'm Detective Gerald Frey. Please have a seat."

Zoey sat down next to Micah with her hands in her lap. Her palms were starting to sweat and her heart raced in her chest. A quick glance at Micah showed he'd calmed down as he sat stone-faced. He glanced at her and gave a small nod. He was attempting to let her know he was okay, but it didn't matter. Zoey was scared. Detective Frey finished going through the report, then peered up at both of them.

"Let me make sure I understand this. You were both downtown in front of the pharmacy together? And you are co-workers? I'm sorry I didn't catch your name."

"Zoey Sanders. Yes, we work up at Mountaintop Search and Rescue. I'm lead medical, and Micah is our dog trainer and handler. We were downtown and he was at the pet store. I was at the pharmacy."

"Alright, so witnesses say there was a woman that matches your description who was knocked to the ground by the victim, Michael Andrews. Was that you?"

Zoey nodded. "Yes. Mr. Andrews shoved me to the ground and called me a bitch."

"Why would he do that?"

Zoey paused. "Detective Frey, I want to be helpful, however, I'm wondering if I need a lawyer?"

"That's up to you. I'm just trying to see what led up to the incident." He met her eyes and smiled. "The report is mainly witnesses, I need to see what direction this took."

Zoey was uncomfortable and too unfamiliar with anything legal to say anything else. She didn't want to risk Micah's safety. She turned to Micah.

"Do you have a lawyer? I do not want to get in too deep here."

Micah raised his hands to sign back to her but he was still cuffed. She knew she'd understand, but the police didn't know that. She put her hand over his to stop him.

"Why is he still cuffed? I was told he'd be uncuffed once he got here, so he could communicate."

Detective Frey seemed embarrassed. He fumbled through keys on his desk until he found the right one and uncuffed Micah. Micah raised one slight eyebrow at Zoey. He rubbed his wrists and answered her previous question.

"No, I do not have a lawyer. You can answer questions about what happened up until, well, you know. I am requesting a lawyer, one who knows ASL."

"Micah is requesting a lawyer fluent in ASL. He does not have one. Mr. Andrews pushed me down because he was drunk, and I asked him why he hadn't learned his lesson."

"Learned his lesson? About what?" Detective Frey asked, meeting her eyes.

"About being drunk and starting the avalanche that killed my brother."

Detective Frey sat back and stared hard at her. "Sanders. Charles Sanders was your brother?"

Zoey sighed, clasping her hands together. "He is my brother."

"I'm sorry about your brother. I remember his name from the investigation of Mr. Andrews. Okay, so you confronted Mr. Andrews and his response was to shove you to the ground and call you a bitch. Did he threaten you?"

"Not verbally, but he came over and was standing above me while I was on the ground."

"At that time, Mr. Byrne, uh... Micah, came out of the pet store?"

"I guess so. All I know is, I was knocked to the ground and Micah got Mr. Andrews away from me."

Detective Frey leaned forward and jotted down some notes. "Look, I know you can interpret but considering you're part of this case, we need to get a court-approved, certified interpreter in here. We have a list somewhere of people we can call. I doubt there is an attorney who knows ASL but if we get an interpreter in, they'll be able to help with that as well. Hold on a sec."

He picked up the phone, hitting a couple of numbers. He spoke briefly to the person on the other end and hung up.

"Zoey, you won't need an attorney as you are not being charged with anything. We do need a full statement from you on what transpired. I've asked for an interpreter to be brought in and a public defender for Micah. Listen, I'm not your enemy. Clearly, this isn't a simple case of assault and battery. However, I pulled Micah's record and it's not the first time he's assaulted someone. Or the second. That's not good. He may have been trying to defend you, but the courts are going to look at everything. Let's get him representation, then go from there. He'll likely go before a judge by the end of the day, maybe tomorrow if we can't get an interpreter sooner."

Zoey sat awkwardly. What was she supposed to do? Detective Frey handed her his card. She slipped it into her bag and looked at him. "What now?"

"Now, we need your statement. You can fill Micah in on anything I've told you. I wouldn't discuss the incident, however. Wait for a lawyer. I need to go grab some forms real quick."

He got up and left the two of them at the desk. Zoey waited until they were alone, turning to face Micah. He watched her for a moment, then winced in shame.

"Z, I am sorry. When I saw you on the ground and him standing over you, I flipped out. I wanted to kill him. I could not stop myself."

"Well, do *not* tell people that," Zoey responded and touched his hand. "I am sure you picked up on most of this, but they are getting you a public defender and an interpreter. They will not let me because I was part of the incident, and it has to be court-approved and certified, I guess. I do not know the extent of the law or how it works. They are saying you might go in front of a judge today if they can get an interpreter here. If not, then tomorrow. I will figure out bail. Kyle is here. He was making a stink in the lobby."

Micah chuckled at this. Kyle had no filter. He sat forward towards her, shoulders hunched, and met her eyes, his sage eyes sincere and apologetic. "Zoey, I know this is bad. Not sure how bad, but probably a lot. Do you know, did he survive? Michael Andrews?"

She shrugged because she didn't. Part of her wished he hadn't, but for Micah's sake, he needed to. "They are still saying assault and battery, so I am guessing so far he has."

Micah took her hands in his. They were warm but cut up and his knuckles were raw. He stared down at them and gave her hands a squeeze. "Now you know."

"I know what? I mean, I saw you break the guy's nose last year. You told me you lost your last job because you hit someone. Each time, something triggered it."

"But I took it too far. I am the avalanche. I cannot stop it once it starts."

"Yes, you can. You have not, but you *can*. You just need a reason to diffuse it. To turn it off. You have to want to." Zoey knew both sides of him. He wasn't a monster and he wasn't a threat. Something would be his trigger point, but he had the ability to stop it.

"Thanks, Z. You have way too much faith in me." He put her fingers to his mouth and kissed them.

Detective Frey came back a few minutes later and sat down. "Alright, so good news, a certified interpreter from the college is on their way. The other option was using a VRS, a video relay service if we couldn't find one. The public defender's office is also sending someone over. Don't take this the wrong way, but Micah's being deaf may help speed this along. Zoey, you'll need to go out front and meet with Officer Christie to give your statement. Micah is going to a holding cell until the interpreter and public defender get here, so he can meet with them. Can you interpret for me?"

Zoey told Micah everything the detective said and he nodded he understood. An officer came to the door and

motioned to Zoey for her statement. Zoey stood up, not wanting to leave Micah's side. Detective Frey cleared his throat.

"Leave a phone number with Officer Christie, we'll let you know when he goes before the judge. You have my card if you have any questions. Again, I'm sorry about your brother. That was a real tragedy and I know your family suffered greatly because of it."

Zoey smiled the fake smile one gives when given condolences. She peered at Micah who looked back at her sadly, knowing they might now see each other again for a bit.

He quickly signed, "I am sorry. I love you."

She gave back the *I love you* sign low and to her side, so only he could see it.

She followed the officer to a desk and gave her statement, careful to only state facts and not say anything about seeing Micah beating the bloody hell out of Michael Andrews. She focused on Michael Andrews assaulting her. When she was done, she stepped back into the lobby and saw Kyle sitting, waiting with his elbows on his knees and his hands clenched together in front of him. He saw her and jumped up, wrapping her in a firm hug.

"Zoey! What the hell is going on?"

"Let's go somewhere and I'll fill you in. I don't want to say anything here."

They both glanced around at the watchful eyes of the police department and stepped outside into the bright sunlight. They walked a few blocks and bought coffee from a cart, sitting at some unoccupied benches in a nearby park. Zoey took a deep breath, trying to process everything that happened. She filled Kyle in on the incident and what the detective told her. Kyle sat

quietly, taking it all in. He waited for her to finish and leaned forward, shaking his head as he let out a long, deep breath.

"We need a plan. First, the county *will* fire him, regardless. I had to fudge things to get him hired in the first place, and those facts will come out. I didn't mention his record. Now that's going to be out there. They'll drop him so fast to distance themselves from the situation. I might be able to hire him as an independent contractor, however, even that is going to be a hard sell, and not likely if this goes badly. If we owned the land, the training facility could just be privatized and he could run that, but I can't afford to buy the land yet. Anyway, that's getting ahead of ourselves. Today. So, if he goes in front of a judge, he can probably make bail. I have some money saved. I'm sure we can drum it up. With the pending lawsuit, the county won't want him on their property. Do you know if he has anywhere he can stay?"

Zoey thought about it and the only place she could think of was to ask her parents. She wouldn't even know where to begin with asking them, however, it was their only option. She'd swing by after she met with Kyle. They'd warned her about Micah's temper, she didn't want this to come back to haunt her. Hopefully, they'd understand.

"Maybe. I'll know shortly. Do you think if we could buy the land and get the training center built, he'd still be able to run that?"

"I can't see why not, that has nothing to do with the county. I mean, right now, they own the land, but they want to sell it because of the whole Maizie Bright lawsuit. If it's private land, they'd have no say. That being said, his days with SAR are pretty much over since that is strictly under them. He's had at

least two different incidents with two different SARs, and no one will want to touch him. He was lucky to get away with breaking the guy's nose last time, only because the guy was waving the gun around in front of the police."

"Michael Andrews."

"Who's that?" Kyle asked, confused.

"The guy whose nose he broke. The guy he tried to kill today. The guy who murdered my brother and four other people," Zoey responded bitterly.

Kyle reached across and took her hand, making her look him in the eye. His eyes held a determination she hadn't seen before. He set his mouth in a grim line and squeezed her hand.

"Oh yeah. Fuck that guy."

22

ichael Andrews survived. He came to consciousness with absolutely no recollection of what happened and a blood alcohol level so high, it was astounding he was ever upright, to begin with. With this information, and the fact that witnesses observed him knock Zoey to the ground prior to Micah hitting him, allowed the charges to be dropped to misdemeanor assault and battery. The judge dropped it further to just misdemeanor battery because since Michael Andrews couldn't remember anything from being so inebriated, they couldn't prove assault. He was cleared by doctors with some stitches, contusions, and black eyes, but surprisingly nothing else. Perhaps, like in drunk driving accidents where the drunk walks away unscathed, being falling down drunk and getting beaten prevents them from sustaining serious injury.

Zoey received the call the morning after Micah's arrest to come pick him up. No bail needed. He was sentenced to probation, a five hundred dollar fine, and anger management

classes. The classes were offered in book form since he was deaf. As long as he completed the course work, he completed that part of his sentence. Zoey hung up the phone and sighed in relief, her hands still shaking from fear. This could've gone so much worse. She ran to let Kyle know and he whistled as he clapped his hands together.

"That's great news! Unfortunately, though, it doesn't change the county's stance on employing Micah, so he's being terminated. He can get his things, but they don't want him on the property as an employee. I'm sorry."

Zoey understood. Regardless, Micah had a history of blowing up and now that it was out in the open, there was no hiding it. The county was doing what any government employer would do in the same situation. He was a risk. They'd have to figure out what the next step was for Micah.

"I talked to my dad briefly last night. I didn't get into details but let them know our situation. They said Micah can stay in their extra room until we get this sorted. I'll keep the cabin, however, I will stay at my parents' sometimes, too. Nights Brandon or Callie can cover. Jake told me he could work with the dogs if they can stay up here. I know Micah will want a say in that, but we can't go without the dogs or a handler."

Kyle rubbed his chin, then bobbed his head. They were in their highest season for the next month with spring thaws and fresh snow. They needed the dogs. If they could just get enough money to get even the tract of land the training facility was on, they could make it work. Grants for the whole camp had been applied for, but grants move slowly and time wasn't on their side.

"I can put in a few calls to other SAR and let them know we're pretty much without a handler. Jake can run the dogs,

however, Micah has a second sense about these things. The dogs also trust him with their lives. Unfortunately, I feel like the dogs would be leading Jake, not the other way around."

"Alright, well I'm leaving to go pick Micah up from the police station now. Is he allowed back here to wrap things up, or do we need to go straight to my parents' house?"

"No, he's fine to come back here. He just can't work or live here. If he ends up staying the night every now and then, I'll turn a blind eye. We'll figure this out, Zo. I have a couple of thousand dollars saved. The training tract is about eight thousand. The whole camp is about twenty-four thousand. I think if we can come up with around ten thousand, we could put that down and finance the rest. I don't have any collateral, but maybe all of our vehicles combined would be enough."

He chuckled. None of them had much to offer. Zoey had a little over two thousand in her account. Together she and Kyle had almost four thousand. Micah had some saved, but having to pay court costs and his fines would probably drain most of that. Now that he was out of work, he needed to hold onto what he could. Jake and Callie were trying to start their lives, so she didn't want to ask them. If she could just come up with another six thousand, they'd be able to buy the training tract at a minimum or put down money on the whole camp land. Right now, she just needed to go get Micah. She ran the dogs out before she left and locked them in the cabin. She could see they were confused and stressed. They needed to see Micah.

When she drove up to the police station, he was already outside with a stack of papers in his hand. He was standing off to the side, leaning against the wall with his head down, reading the papers. His hair was loose and hung down in front of him like a

shield. He saw her pull in and stood straight up, a mixture of exhaustion and relief on his face. He climbed into the passenger side and glanced at her, trying to read her face.

"Hey. The dogs missed you last night." Zoey met his eyes.

"And you?" he asked.

"Of course, I did. I did not sleep much."

"Me either," he agreed.

"The county terminated you. You are not allowed to stay at camp anymore, however, my parents said you could stay in their spare room while we figure out what to do. We can go to camp to get your things and see the dogs. My parent's place is too small for all of them but we can rotate one at a time. Jake and I can work with them on SAR until we-"

She trailed off. Until they what? That was the real question. Everything was up in the air. If they could get the land it would change everything, but that didn't seem possible yet. Micah reached out and took her hand.

"We will figure it out," he signed with the other.

They drove back to camp to see the dogs and sort things for the time being. Kyle needed to have an official meeting with Micah, per the county, to terminate him and lay out expectations. Once they got there, Kyle was out on patrol, so they slipped into the cabin to be alone. As soon as the dogs heard Micah, they were beside themselves with joy, climbing over each other to lick him and sniff the different smells on him. He sat down on the floor with them and rubbed all of them. His face relaxed around the dogs and for a moment things didn't seem so bleak. Zoey made them breakfast while Micah gathered his things. They took a shower together and tried to forget

everything for a little while. Micah was relieved to get in clean clothes and wash the blood off of him.

Shortly after, a knock came at the door. It was Kyle to have their official meeting per the county's requirements. He looked grim. Micah nodded and they walked out together. Zoey watched them head off, biting back tears. The county was within its rights, but they were hurting the whole SAR team by getting rid of Micah.

When Micah returned, he added his termination letter to the stack of papers from the court. Jake came by and went over some training with Micah for the dogs. They'd worked together over the last year and Jake had a good handle on commands and guidance. He didn't have Micah's presence, though, and the dogs still looked to Micah for confirmation. Trek was the strongest of the three dogs now, so he'd stay back the majority of the time. Micah would bring him only on their lighter weekdays or stay over to make sure Trek didn't feel abandoned. Chef was slowing down, but was mostly Zoey's dog now and would only go to her parents' house when she did. Spin was catching on quickly but still needed Trek to show him the ropes. He could go with Micah the most, and probably more for Micah than anyone.

Micah shook his head and peered around the cabin. This was it. Unless they could buy the land, he couldn't call it home anymore. The training facility would continue to get built in the hopes he'd be back as the facility manager and basic owner. They'd thought they had plenty of time to get it going and now summer, and countless clients, were beating down their door. Zoey asked if he wanted to stay longer or wanted to head to her parents' house. He took her hand and led her to the bed where

they lay and held each other for some time. Finally, they got up and loaded his truck. She'd follow him into town, so she could get back out to camp for her shift in the morning.

Chef came with them for this round since they were going to stay at her parents' that night. She'd give him time to adjust, then Spin would come and stay for a few days. The schedule wasn't nailed down yet, but at this point, they just wanted to get through the day they were on. Chef rode with her, taking up most of the back seat. It was afternoon when they got to her parents' house and Zoey realized they'd skipped lunch. The house seemed even smaller now that they weren't there for a social visit. Her mother greeted them at the door and gave them each a hug. Her father had run to the store for some things, so Zoey's mother showed them to the room for Micah to put his things in. They unloaded his few boxes and sat on the bed. It had been Matilda's bed growing up and thankfully was a full-sized bed. The room was tiny, fitting just the bed, an end table, and a four-drawer dresser. There was enough space on either side of the bed to maneuver but that was about all. They would share a bathroom.

"You okay?" Zoey asked Micah.

He gave a stoic look and cocked his head. "Yeah. I truly appreciate your parents taking me in. I am pretty much broke after all the fees and stuff. I do not know how I will repay them."

"They are not expecting you to."

"I know, but I want to."

She reached out and ran her fingers through his hair, which was now down to almost the middle of his back. It was soft but thick. Almost wiry. He smiled at her a little defeated. If they just hadn't gone downtown. If they just hadn't seen

Michael Andrews. There was no going back. They heard Zoey's father pull in and went out to greet him. He had bags of groceries, so they each grabbed a couple and brought them in, setting them on the counter. Zoey's mother came in to help unload and within minutes everything was put away.

"Mr. and Mrs. Sanders, thank you so much for letting me stay here. I do not know what Zoey has told you, but I appreciate your kindness," Micah expressed to them.

"First, call us Isa and Burt. Mr. and Mrs. Sanders will get old fast with you staying here," Zoey's father joked. "Second, I know you were arrested for hitting the guy who started the avalanche, but I'm guessing there is a lot more to the story than that?"

Micah nodded. They moved to the table and Micah began telling them what happened, including his past history and his breaking the guy's nose the day of the avalanche. Zoey and her mother interpreted for her dad, who still didn't know much sign language. He listened thoughtfully but didn't respond right away, which Zoey could tell made Micah nervous. She pressed her knee against his under the table and felt him squeeze her leg in gratitude. Finally, her father spoke.

"Let me say, thank you for protecting my daughter, what sounds like twice. Michael Andrews is a piece of shit and deserves whatever is coming to him. He's one of those people who skates through life hurting other people and never paying the price. I'm glad to hear you won't do jail time. You're welcome to stay here as long as you need, but I'll require your help. Trying to put up some fencing and other projects around here. I know Isa would appreciate your help, as well. We're busy people, always got things going. What are your plans?"

Zoey responded to show she was part of all of this. "Kyle and I are trying to figure out a way to buy the land the camp is on. The county is willing to sell it, however, it's twenty-four thousand and between us, we have four thousand. If we can buy the land, Micah can run the training facility we're building out there, as then it will be private land, and he won't work for the county. We're already booked for summer and almost full for the fall. If we can get the land, Micah has a job and place to live. If we can't, not only will he not, but we'll have to cancel all of the clients coming in for training."

Her parents glanced at each other, a silent message passing between them. Burt got up and began cutting vegetables for dinner. Isa reached out and patted Micah on his hand.

"It will all work out. You were doing what you thought was right. There are many different paths to the end," she told him and got up to help Burt.

Zoey set the table and showed Micah where dishes and silverware were. He helped her set the table. Once they were done, he took Chef out back to sniff around. Zoey watched her parents work in sync with each other and offered to help. Her father set down his knife on the counter and stared at her.

"Zoey, first let me say, I like Micah. I can tell he has a good heart and is a hard worker. But how deep in this are you?"

Zoey flushed, feeling like she was a teenager again. "Dad, I love Micah. At this point, we intend to be together but I'm no child. I know things can fall apart. I've seen his anger. Not personally, but I was there when he beat up Michael Andrews. Both times. I've seen him flip the switch. He's never done it towards me, the dogs, or anyone we know. It's always been directed at someone who instigates it. I'm not making excuses for

him, I'm just trying to answer the question I think you're trying to ask me."

"We just want you to be safe," Zoey's mother said softly. "I believe Micah would never hurt you or anyone he cared about. He's not like that. But whether or not the fist is raised at you, you can still end up paying the price for his temper."

Zoey knew what they meant. Micah wouldn't strike her, but his blows could unintentionally bring them both down. Like it almost had downtown. He needed to get ahold of his anger before it destroyed them both. He was aware of it, however, hadn't developed the skills to stop it before it was out of control.

"Micah has had a hard life, and that's no excuse, but he is dealing with a lot of rejection and abandonment issues. He's working on it, though. He doesn't have a supportive family. His adoptive parents love him, but they have biological grandkids now they give all of their focus to. His birth father is dead and his birth mother wrote him off. He has a lot to be angry about. I promise he's aware. He doesn't excuse it." She didn't know what else to say.

Her father looked at her, then smiled. "You were always that little girl, trying to save the bird with the broken wing."

"Dad, he's not a bird with a broken wing. He's a man who's trying to overcome situations he'd no control over. Hurt other people inflicted on him. He began fighting to defend himself, and he knows he needs to stop. He is the most caring and giving person I know."

"Fair enough. We're here for him and we're here for you, Zo. I need you to understand where we're coming from. This isn't your husband or someone you've been with a long time. The risks are high. We care for Micah, but you're our daughter

first. Your best interest is what we're looking out for. Micah has a safe place with us as long as you say so. The two of you need to figure out what you're going to do, what your direction is."

"I know, Dad. We both appreciate your generosity. I don't know what is going to happen, but I do know we're planning to be in this for the long haul. Maybe one day something will happen which will make us decide sooner, or for something different, but for now, we're both okay with the way things are."

Little did Zoey know, a couple of weeks later everything would be put to the test.

amp wasn't the same without Micah, and everyone was feeling it. The calls were steady and both Kyle and Jack were taking the dogs with them, even on calls where they didn't need to search for people. This helped to create a bond between them, and kept the dogs' minds off where Micah was. Zoey was exhausted and struggled through her days, feeling like she was just working or sleeping. So much had happened, she figured it was all finally catching up with her. Plus, trying to split her time between camp and her parents' was taking its toll. Micah was helping her dad, but within a week they'd caught up on most projects. The team needed him back.

The lawsuit put everyone on edge and the county pushed the issue of selling the land. Grants were hitting a dead end or locked up in red tape. Kyle mentioned what could happen if the county sold the land out from under them. Those who were paid employees would keep their jobs but would need to move to work out of the nearest firehouse. This would cut their response time dramatically. Volunteers would just be call-ups and wouldn't be of much use in critical situations. Other SARs did it, but Mountaintop SAR always prided themselves on being on the scene first.

Zoey was closing down her shift in triage, restocking supplies and sanitizing everything when Brandon came in for his weekend shift. She was relieved to see him. He looked at her, raising his eyebrows.

"You alright, Zoey?"

She sat down and shook her head. "I'm just tired. Not getting much sleep and now I have a stomach bug. Burning the candle at both ends, you know?"

Brandon nodded. "Things okay with Micah?"

"He's depressed, obviously. He's made a few calls but as Kyle said, no one wants to hire him now with his record. He's got a lead on construction work for now."

"Damn, I'm sorry to hear it. You two have been through the wringer."

"Yeah."

She pushed down the nausea that was threatening to bring up her lunch. She was pushing too hard and stressed most of the time. She needed sleep but when she'd lay in bed at night, all the possibilities of things falling apart crept in. Chef started sleeping in the bed with her, sensing she was on the verge of a breakdown. Suddenly, she felt she wasn't going to be able to keep her stomach contents in and ran outside to vomit around the side of the building. Brandon followed her out and handed her a paper towel.

"Why don't you head out? I can finish up. Go get some rest. Broth, water, crackers. Stay hydrated."

She chuckled at Brandon telling her stuff she already knew. It was nice to hear, anyway. She wiped her mouth and threw the paper towel in the trash as she went to the cabin. She climbed into bed and fell asleep for a couple of hours. Panic woke her up out of a dead sleep and she sat up in bed, attempting to settle her heart. Timelines were forming in her head. She'd been busy and stressed, not even thinking of the possibility. Her mind counted back trying to recollect what was going on the last time she'd had a period. What was the weather like, when had it started? How long had it been? She couldn't recall.

She remembered having it but not exactly when. It'd been during a storm, she was worried she didn't have enough supplies. Horror came over her when she realized it'd been at least six weeks. She got out of bed and grabbed a pad of paper and pen. She began noting what she remembered about what was going on. She'd been feeling under the weather for a couple of weeks but chalked it up to everything going on. Finally, something clicked and she looked at the calendar. It'd been two months. She was a month late.

How had she not noticed?

She calmed herself. Stress could stop periods, she knew that. She'd gone through physical stress for at least a month after being rescued. It was common for women who go through physical trauma to skip a few periods. That was probably more likely. They used birth control, she reminded herself. Taking deep breaths, her mind and heart settled. She was scaring herself for no reason. It wasn't that she didn't think about having children with Micah, because she had... in the far-off future. With him being out of work, the lawsuit, and possibly losing the land, now was just not the time.

Besides, they were still working on their relationship and with everything they'd gone through, that still needed some tending. She'd take a pregnancy test to rule it out but felt confident her body was just reacting to all it'd endured over the last year.

To start de-stressing, she meditated for twenty minutes and felt more at peace after. She took a hot shower and put on slippers and a robe. She texted Micah to let him know she was going to stay at camp and try to get some sleep. He responded for her to please take care of herself and that he loved her. She made broth, sipping on it by the fire. Chef rested on her feet and sighed. Much to her surprise, she started to fall asleep by the time it was dark and climbed into bed. Chef laid next to her and she rubbed his thick fur. She texted Micah, "good night," and dozed off to sleep.

The next morning, she woke up with her stomach doing flips. She took shallow breaths until it settled and skipped coffee. Brandon was still on until the afternoon, so she drove to the pharmacy in town. It'd only been a little over a couple of weeks since Micah beat Michael Andrews outside those doors and she half expected to see bloodstains on the ground. She didn't and people passed by without a thought of the events of that day. She didn't just want to buy a pregnancy test, so she grabbed supplies for triage and a few snacks. Once she checked out, she considered if she should go by her parents' house and take the test but didn't want to alarm anyone. She drove back to camp and took the test over the composting toilet in her cabin.

She was for sure it'd be negative and she'd be able to put that fear to bed. The test said to wait five minutes, so she took it with her while she made a cup of tea. Once she got the kettle

going, she glanced at the test and her heart started racing. She grabbed the box and read it. One line not pregnant, two lines pregnant. Whether or not she wanted it to be true, there were two lines. She sat down at the table in shock. They'd always used birth control. Right? She put her head on the table and bawled. What were they going to do? She cried until her eyelids hurt and sat back in the chair, feeling numb. They had no way to take care of a child right now. Micah was out of work, she might be if the lawsuit went through.

Chef came and put his head in her lap, staring up at her with his big, droopy eyes. She mindlessly stroked his head and let her mind run over and over the reality. She was pregnant, around two months or so. She'd spent her early twenties trying to figure out who she was and what she wanted to do with her life. Then she went to school to become a paramedic. She just now felt like she had a handle on that. Her thirties were when she thought she'd have a family... with her husband. Here she was, unmarried and the father was unemployed. Panic welled up in her and she took deep breaths, attempting to keep it in check. Chef put his paw on her leg and she looked at him gratefully. It really did help to have him there as she rubbed his head and counted over and over in her head.

How would she tell Micah? Would she tell Micah? He was trying to put his life back together just for himself at this point. No, she needed to tell him. This affected him, too. What would her parents say? They knew she and Micah lived together, so they knew they were intimate, but the timing was terrible. What would she do, raise a child in this cabin with Micah somewhere else? He wasn't welcome back and she needed to be here for her job. It all just didn't work. She needed a friend to

talk to. She chewed her fingernails, trying to not freak out and to decide what to do. She got up and went to the one person she knew would be a good barometer.

She knocked on Kyle's cabin door. He opened it, surprised to see her so early.

"Hey, Zoey! What's up?"

"Can we talk?" She felt tears creeping up and Kyle saw it, too.

He ushered her in just as the tears made their way out. "Whoa. What's going on?" He gave her a tissue and guided her to the couch.

Zoey took deep breaths until she could compose herself. "I'm pregnant."

"It's not mine, is it?" Kyle joked, but his eyes were wide.

"Haha, funny. I haven't told Micah yet."

"Man, that's heavy. Do you want the baby?"

The baby. Even that sounded foreign. That was about the only question Zoey hadn't considered. She closed her eyes and thought about the possibility. Did she want to keep the baby? Ultimately, she did or thought she did. It wasn't that she didn't want to be a mother, she honestly wasn't thinking about it at this time.

"I mean in the long run, yes. Just not now."

"So, ask yourself, what's different about now? Yeah, I know, Micah's out of work, we're being sued, blah blah blah. But take all that out of the equation. Would you love a child, now? If someone walked up and handed you a baby, your baby, on the street and walked away, what would you do? Would you drop it at the fire station or take care of it yourself?"

That was a good question.

She imagined the scenario and knew she wouldn't have the heart to drop it off at the fire station, she'd take it home and care for it. Wherever that may be. "I'd keep it."

Kyle nodded. "Zo, having a kid is never easy. Trust me. I was married and employed when we had our son. It was still the most stressful, exhausting time in my life. But I would've and still would kill for that boy. Our marriage didn't last, but he is the best thing that ever happened to me. I know this is an abstract concept right now, however, babies are born all over the world to people with less. We'll take care of you, of your child, if this is what you want. I'll build you a nursery. And a crib. But know I support you, no matter what you need to do."

Zoey smiled. Kyle always got it and said the right thing. "Thanks, Kyle. That makes me feel better. If we lose all of this, you'll have no place to build anything."

Kyle shook his head. "Don't remind me. If I can just drum up another eight thousand, the bank will finance the rest. Maybe it's time to rob a few banks."

"I have two thousand I can spare if it means I have a home. If not, then I need it to find a place to live," Zoey offered.

"Okay, so six thousand more. One less bank maybe."

Zoey laughed and shoved him playfully. She needed to talk to Micah and her parents. It was time for her shift, so that would need to wait. She stood up and hugged Kyle. He'd helped her sort out what to do, at least for the time being. She headed for the triage tent to relieve Brandon. He'd everything prepped and hopped up when he saw her.

"All good to go, Zo. Hope you have a quiet night," he said, scooping up his bag. His wife was expecting and he didn't like being gone for too long.

"Thanks, Brandon. Tell Missy I said hello."

"Will do! See ya!"

After he left, she sat down to dig through medical books on pregnancy. Of course, she knew the basics but didn't deal with it in SAR. At least not yet. Besides, seeing the pictures made it more real. She was two months along based on her last period. She flipped to what a baby looks like at two months along. Kind of an alien. She stared at her stomach, trying to imagine it in there. Yup, alien seemed about right. She sighed and closed the book. Her due date was the end of November. That'd give her some time to try and make sure her life wasn't such a wreck. She'd tell Micah, however, she needed time to let the idea become more familiar in her head first. She tried to drink coffee but it smelled and tasted like dirt. She poured it out and drank tea instead. A little while later, Kyle came by with some peppermint candy disks.

"These helped my wife during her pregnancy. Thought you might like some."

Zoey took them gratefully. "Hey, it looks like my due date is the end of November if I calculated right. In case you need to find someone to replace me."

"Well, we'll get you covered but not replace you. You can always bring the baby here," Kyle only half-joked.

Zoey glanced around at all the dangerous things a child could get into and shuddered. "I think not."

Kyle shrugged, then snickered. "My kid was always with me once he could walk. I'm sure my tactics would be frowned upon but, hey, he's still kicking."

"Yeah, but he's your kid. You're invincible."

"I don't know, Zo. You're invincible. Remember, I pulled you out of the water and you fought all the way through. People like us, like Micah, we're different. We're survivors." He grinned and waved by the door before heading back to his cabin.

Zoey thought about what he said. They were survivors. All of them. It's what drew them to Search and Rescue in the first place. They didn't seem to comprehend their own mortality. And they were fighters. Ready to take on anyone or anything that got in their way. The one reality seemed to encourage the other. Maybe that was the problem.

They didn't know when to quit.

24

sa and Micah were tilling a plot for a vegetable garden when Zoey drove up. She stayed in the car and watched them, smiling to herself. They were having a vibrant conversation with what seemed to be about peas and Isa's childhood, from what Zoey could make out. Her mother had always been somewhat reserved with her children. Loving and firm, but never really open about her life before being a mother. It was interesting to see her interact with Micah because he wasn't one of her children, but was still her children's age. She communicated with him like a cross between a mother and an auntie. Micah appeared to be getting a lot out of the relationship as well. Zoey took a deep breath and got out of the car. She'd waited almost a week before being ready to tell Micah or her parents about the pregnancy, to make sure she was set with what she wanted to do.

Micah saw her come up and practically ran over to hug her, almost tripping over Trek, who was equally excited to see her. They hadn't been apart this long in a while, and even seeing him made her heart flutter. She knew she'd spill the beans before she was ready, so she'd made excuses as to why she couldn't come into town. Chef wagged his tail and went to sniff the dirt plot with Trek. Micah kissed her, pushing a strand of hair out of her face.

"I missed you!"

"I missed you, too, Micah. It is lonely out there without you. Hey, can we take some time to talk? Maybe take a ride to the lake?" She knew she needed to get it out soon because she was horrible at keeping secrets for long.

He watched her concerned, attempting to read her face, then nodded. "Of course. Let me make sure Isa is set for me to go."

He walked over and Zoey furrowed her brow at him calling her mother Isa. It was so familiar and so weird. Her mother waved at her, then went back to work on the garden. Micah came over, followed by the dogs, and took her hand. It was so strong around hers, she hoped it'd be enough to get them through this. They headed to his truck, Chef and Trek jumping in as soon as the door opened. Zoey got in the passenger side, enjoying the familiar smell. Micah got in and smiled at her, watching her from his side. He was just so beautiful. She smiled back, trying to quell the butterflies in her stomach.

They drove to the lake and parked near a trailhead. There was a nice hiking trail around the lake, so they started around, enjoying each other's company. The dogs ran ahead, excited to play together. They took a side trail down to the water's edge and stared out. It was the beginning of May, signs of life were beginning to appear all around them. They'd likely still

get snow, however, spring was making an effort to break through.

Micah turned to her. "Did you want to talk now? Is it about camp?"

Zoey nodded, then shook her head. "Not exactly. Can we sit on that rock over there?"

Micah looked confused but moved over to the rock and sat down. Zoey sat next to him, relieved when he took her hand. She chewed her upper lip for a moment, then faced him. He met her eyes and she could see he was worried.

"Micah, I love you. Let me say that first because I do not want you thinking this is anything it is not. I want to be with you no matter what, so do not worry about that."

He visibly relaxed. "Okay, so what is going on?"

Zoey couldn't decide if she should build up to it to prepare him or just blurt it out. Either way, it was going to be a shock. She chose the middle ground. "So, I have been feeling ill lately. Exhausted, vomiting, weak. I thought it was stress from everything, but needed to rule some things out," she paused, calling up courage.

Micah was worried. Was she sick? "Z, what is it?"

"I am pregnant."

Micah stared at her, trying to register what she'd just told him. His mouth hung slightly open and he shook his head. "Jesus, Z, I thought you were going to tell me you were dying."

Zoey looked at him in disbelief. That was it? This was his reaction to the news? He wasn't freaked out like she was. "Micah, I am pregnant. We are going to have a baby," she tried to convey it in a couple of different ways to make sure he understood.

He nodded. "I understand. I mean, I get with me being out of work this is not ideal, but at least you are not dying."

"Micah! I have been stressing this for days, trying to figure out how to tell you, thinking you would freak out. This does not make you freak out? I was. I still am."

He watched her, then squeezed her hand. "I always knew from day one we were going to be together and maybe have a family. This just makes me have to work harder to make sure when this baby comes, we are ready to go. I love you, Zoey. The plan is all out of whack, however, it is still the plan. Right? You want this with me, right?"

Zoey was at a loss for words but bobbed her head in agreement. She stared out at the lake as a blue heron flew like a dart across the surface. She gazed at it until it disappeared on the other side of the lake. Micah was on board, she was on board. They had Kyle's support, whatever that ultimately meant. They had almost seven months to get things in order. She didn't want to presume anything, but they needed to lay out a plan of action. She shifted her eyes back to his.

"I have to tell my parents. I need to know how to present this to them. About us and our future. The world is different than in their day, but I want us all to be a family."

"Zoey, we are a family. I would marry you today if that is what needs to happen, and you would have me. I will love you until I die, anyway. I do not need a piece of paper to tell me that. But if you will have me as your husband, I would be honored."

Zoey thought about his words. It'd always seemed right between them, natural. Bringing a child into the world certainly changed the timeline, but not the intent. She nodded and leaned in to kiss his cheek. "I think I would like that. For you to be my husband."

He blushed and grinned, sliding his arm around her. They stayed at the lake a while longer, enjoying the serenity. The temperature began to drop and they walked back to the truck, Chef and Trek trailing along behind at their own pace. Micah paused at the truck and embraced Zoey, kissing her on the mouth. He pulled his head back and looked into her eyes, his own eyes shrouded in thought. He stared off for a moment and then back.

"You are all the family I need. Well, you and now the baby. Your parents have been like family to me and I was on the way to considering Charlie a brother. You all made me feel part of something right away. I do not want you taking my last name. It does not mean anything to me. I want you to keep your last name and if you are okay with it, I would like to take it as my own."

Zoey raised her brows. She'd never thought of that, but with the way his adoptive parents had basically shunned him recently, she honestly didn't want their last name, either. Micah Sanders. It had a nice ring to it.

"Micah, that is beautiful. I am touched that you thought of that. I would love to share my last name with you. Plus, it was Charlie's, too. I guess we need to go tell my parents. Not sure how they will react to all of this. We keep springing things on them."

"I am ready if you are. Wait, when are you due?"

"End of November."

"A winter, holiday baby. That is good. It will give us some time to work this out."

They loaded up and headed to her parents' house. Zoey was nervous about their reaction. Her parents were practical and old school. They'd already had dinner and left food on the counter for Zoey and Micah for when they came in. They were in the living room reading, with classical music on the record player. Zoey didn't think she'd be able to eat until they talked, if then. She and Micah sat on the couch across from the chairs her parents were sitting in. Her parents both glanced up and put their reading down, her father peering over the top of his glasses at them. Zoey cleared her throat, looking at Micah for reassurance.

"We have something to tell you. I know everything is a mess right now and this is not the ideal time, but it is what it is. We are expecting a baby." Zoey internally winced with the last words.

Her parents stared at both of them and then at each other, conversing with their eyes. Micah, not wanting to let it sit for too long, continued.

"We are going to get married."

Her parents' faces didn't change. They hid their emotions while processing the information. Finally, her father sighed and rubbed his nose.

"Well. That is some news," he said dryly.

"When?" her mother asked, her voice above a whisper.

"Uh, well the baby is due in November. We have not set a date to get married or anything," Zoey fumbled through her words.

Micah took her hand, covering it with his own. He glanced at her and signed, "Soon?"

Zoey nodded. She didn't want a fancy wedding or months of planning. The courthouse would be fine. "Okay. Courthouse?"

He shook his head vehemently. "No, something nice. Maybe a small gathering at camp?"

Zoey thought about it. They were family, too, so she did want them there. She shrugged. "June?"

Micah considered that, then bobbed his head. "June 7?"

They had a date. Her parents watched the conversation, her mother interpreting for her father. They all stared at each other and a mutual sense of agreement was reached. Regardless of how this all happened, Micah and Zoey were getting married and a baby was coming. They needed to move forward to get everything planned.

Isa stood up and came over to Micah, embracing him. "Now, you will be my son."

Micah flushed at this, then grinned. Her father was less forward, but he felt the same. He motioned to Zoey to speak with her alone in the kitchen and she followed him in.

"Zoey, your mother and I support you. I know you weren't expecting this and it only adds to your stress. You mentioned before, if you all could raise enough money to buy the land the base camp is on, Micah would be able to run the training center, right? How much money?"

"We have four thousand, now. Kyle said the bank would finance the balance if he could put ten thousand down."

Her father thought about this, running his hand across the top of his head.

"When we sold the farm, we made a good profit since it was paid off. Your mother and I talked about giving each of you kids a portion since we couldn't leave the farm to you. I'd like to give you and the baby part of your portions now, to do with how you see fit. We could give you five thousand, the baby three thousand, and save some for later when they are older. This would give you eight thousand to work with. I'd want your name on that land now, though. So, you at least partially own it."

Zoey was floored. It was a risk her parents were taking to give her the money. She couldn't turn it down, though. She hugged her father, wiping away a tear that escaped down her cheek. "Thank you, Dad! I promise this is an investment. It will get Micah back to doing what he loves and take the pressure from the county off us."

"You're a smart girl. We're so proud of you and your determination. And your big heart." Her father ruffled her hair and went back into the living room. Zoey took the chance to call Kyle and let him know.

Kyle answered, sounding half asleep. "Kyle here."

"Kyle, It's Zoey. I have the money! My parents are giving me money from the sale of the farm. The agreement is, we need to go in on this together. I'll pay you to build a room onto our cabin and give you the other six thousand outside of that needed for the down payment. We can be co-owners of the land. I've so much more to tell you, but how soon can we get this rolling?"

"Well, I can put the offer into the county tomorrow. If they accept, we can finalize the loan with the bank pretty much immediately. When are you back to camp?"

"Day after tomorrow. I can meet you in town sooner if need be. Let's do this!"

Kyle laughed and sighed with relief. "Best news I've heard in a while. You tell Micah about the baby?"

"I did. He was weirdly fine with it."

"Sounds like Micah."

"Okay, I'd better go. Let me know when and how to get the money to you. Get ready to start building that nursery," she teased.

"You know I'm so on it. We're going to have us a little camp baby."

They hung up and Zoey went to the living room. She got Micah's attention by waving at him. "Hey, I am tired. Can we go lay down?"

He nodded and stood up, saying goodnight to her parents. Zoey waved at them and went to Micah's room. Chef and Trek followed, lying on the dog bed on the floor. Chef understood he only slept in the bed when Micah wasn't there. Zoey was exhausted and could hardly keep her eyes open. She stripped down to her long john bottoms and a tank top, peering at her still flat belly. She rubbed her hand across it, trying to connect with the being growing inside. It was still a foreign concept.

Micah came over and put his hand over hers. That seemed a little more concrete. She climbed under the covers and yawned. She filled him in about the money and her conversation with Kyle. They could be back to camp in just a few weeks, as soon as the land deal went through.

Micah leaned up on his elbow and stared at her. "Seriously?"

She nodded half-heartedly, attempting to keep her eyes open. She placed her hand against his cheek.

Micah grinned and kissed her. "This day keeps getting better and better."

He burrowed down next to her and gathered her in his arms. He placed his hand over her belly and left it there. She felt him move his hand into the *I love you* sign on her belly. Then he moved it up to her heart. She wearily tried to give him the sign back and accidentally hit him in the nose. She heard him chuckle, resting his head against hers as she fell asleep.

25

 yle and Zoey signed papers on the land two weeks later, moving from being county-owned land used by SAR, to a small community where the members of SAR lived. This allowed more freedom, not needing county approval for everything they did. The county was happy to offload the land as they were hoping to settle with the family of Maizie Bright as soon as possible. The family wasn't buckling, however, and denied any settlements up to this point. The county also refused to pay salary for another handler as they were cutting their funding for SAR as a result. They were pushing to move to a more volunteer-based team, although the team knew that wouldn't go over well in the long run. For the time being, Kyle, Zoey, and Jake were safe with their positions, but the part-time positions were cut as well.

Once the papers were signed and the sale of the land finalized, Micah was able to move back home. By the time Micah came back, walls and a roof had been put on the training center

and Kyle was working on the inside. Micah jumped right back in to help, so they'd be done in time before the first class. With longer days and warmer weather, they were able to move quickly and soon a formed center sat on the edge of the training field.

The first group coming for training was in late June, so they had around a month to get the center completed and everything in place. Since Micah could no longer work for SAR, his focus was mainly on getting the facility completed. The training center no longer fell under SAR and it no longer qualified for non-profit grants, now running as a private training center adjacent to the camp. Kyle's cabin became his own private property as did Zoey and Micah's. The rest of the camp was jointly owned by Kyle and Zoey. For insurance reasons, the county technically rented the triage area from Kyle and Zoey, and any area where they stored their equipment or volunteers stayed. This included the bunkhouse, giving a little funding towards land payment back. Jake's cabin still belonged to Kyle and Zoey since he lived there full-time, but the county didn't have that as part of the job requirement. He wasn't sure if he'd live there long-term, so they let him stay but retained ownership. The total land acreage they purchased was almost eleven acres and was still surrounded by county and state land. Zoey made sure Charlie's memorial was included in the purchase and planned to add gardens around it over time. Her parents had yet to see it, so she wanted it to be special when they finally did.

Morning sickness took ahold of Zoey around the clock. She felt like once she knew, it was somewhat partially psychosomatic as it got much worse than it'd been prior to her taking the test. A visit to the midwives confirmed her timeline and she discussed having the baby at home, being aware of the

risk of infections in hospitals. She found a pair of midwives who assisted home births in the town, and they were willing to drive up to the camp when the time came. Micah was nervous at the prospect but supported how she wanted to give birth. Zoey was nervous as well, however, as a medical professional she felt better being home.

They planned a simple wedding, using the training field and setting up a few tents for food after. It was short notice, so Zoey was not surprised when her siblings declined and was secretly relieved. Micah chose to let his adoptive parents know after the fact, as he felt they might make an issue about Zoey being pregnant. This left Zoey's parents, Kyle, Jake, Callie, Brandon and his wife, a few friends, volunteers, and local rescue personnel they'd become friendly with. All in all, around twenty to twenty-five guests. They set up chairs and lined the path with flowers. Kyle built a small arbor for them to stand under to say their vows. They found an officiant a few towns over who knew ASL and chose to write their own vows.

On the day of the wedding, Micah and Zoey woke up and had breakfast, both fighting butterflies. Not over marrying each other, but over the whole public event. After breakfast, Micah went over to Jake's cabin to get ready, leaving Zoey in their cabin. She was wearing a long, off-the-shoulder sundress with sandals, and Callie offered to weave flowers through her hair. Callie showed up about an hour before the ceremony with a basket of delicate, small, white, pink, and yellow flowers. Zoey was dressed and sitting, trying not to bite her nails when Callie came.

Callie brushed out Zoey's waist-length black hair and curled random strands at her hairline with a few all the way around. She then took the flowers and weaved them through with a needle and thread. When she was done, Zoey looked in the mirror and was taken aback. It was beautiful. She mostly wore her hair in a ponytail or braids for work; Callie made it look stunning. Zoey didn't wear makeup, so Callie only dabbed on glistening lip gloss and a little shimmer on her upper cheekbones and eyelids. This brought out Zoey's large, dark eyes and high cheekbones, making her appear like a mythical fairy queen. Zoey admired herself and smiled.

"Thank you, Callie! You made me look so pretty."

"You're easy to work with. Women put on makeup to look like you when you don't." Callie laughed. "You have thick black eyelashes I'd kill for. Plus, you have those full lips and high cheekbones. You'll never age."

Zoey had never thought of herself in those terms. Racism was still prevalent in the area, growing up she'd been treated like an outsider. No one asked her to prom, boys she liked wouldn't give her the time of day. While part of her knew it was because she wasn't white, part of her still felt ugly because of it. Most kids didn't know her ethnicity because she was both white and Chamorro. They assumed she was Hispanic and she'd been called every Hispanic racial slur imaginable. She didn't bother correcting them that she wasn't Hispanic because they didn't care about her race, they only cared she didn't look like them.

Over time, the town grew and by the time Charlie was in school, the racist, white kids weren't so blatant, but it still existed. Charlie was in people's faces, though, and had a large group of friends. If anything was said about him, it was likely behind his back. He and his friends wouldn't have tolerated open bigotry and were a force to be reckoned with.

Zoey had one more thing she wanted to wear and grabbed the ghost necklace Charlie snagged from her when they were kids. She slipped it over her neck and wrapped her fingers around the ghost. She also wore the pawprint necklace Micah had given her, seashell earrings from Guam her mother brought back, and her grandmother's mother-of-pearl bracelet. Callie handed her the bouquet and smiled. It was time.

The arbor Kyle made was intertwined with flowers and light yellow ribbon. The officiant and Micah were already at the arbor and Zoey stopped to stare at Micah. He was wearing a cream-colored linen suit over a white button-down shirt. No tie and his top two buttons were undone due to the summer heat, showing a peek of his red chest hair. He was clean-shaven and his eyes stood out, matching the landscape behind him. His long, loose red hair against the suit was striking and he took her breath away.

He smiled at her and signed, "wow."

She signed back, "Same."

Her father walked Zoey to Micah, and she handed her bouquet to her mother sitting at the front to hold. Trek, Chef, and Spin lay patiently to the right of the altar, each freshly bathed with matching collars. The gathering was intimate with only three rows on either side. A light breeze was keeping everyone cool and Zoey admired how it blew strands of Micah's hair back. She resisted the urge to reach out and catch one. She met his eyes, keeping hers locked there for stability. Everything would be in ASL and Zoey's mother offered to interpret for the guests. She stood up to the side of the arbor and began interpreting as the ceremony began. The officiant did the initial readings, then signed it was time for them to read their vows.

Zoey chose the go first. "Micah, you have been my best friend and my rock since shortly after we met. I was drawn to you the day you stepped out of the truck and into our team. I was terrified to try to converse with you because all I knew was some of the sign alphabet. But you made me feel comfortable right away. I wanted to learn ASL as quickly as I could, so I could communicate fluently with you. Everything with you is so natural. When Charlie died," Zoey paused as she felt tears welling up.

Micah reached out and brushed a stray tear from her cheek with his thumb.

She took a breath and went on. "When Charlie died, I was devastated, so lost. I was drowning. You came out to save me and even when I pushed you away, you did not give up on me. I celebrate every day you are in my life. I do not know what I did all those years without you. It was like I was always searching, but I did not know what for until the first time you kissed me. Then it all made sense. I cannot believe we get to start a family together in this place. I know you will be an amazing father, and our children will be lucky to have you in their lives. You are my everything. Thank you for choosing me. I promise I will be forever yours."

Micah now wiped a tear from his own cheek and met her eyes with such sincerity, Zoey held her breath. Her mother blew her nose and wiped her eyes in the pause. Micah took a deep breath.

"My Zoey. I say that because you were mine the second you stepped out of the triage tent into my life. I knew then, I would marry you. I knew then, we would have a family one day. I just needed to convince you." He smiled and a chuckle ran through the crowd. "I knew it was not appropriate to ask to kiss you at the time, however, I wanted to every moment I was around you. I found reasons to be around you. Then you let me kiss you and I knew I was in. When Charlie died, I watched the person I love most in this world, go through a hell she could not find her way out of. It tore me apart, not being able to help you. But you are amazing... so strong... and you found your way back to me. I swore I would protect you for the rest of my life. The day you were washed down the river, I truly thought I lost you and my heart shattered. I can never thank Kyle and Chef enough for saving you... thus saving me. I have been wanting this day my whole life, I just had to find you. I did not choose you, you were my destiny. I swear on my life, I will put you and our children above all. You are my life."

Not a dry eye was left after their vows. Zoey's mother sat down and cried into her tissue. The officiant handed Zoey and Micah each a tissue and they wiped each other's eyes. Once everyone was composed, they exchanged rings. Delicately carved hardwood rounds Kyle made for them. Once the rings were exchanged, the officiant made the legal announcement, which surprised a few in the crowd.

"I now pronounce you husband and wife. You may now kiss each other. Please officially welcome the new Mr. and Mrs. Sanders."

Zoey's parents stared at each other shocked, then clapped happily. They didn't know Micah was taking Zoey's name. This would mean their grandchildren would also have their last name, continuing the family bond.

Zoey met Micah's lips and sighed. He put his hand on her lower back, pressing her against him. The crowd gave their applause in sign and hollered. They laughed and drew back, meeting each other's eyes. Rock and earth. Micah took her hand firmly in his and they walked down to the tents set up by the center fire pit. One tent had long tables of food and drinks, the other had tables to sit at and a dance area. Zoey made sure speakers were set directly on the laid dance floor, so Micah could feel the vibrations for their first dance. The crowd came down and everyone grabbed plates of food, congratulating Zoey and Micah as they came by. Zoey's parents came up to them and Isa embraced Micah.

"I told you, you are my son. Now you share our name, which is the greatest honor," she told him.

Micah leaned down and kissed her on the cheek. "You do not know what that means to me."

"I do because it means the same to me," she replied.

Burt shook Micah's hand, then to Zoey's surprise, embraced him as well. "Welcome to the family. I'm proud to call you *son*."

Zoey thought she might lose it at that moment. Her mouth hung open and she shook her head, shocked.

"Zoey, dear, close your mouth before something flies in there," her father teased.

She snapped her mouth shut, then grinned. Glancing at the food, she decided to stick with fruit and seltzer, so she could make it through the evening without puking. Micah saw her expression and nodded. He knew and would get her the right things. She made her rounds, saying hello to Brandon and his very pregnant wife, Missy, then the rest of the guests. By the time she made it through, she was tired and searched for Micah. He was just coming around with their plates and guided her to a table. Grateful to sit, she slipped off her sandals and rubbed the grass under her feet. Micah glanced over at her, then smiled.

"Well, no backing out now," he signed.

"I would not dream of it. Who would take care of me?" she replied, placing her hand on his cheek. His eyes were like the universe calling to her.

He leaned over and kissed her softly, letting his lips stay for a while longer. Heat flushed in her cheeks and she drew back, biting her lip to quell the desire.

"Later," he joked.

They ate and Zoey felt like she'd be able to keep the food down. Jake turned down the music, calling Kyle out to the dance floor for a toast. Kyle came up, already a little buzzed, and raised his glass high into the air. He set his glass down on a nearby table, so he could sign what he was saying.

"To two of my favorite people and two damn expert rescuers. Zoey, I took you under my wing when you joined the team, but you quickly showed me a thing or two. Micah, I took a chance on you and you proved to be the best dog handler I have ever seen. Most importantly, you have become family and I am happy it continues to grow. Here is to you two, and the family you are starting. Cheers!"

Everyone raised a glass, signing cheers with their other hand... something that must have been Kyle's doing. Micah blushed, nodding his appreciation. Jake came back up and pointed at them.

"Time for that first dance."

Zoey got up and led Micah to the floor. They stood feeling the music as Micah drew her in close to his chest. She wrapped her arms around his neck, laying her head against him.

He rested his head against hers and they began to sway to the rhythm. Everyone around them disappeared and for the first time, Zoey felt aware of the child growing inside her. Not physically, but emotionally. She felt the connection between the three of them. Micah placed his fingers on her chin and turned her face up to meet his, his eyes saying everything she was experiencing. They were a family now. He kissed her long and slow, taking her breath away.

The dance ended and others came out to the floor. They stayed for a couple more dances, then stepped away. Zoey was beginning to feel all of the emotions and stress of the day wearing her down. She looked at Micah and he understood. Kyle was building a fire in the center fire pit and the crowd was starting to get a little rowdy. Micah made his way to Kyle to excuse them. There was plenty of food and drinks for everyone to stay, but Zoey needed to lie down for a while.

Zoey let her parents know she was going to rest and they took this chance to take their leave. The party was for the younger people. They embraced and kissed her, then made their way over to Micah. They conversed with him for a moment and hugged him goodbye. She saw them to their car and went to find Micah. He was waiting for her by their cabin and she gratefully followed him in. It was cool and quiet inside, peaceful. The crowd was ramping up outside, so Zoey was glad for the break.

Micah led her to the bedroom and took off his jacket, placing it on a chair. Zoey slipped off her jewelry and shoes and lay next to Micah. He put his arm around her, nestling her hair. She rested her head against his, breathing out all the stress of the day. Later they could consummate the marriage, but for now, they only wanted to hold each other as husband and wife.

26

hen Zoey awoke, it was dark and Micah wasn't in the cabin. She checked the time and it was pushing almost ten at night. She'd been asleep for hours. Her stomach growled, the evening being the only time she could eat full meals. She crawled out of bed and went to the door to peer out. Almost everyone had left except Kyle, Jake, Callie, and a few other guests who were sitting around the fire. Zoey could see the ambulance driver Martina, who went by Marti, sitting over by Kyle, clearly flirting. Marti was in her forties and a firecracker. She loved her job and much like Kyle, it'd caused her marriage to end. Her children were grown and married with kids of their own. Zoey liked Marti because she lived her life with honesty and compassion. Marti had immediately taken to Zoey when she joined the team and made sure she was taken care of. Zoey considered her a mentor and a friend.

Zoey noticed Kyle's son, Christian, had joined the group and must've come after, as he'd not been at the wedding. Sitting on the other side of Kyle, he was the spitting image of his father. They were both sitting, leaning back in their camping chairs with their long legs stretched out in front. Zoey scanned for Micah but didn't see him in the group. She didn't want to go out as she was half-dressed and barefoot but wanted food from the tent. Her eye caught motion in the tent and she could see Micah grabbing stacks of food and drinks. He was precariously balancing dishes in one hand and drinks in the other, using his chin to keep the plates from falling over. As he wound carefully around the fire area, Zoey could tell Kyle was giving him shit about something and Micah laughed, trying to not drop the plates. Zoey swung open the door as he got close and snagged the drinks out of his one hand, so he could use it to steady the food.

Once inside, he set it all down and spread it out. Zoey was ravenous and began to dig in. They'd agreed on vegetarian fare, allowing them to eat the leftovers. Zoey scooped onto her plate chickpea salad with crackers, bean enchiladas, and a Chamorro spinach in coconut dish her mother made. They'd forgone a wedding cake, knowing it would probably make Zoey nauseous, instead having cupcakes with daisies on top for the guests. Micah brought two of them back and put them in the center of the table. Zoey ate as much as she could, to make up for the rest of the day she was barely able to keep anything down. She was just about three and a half months along, hoping morning sickness was on its way out.

They polished off all the food Micah brought in, except the cupcakes, and sipped on the lemonade he'd brought. Zoey got up and lit candles, turning off any lights. This gave the cabin a soft glow. The dogs were all curled up together sleeping and didn't move at all. Zoey came behind Micah and wrapped her arms around him, kissing him on the neck. He put his hand on her arm and leaned back against her shoulder. She came around and picked up a cupcake, setting the daisy back on the table, and peeled the paper off. Micah stood up and took the other, doing the same. He put his out to her and she took a bite and put hers out to him. He took a bite, meeting her eyes. They set the cupcakes down and came together to kiss, tasting the sweetness on each other's mouths. Zoey ran her fingers through his hair and sighed, pressing against him. Micah pulled his head back and watched her.

"My wife," he signed.

"My husband," she replied, then laughed softly, biting her lower lip. "Well, not quite officially, yet."

His eyes locked on hers and heat rose between them. He led her to the bedroom and they stood staring at each other, taking in the commitment they'd made. He reached up and slid her dress off her shoulders, letting it drop to the floor. This left Zoey standing naked except for her underwear. She unbuttoned his shirt and slid it off his shoulders. They moved slowly, savoring the first time as a married couple. Micah came towards her, slid his arms around her, and leaned in to take her breast in his mouth. Zoey felt her knees shake and let her weight fall against him. They moved to the bed and he laid her gently back against the pillows. He slid off her underwear, then his pants. She ran her hands down his chest and drew him towards her.

As he entered her, he moved cautiously, making sure she was alright. She couldn't wait any longer, kissing him hard on the mouth and driving him into her. They moved together in a pulsating rhythm as they did on the dance floor, matching each other's every move. As Zoey felt Micah release, she was overcome

with a sensational wave of joy. She cried out as she clung to him, her muscles giving way to trembling. They lay together, not wanting to let go of the moment. Micah braced himself and met her eyes, pushing sweat-moistened strands of hair off of her face. She wrapped her fingers in the damp hair at the base of his neck. He kissed her gently and they separated. He rested on his side and looked at her.

"My wife."

"My husband."

This time it was official. Neither of them could sleep, so Zoey slipped on a nightgown and Micah put back on his pants. They went to the kitchen and finished off the lemonade and cupcakes. A glance outside showed everyone had dispersed and the fire was out. They slipped out to the cabin porch and sat in the chairs. The stars were bright and it reminded Zoey of the night Micah had asked her to go hiking. He must've been thinking the same and turned to her.

"You want to go?"

Zoey nodded, grinning. "Absolutely."

They quickly got dressed. They packed sleeping bags and backpacks with snacks and water. This piqued the dogs' interest and they waited by the door, ready to go. They headed out into the night, holding hands and watching the stars. The dogs would run off on the hike, then come back in a different direction, chasing each other and barking. They headed to the grove and built a fire. It was summer, but late at night still was cool enough to enjoy a nice fire. Once the fire was going, they laid out their sleeping bags and sat together watching the flickering lights. They conversed into the night about the baby, the training center, and their future. The dogs, worn out by their romps

through the woods, came and surrounded them to sleep by the fire.

"Have you thought about names?" Micah asked her.

Zoey hadn't. She was just now coming to grips that a real person was growing inside of her. She thought she noticed a small bulge low on her stomach but wasn't completely sure. They'd heard the heartbeat and had an ultrasound scheduled in a couple of weeks. She shook her head.

"No, you?"

Micah nodded, then blushed. He'd clearly given it a lot of thought. "I was thinking, either way, if it is a boy or girl, we could name it after your brother Charlie. Charles if it is a boy, Charlotte if it is a girl. Then Charlie would work as a nickname for either."

Zoey didn't know if it was pregnancy hormones, the emotions of the day, or just how absolutely thoughtful that was, but she burst into tears. Micah, thinking he'd said something wrong, wound his arms around her and hugged her tight. He lifted her chin to meet his eyes.

"Z, I am sorry if I was out of line. I did not mean to be."

Zoey shook her head, rubbing her nose on her sleeve. She coughed to clear her throat. "Micah, that is the most beautiful thing you could have said to me. The fact you even thought that touches my heart in a way I cannot explain. I love it."

Micah's face washed over in relief. "So, Charlie?"

"Charlie," Zoey whispered the name, finding a spark of joy the name hadn't brought her in so long.

She placed Micah's hand on her throat and said it louder. Charlie. His eyes lit up and he repeated it in a raspy whisper. Charlie. He traced the letter C over her stomach. Zoey kissed him hard and made the *I love you* sign on his chest. Micah had come into her life out of nowhere. She'd pushed him away and injured him so badly, he should've never forgiven her. But here they were out in the woods under a veil of trees and sparkling stars, picking the name of their child. It was almost too unreal. Zoey held his hand and rested back on the sleeping bags, watching the stars through the trees. An owl called out in the distance and another replied. Micah lay down next to her, gazing up. Chef came over and put his head on Zoey's belly and sighed. Zoey petted his head, chuckling.

She wasn't sure when she dozed off, but when she woke up it was morning. Micah was up feeding the fire and making tea. He saw her sit up and came over to kiss her.

"Good morning. How are you feeling?" he asked, rubbing her neck.

"Surprisingly good. Not queasy. Yet." Zoey stretched and yawned.

The dogs were already out playing outside of the grove and she could smell Micah making food.

"Pan toast and jam if you can stomach it," he answered her unasked question.

She tipped her head. It actually sounded good. He went over to make her a plate and brought her a cup of tea. Zoey nibbled the toast and was happy it seemed to be staying put. Micah sat down with her cross-legged and sipped on tea. They let the fire die down and went to a nearby creek to douse it before they headed back to camp. Brandon and Callie were covering to give her a couple of days off to enjoy her new marriage. Once the

fire was out, they took their time to get back to camp, reveling in their alone time.

Micah had trainees coming in two weeks for the facility and was leading back-to-back classes until October. Even then, he already had some classes booked. Zoey talked to Kyle about working right up to delivery but taking a couple of months off after to adjust to motherhood. The county approved coverage and Callie agreed to cover at that time. She was done with classes and was taking time to decide what route she wanted to go. This would allow her paid time to figure it out. Micah also had no classes scheduled from mid-November until the end of the year. But until then, they were both going to be busy.

Camp was quiet when they came in. Callie was in triage and Jake was out chopping wood. Kyle must have run to town because his truck was gone. All the leftover food from the night before had been doled out and a cooler's worth was sitting on Micah and Zoey's porch. They brought it inside and moved it to the fridge, putting the cooler back in storage. The tents had been collapsed and the arbor was placed on the pathway to their cabin. They paused and kissed under it.

Micah had some paperwork to file, so they wandered over to the training facility, which was now complete with four attached bunkhouses. Each with its own fenced yard and kennel area. The office at the end also had a fenced yard and a row of six kennels off of it for Micah to be able to rescue and train dogs. The bunkhouses were basic with a composting toilet, wood stove, and bunk beds. There was a shared kitchen and shower in a separate building behind the bunkhouse.

Kyle's son, Christian, was part of the first training group, but since he didn't have a dog to work with, he'd be

working with a rescue Micah brought in. Christian expressed an interest in dog handling and Kyle jumped at the chance to bring his son into the fold. He was quiet, unlike Kyle, and seemed to have a natural affinity for dogs.

Micah had two rescues he'd adopted and gotten through their initial getting used to their environment phase. One was a female hound mix named Bean and the other a Jack Russell, Terrier mix named Razz. Razz was the dog Christian would train with. Bean was still dealing with human fears. Micah had taken her under his wing. Jake started working directly with Spin, so the SAR still had a dog to take out on rescues. Spin had begun to bond with him. Micah discussed making Spin officially Jake's dog, having him move in with Jake to further the bond. Jake was excited and chose to go through the first class, so he was completely on board.

Micah prepped the papers for mailing and checked on Bean and Razz. Razz liked to run at the kennel wall and leap off it. He was a small dog with tons of energy. Christian was going to have his hands full. Bean came over and licked Micah's hand but eyeballed Zoey, unsure. Zoey sat on the ground and Bean came closer, finally letting Zoey pet her. They played with the dogs, building their trust and getting them used to boundaries until Zoey felt her stomach growl. This baby was making high demands of her body.

They left the training facility just as Kyle and Christian were coming in from their run to town. Christian started to unload the truck, but Kyle made a beeline for Zoey and Micah, practically running. He got to them and paused to catch his breath, his eyes wide. He put a finger up while he coughed and shook his head. They stared at him, confused.

"You are not going to believe this!" he exclaimed, signing rapidly. "I just heard when we were in town. It's all anyone is talking about."

Zoey and Micah glanced at each other, then back at Kyle.

"What?" Micah asked.

"Michael Andrews, the guy you beat the crap out of? He is dead. Hit by a truck."

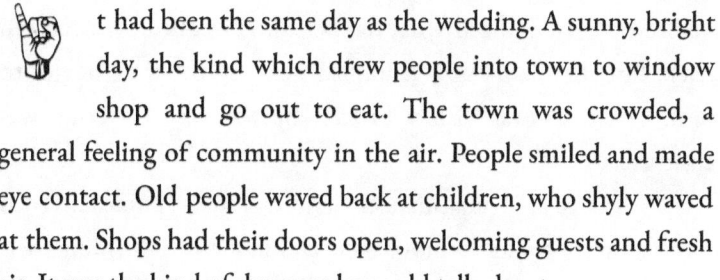

t had been the same day as the wedding. A sunny, bright day, the kind which drew people into town to window shop and go out to eat. The town was crowded, a general feeling of community in the air. People smiled and made eye contact. Old people waved back at children, who shyly waved at them. Shops had their doors open, welcoming guests and fresh air. It was the kind of day people would talk about.

Just not for this reason.

Witnesses say Michael Andrews was stumbling around downtown. Drunk and trying to hit up conversations with whoever would make eye contact. He wasn't being rude or belligerent, but it made people uncomfortable and they moved their children away. When asked what he was saying, no one could quite remember. Something about life and not taking things for granted. Maybe. It was as if his words disintegrated the moment they left his mouth. Everyone said the same thing. He was around all afternoon, going up and down the street talking

at people, not really caring if they were listening. His eyes were glazed and he wasn't all there... until he was, in the moments before the truck hit him.

Numerous witnesses said he stumbled away and stood quietly for a bit. Then, as if he transformed, he stood up straight, his eyes focused and clear, and walked towards the busy street. He paused at the curb for a moment and as a large delivery truck came barreling down in the lane closest to him, he simply stepped out in front of it. Intentionally. The delivery driver said it was like when a cat darts out from under a car in traffic, there was no chance to stop it. He didn't even have a chance to hit his brakes to see if he could move over. The lane he was in was clear, then like a magic trick, a man appeared and was under his truck before he even realized what happened. He pulled over and ran back, but the man was a crumpled heap by the time he got to him. His neck was visibly broken by the way his body was contorted.

Police and ambulances arrived almost immediately as mothers were trying to move their children away, shielding their eyes from the horrific scene. He was pronounced dead on the scene, killed instantly by the impact. People filtered away as the area was closed off and police prevented anyone from coming too close. Eventually, the town settled and people left for dinner. Just another homeless guy, just another drunk. It was easier to accept if they thought about what happened in those terms. Not a real person to them. Deny connection and it couldn't happen to them or anyone they loved. Simply another story to tell around the dinner table.

Except Michael Andrews was not homeless. Far from it. He owned a successful construction business. He'd been married

with two children and lived in a nice neighborhood. His wife left him a few years earlier because of his drinking and womanizing. He'd spiraled off the deep end after that. He'd lost any chance at custody and his employees said the business did better when he wasn't around. But he had money and a big house. Men's toys... like guns, boats, and snowmobiles. Too much time on his hands he drank away. Most of his friends kept their distance as he spun out of control. He'd been an after-work drinker, they said. Then he started cheating and drinking more. His wife found out and left. Packed the kids up when he was at work one day... got in the car, and escaped. She didn't want the house or his money. She simply wanted out. After that, he drove everyone else away.

Zoey wondered if this had been a final act of a guilt-ridden man. Or maybe he was just tired of his life. He never showed any remorse for the five lives he took. He didn't even seem to register it ever happened, the day on the street he pushed her down. Alcohol had taken his brain. He was a booze-soaked skin of a man. She didn't feel sorry for him. After all, he did it to himself. Then he took innocent people down with him. She felt for his children, who'd probably been robbed of a father most of their lives, and hoped they'd have someone decent to step in and guide them. She bitterly thought they were better off, anyhow.

No charges were placed in his death as from witness accounts, it was suicide. The delivery driver hadn't done anything wrong, even though he'd be haunted by the sound of his wheels rolling over the body for the rest of his life. Michael Andrews wouldn't be missed. After it was determined his estate was worth a substantial amount of money, everything was sold off. A portion was given to his children. The majority was paid out to Maizie Bright's family.

Once Michael Andrews was dead, Maizie's family was willing to settle the lawsuit, losing steam over someone paying the price. The one person they were truly angry at no longer existed and couldn't feel their wrath. Not that he ever had. The county paid a small portion and the rest was paid out by his estate. The case was closed and that chapter in all their lives was over. By the time it was all said and done, July was coming to end and everyone all but forgot about Michael Andrews... and sadly, Maizie Bright.

During all of that, Micah and Zoey found out they were having a girl. Charlotte. Micah was beside himself with joy and Zoey was secretly relieved, afraid a little boy would remind her so much of Charlie, she'd be chasing his ghost. She let her parents know and they were already showering them with presents. Micah wrote to his adoptive parents, letting them know about marrying Zoey and the baby. They sent back a generic congratulations card and a check for a hundred dollars. They weren't unkind about it. They just weren't involved. Their life was in Florida.

Zoey continued to work and once morning sickness passed, she felt like she could take on the world again. The guys were always telling her to take it easy, to which she brushed them off and got back to work. She was showing now and moved to bigger scrub tops to make room for her belly. Luckily, scrub bottoms had a drawstring, so little by little, she kept tying them looser. The summer was hot and she was uncomfortable but as long as she could eat, it was bearable. She was moving into her sixth month of pregnancy and the baby was super active. She especially kicked when Micah put his warm hand on Zoey's stomach.

The training center kept Micah busy and they were already getting requests for the following year. He only wanted to run it from April through October to avoid the heavier snowfall months. Kyle was able to confirm the county would allow him to use Micah as a contractor for rescues as long as he wasn't employed by them or fall under their insurance. This would allow him to assist during the busier months. Jake had officially taken on Spin, and Christian trained and was working with Razz. Bean replaced Spin in the pack and Chef was allowed to retire, though he still liked to get in on the action now and then.

The camp successfully brought back its volunteers over the summer and the bunkhouse was often full. At times between the training facility, volunteers, and staff there were up to thirty people milling around. Kyle started a preteen and teen day camp in basic safety and rescue, so when the volunteers weren't out on a call, they were working with the kids on wilderness survival, first aid, and dos and don'ts. Kyle was almost finished adding a room onto Micah and Zoey's cabin and was cutting a door into the existing wall. The room was almost the full length of the cabin and separated by a divider halfway down. This allowed for one half to be used for the baby and the other half to be used for whatever they needed. This way if they had another child, they still had plenty of space.

Kyle began seeing Marti, though they both liked their space and privacy, so she kept her place in town. Neither of them was looking for marriage, or to spend all their time together. They'd done that in the past and it hadn't worked out, so they decided what they had was perfect. Brandon and his wife had a baby boy, making Brandon absent for the rest of the summer.

Jake and Callie set a wedding date for the following year, still just happy to have locked each other down.

As summer came to an end, the team started to think again about winter, how to prepare camp for impending storms and rescues. Zoey was going to be out at least for December. Brandon didn't want to take on additional responsibilities with the new baby but promised a weekend a month to offer some relief. Which left Callie almost solely covering triage. She assured them she'd be fine, but it put everyone on edge. Brandon offered to at least be on call for a real emergency and Zoey assured them if things got bad, she could load up the baby and come over to help. To which Micah gave her a stern eye, shaking his head.

"Over my dead body," he insisted.

"No worry, Micah, I would never let her do that," Kyle told him. "I think with all of us having first aid training, we will be fine."

Zoey pouted and glared at Micah. He met her eyes, grinning. Her stubbornness wasn't going to win this battle. She sighed and kicked him under the table they were sitting around. He winced and rubbed his leg, giving her the *I love you* sign. She begrudgingly gave it back. He was right, though. They needed to focus on their new family and rest when they could. There wouldn't be time or energy for extras.

After Labor Day, many of their volunteers had to go back to school and the kids' camps ended as well. Zoey was relieved; so many people around all the time was exhausting, and they had *so* many questions. Now, the focus was on prepping for winter, getting the woodshed stocked, and making sure all equipment went through maintenance. Zoey taught refreshers to the team on first aid at their request.

Typically the heaviest snows came November through March, however, year to year was different. What none of the team expected that year, was for it to start snowing steadily by mid-September. By the end of September, it had snowed so much, they were already getting calls of stranded people and injuries. It was going to be one of those years. The years where the calls never stop. This made Zoey nervous. Having a baby was stressful enough, having a baby in the winter with early snowfall on a mountain, much more so. Her midwives assured her they had four-wheel drive and were used to coming out in bad conditions. Marti told her if she needed to get the ambulance up there, she'd figure out a way.

The baby's room was finished by the end of September, and they held a housewarming of sorts to show everyone. The team surprised Zoey with an impromptu baby shower during the housewarming. Kyle, as promised, made the baby a crib, meeting all safety specifications. Jake and Callie gifted them a rocking chair to go in the nursery, and Brandon and his wife sent over a set of baby blankets and towels, not being able to make the event with a baby and the unpredictable weather. Zoey's parents came to the housewarming with a ridiculous amount of baby items. Before long their once basic cabin was exploding with pinks, blues, greens, and yellows.

Kyle proudly showed off his handiwork by opening the door to the new room. They all walked in and were able to fit into the space easily. The space was set as two separate areas and in a clever last-minute thought Kyle cut and installed a sliding window in between the baby's area and Micah and Zoey's bedroom, so they could keep an eye without having to go in.

Zoey planned to have the baby near her until she could determine a schedule, then move the crib to the nursery.

After the eventful gathering and everyone left, Micah led Zoey to the couch and sat her down. He went to the kitchen and made them tea to have by the fire. He let the dogs out and they could feel the winds blowing, bringing in another storm. The dogs did their business quickly and bolted back through the door. Micah shut the door firmly, shaking his head. They all knew it was going to be a tough winter. He sat down, setting Zoey's feet on his lap, and began rubbing them. She sighed with relief.

"Magic hands," she signed and leaned back on the couch arm.

He laughed, massaging her swollen legs. Being on her feet all day while pregnant was taking its toll. Her back ached most of the time, now nothing was starting to fit. She still had two months left and already felt like she was bursting at the seams. She shifted uncomfortably, trying to make room to breathe. No matter which way she moved, the baby moved, too. It was a battle of wills and Zoey was most definitely losing ground. She stroked her stomach, sighing.

"Are you ready for all of this?" he asked her.

"Not even close. Brandon was smart having his baby in the summer when it is less busy and we have too much help. I am a little scared, to be honest. It seems so monumental."

"Hey, we have each other. We can do this. Besides, it is not like we planned to have a baby in the middle of winter. She just had a mind of her own, our Charlotte." He looked happily wistful and rubbed her legs.

Zoey nodded, not feeling so enchanted at the prospect of the little willful being inside her. "I have a feeling it is foretelling her personality since she is coming in with such a bang. I am glad I have you, Micah. I truly do not know what I would do without you."

Micah squeezed her leg and smiled. "Luckily, you do not have to."

28

---

he snow continued to come in hard and heavy through October. The only benefit was that it didn't let up enough for too many clear days, which kept tourists away from the slopes. The calls were still heavy but no deaths had been reported. The team finally got a break from the storms near the end of October and unseasonably warm days for about a week. During this time, Kyle started laying out the framework for a community lodge and kitchen space. The plan was to expand the triage space into the warming area with additional beds and emergency areas. He worked quickly and with Micah's help, they got the frame, walls, and roof on before it began to snow again.

By the second week in November, conditions on the slopes were unstable and warnings were put out all over the county. Zoey's midwives started driving out for her weekly prenatal visits, ensuring they could traverse the roads, to keep her on the mountain. She was showing no signs yet of being ready to

give birth and although she was uncomfortable, she was fine with waiting a while longer. Training classes stopped for the season, so camp was in shutdown mode except for the rescue calls they had come in. Micah took this time to work with his newer rescue dogs to get them up to speed in the downtime.

Bean had begun sleeping in their cabin now that Spin had moved to Jake's. She was still timid, but once she was out searching, she came alive. Trek became the lead dog, having grown out of his puppiness, and was quick to get other dogs on track. He never left Micah's side. Four new rescues were brought in and were getting acclimated to the environment. Now that Zoey was almost ready to give birth, Chef was her constant companion. He seemed to sense the impending change, underfoot at all times.

The snow let up for a day, so Micah wanted to get Bean out for some deep digs to get her accustomed to having to search and find. She'd only worked close to the center and she needed to gain confidence to become stronger. He went out in the morning and buried fabric scraps with scents. He came back a little while later to eat and relax before he took her out. The sun was shining for the first time in days. Zoey was deep cleaning the cabin when he came in.

"Nesting?" He kissed her on the cheek, his lips cold and chapped. He'd been reading the pregnancy books, too.

"I guess, really just getting stir crazy. Here put this on your lips." She handed him a tub of coconut oil and he rubbed some on his lips and face.

"She will be here soon. Come here, let me massage your back." Micah went to the couch and motioned to her.

Zoey came over and sat with her back to him. His strong fingers began working out the knots in her lower back and she breathed out with relief. It was two weeks until her due date, but the midwives said to plan on the probability of going over since it was her first birth. There was no room left inside of her and she couldn't fathom how something this big would get out of her body. She dropped her head forward as Micah rubbed her neck. He leaned in, sliding his arm around her belly, and kissed her neck. She rested back against him, letting him hold the weight of the baby for a moment.

They made lunch and Micah began loading his pack to take Bean out for training. He was taking Trek, too, to help Bean understand the process. Trek would keep her focused and on task.

"Will you be back for dinner?" Zoey asked as he finished loading his things.

"For sure. Bean is doing good. I think she will find what I buried quickly. I am going out on foot to give her a chance to stay on track. Besides, I do not think it is wise to take out the snowmobiles if we do not have to. Keep things as stable as possible out there. I have my radio if you need me sooner. I will not be far."

He came over and wrapped his arms around her, kissing her deeply. The baby, wanting more room, kicked against him, making them both laugh. He put his hand on her belly and the baby kicked his hand even harder, causing Zoey to wince. Battle of wills.

"She is getting so strong!" she said, massaging her stomach. She swore there were bruises on the inside from the child's feet.

Micah chuckled and brushed his lips against her cheek. "Be back soon. I'll keep my radio on."

He was out the door when Zoey realized he'd forgotten his inflatable vest. She ran it out to him as he slipped on snowshoes. He grinned and took it.

"Cannot forget that," he signed, shaking his head.

"I love you," Zoey told him.

"I love you, Z," he replied and headed out with Trek and Bean. She watched him disappear over the hill and went back inside.

Zoey made sure everything in the nursery was set. They'd found a small dresser at a thrift store in town and Kyle added rails to the top, so it could double as a changing table. The top drawer was filled with diapers and the bottom two with clothes and blankets. Zoey planned on breastfeeding and the midwives had given her a basket of items to help adjust to that, including creams, pads, and the like. She was nervous her body wouldn't be able to perform such an incredible act but was determined to try.

The house was clean and the nursery was set within a couple of hours. She knew Micah would take over all of the cooking and cleaning once the baby was born until she could chip in again, however, she wanted to make sure everything was ready until then. She sat on the couch and put her swollen feet up. She wouldn't miss that. Chef pawed at the door and started whining. That wasn't like him and he'd gone out when Micah left. She called him over to her but he stood staring at the door. He whined again, pawing at the door. Zoey got up and looked out, seeing nothing. He wouldn't stop, getting louder and more desperate.

She got up to let him out and he took off up the hill. He stood at the top and barked at her incessantly. She quickly put on her boots and coat and went outside. No one was around except Callie in triage, so she followed Chef up the hill. Zoey clicked on her radio to see if there were any alerts. An avalanche but no reports of anyone involved, and it was out a decent way from them. Too far out for any of them to be near. Another SAR was checking it out, but it sounded like it was clear. As soon as she got to Chef, he whimpered again and went farther out. He was wanting her to follow, whining and staring at her.

Micah.

She sent him a message in morse code on the radio but it wasn't returned. Panic rose in her. She scanned back at camp to see if she saw Jake or Kyle. Neither were around. Jake's vehicle was gone, he must have headed to town for supplies. Kyle might be out on patrol. She radioed him.

"Kyle, come in. Where are you?"

The radio crackled and he gave his coordinates. Shit, he was the other way. She'd move too slow on foot. She let him know she was going out to search for Micah, who wasn't responding. She was taking a shovel and snowmobile.

"Where did he go?" he responded.

She wasn't a hundred percent, but he typically took the dogs around a specific area to train. "He took Bean out to train, I assume where he usually does on the east end. I'm going that way."

"On it. I'll head that way from here, as it would take me longer to get back to camp than over there. I'm on skis, though. I'll move as fast as I can. Once you get there, give me exact the coordinates."

Zoey made it to the snowmobile shed and grabbed a pack with a shovel and blankets. One of the snowmobiles already had a toboggan attached, so she fired it up and headed out. Chef ran in front of her leading the way, showing his true form despite his age. She was unsteady in her body and felt like the snowmobile would tip a few times but knew time was of the essence, so she kept pushing.

As they drew closer, Zoey could see the avalanche away off had triggered a sympathetic avalanche in their area. Her heart dropped when she saw movement at the edge of the avalanche. Bean was limping towards her. Chef ran into the center and was digging with all of his might. Zoey radioed Kyle the coordinates, then moved as fast as her body would let her towards Chef, shovel in hand. She stuck a probe down and hit something. She trusted Chef's instinct. She started digging downhill of the probe but was moving too slowly.

"Please, Kyle, hurry," she whispered to herself.

Within minutes, Kyle was at her side out of breath and began digging. Zoey scanned for Trek but he was nowhere to be seen. Bean remained at the edge, her eyes tired and scared.

"I radioed Jake, too. He's coming back from town but won't make it in time. The ambulance is on its way," Kyle said between shovels of snow as he dug as hard as he could.

Time... how long had it been? When had Chef whined at the door? How long had Micah been buried? Zoey pushed down the fear and kept digging. All of a sudden, they saw a shock of red hair. As they dug more, they could see he'd deployed his inflatable vest, creating an air pocket around him so he didn't suffocate, keeping him closer to the surface. They cleared the snow around him. He was unconscious and extremely cold. Zoey

found a strength she'd never known, putting her arms around him and tugged as Kyle grabbed the other side.

Trek was still missing, but as they pulled Micah from the snow, Chef was already digging in another area. They knew they needed to get Micah warm as soon as possible. Time was everything. She could feel a faint pulse, however, he was in shock due to hypothermia. They got him to the toboggan and laid him on it.

They were running out of time.

"Kyle, we need to get his chest free of wet clothes, so I can make skin-to-skin contact. You need to drive the snowmobile back," she instructed as she began removing her coat.

"No, Zoey, you're pregnant. I'll do it and you drive," Kyle said firmly.

"Kyle!" she yelled at him and he flinched. "Fucking listen to me! I'll tip us. I need you to go as fast as you can. I'll lay with him to make skin contact. I have a few warming packs I can slip around us. You cover us with blankets and cinch us down. Now!"

Kyle followed her orders. Zoey pulled off her coat and unbuttoned her shirt, not caring what anyone saw. She put the warming around packs under Micah and behind him. His chest was exposed, so she lay facing him, wrapping her arms around him with her chest and belly pressed up against him. He was so cold it made her shudder. Kyle laid blankets on them and threw the straps over, cinching them tightly. They were in a cocoon and Zoey prayed it was enough. She heard the snowmobile fire up and they jerked forward. Kyle ran it at full speed towards camp. She heard another snowmobile pass them. Jake, going to pick up the dogs and equipment. The dogs were part of the team and

Jake would do more good going to get them than to help Kyle and Zoey.

The baby kicked initially but stopped shortly after being pressed against her father's cold body. Zoey moved her arms the best she could against Micah's back, attempting to create friction for warmth. She shivered as his body drew heat away from hers. She knew it was a risk doing this pregnant, but she needed to. It was his only chance.

She felt the snowmobile come to a halt and almost immediately hands were grabbing her and Micah off the toboggan. Blankets were thrown around her and she was brought into triage while he was whisked away to the ambulance to get him off the mountain. She was sat down and quickly checked over. The baby's heartbeat was good. Her temp was low but not dangerously so. A hot drink was shoved in her hand and she was told to drink. She glanced up into Brandon's eyes. He'd heard the emergency call and headed immediately for camp. The team took care of their own. He finished checking her over and confirmed her temp was rising. He sighed, sitting down next to her.

"You take too many chances, you know? Your heart is bigger than your brain," he admonished.

"I had to. I can't lose him."

"Zoey, he doesn't look good," Brandon said softly. "He may have been down there too long. You need to prepare yourself for what might happen."

Zoey burst into tears and the baby kicked in her womb. This couldn't be happening. They'd already been through too much. They'd already paid the price. It wasn't fair. She

remembered her first thought about what it would be like to be in pitch black being deaf and her heart twisted.

Brandon put his arm around her. "Hey, hey. Sorry, I just know you need to know what's going on. You know I wouldn't lie to you. We are paramedics first and I wanted you to understand what Micah is up against."

Zoey stood up and buttoned her shirt. She grabbed her bag and met his eyes firmly. "I have to go."

Brandon put his hand on her arm. "Zoey, you're nine months pregnant. You don't want to put yourself into labor."

"Brandon, my husband is on the way to the hospital and may not make it. I need to fucking go!"

Brandon nodded and went out to find Kyle. He knew Zoey wouldn't listen to him and Kyle was the only voice of reason. Kyle came in, took one look at her, then shook his head.

"Alright, let's go." He handed her a coat and grabbed his keys.

29

he drive to the hospital seemed to take forever. By the time they got there, Zoey had chewed down all of her nails. Kyle dropped her at the emergency room and went to park. The nurse at the front took one look at her, thinking she was in labor, and started asking for her info.

"No," Zoey said firmly. "My husband was just brought in by ambulance. Micah Sanders."

The nurse checked, then took her back to another room. Kyle came in shortly after and they sat waiting. Zoey called her parents, they'd want to know. After what seemed like too long, Kyle went in search of someone he might know who could give them answers. Finally, a doctor came in and sat down with them.

"Can you tell me how long he was buried in the snow?" he asked, looking at a chart in his lap.

Zoey shook her head. "I don't know. He'd left hours prior. Our dog, Chef, started pawing at the door. I guess I got up there in about twenty minutes. I don't know how long he'd been buried already. The avalanche over from us triggered about ten or fifteen minutes before our dog was pawing at the door. That avalanche caused this one. As soon as I got there, I started digging. It took us about twenty minutes to get him out. So, I'm guessing around an hour. When we got him out, I made skin-to-skin contact and put warmers around him in the toboggan."

The doctor met her eyes, after glancing at her very pregnant belly, then cocked his head. He noted the chart and closed it. "He's alive but comatose. He's severely hypothermic and probably wouldn't have survived had you not taken those steps. I hope he'll pull through, however, we aren't sure to what extent, if any, long-term damage he'll have."

Kyle took Zoey's hand and squeezed it.

"Can I see him?" she asked quietly.

"Shortly. We're doing some treatments to deal with the hypothermia. I'll send a nurse in for you when you can come in." He got up and left them alone.

Kyle turned to her. "Hang in there, Zo. Remember, you made it when I pulled you out of the river."

"Yeah, but, Kyle, you got me out in minutes, he was buried for an hour."

Kyle dropped his head, then sighed. They knew the dangers and the timelines. Micah at least had air from the vest, a lot of victims didn't. He'd been so cold. Like, dead cold. Zoey's parents came into the room and at that moment she was a little girl, sobbing on their shoulders. The baby, distressed by her mood, kept kicking forcefully.

Jake called Kyle to update him on camp issues. He'd been able to get Bean and Chef back to camp. Jake told Kyle Trek

hadn't survived. He'd dug him out and brought his body back to camp. Trek's paws were bloody from trying to dig himself out. Jake found Micah's radio a few feet from where they'd found him. It must've been knocked away when he was hit by the avalanche, preventing him from calling for help.

The first avalanche had triggered a sympathetic avalanche and it hit Micah and the dogs before they had a chance to react. Trek had been closer to Micah and had gotten buried about six feet away. Bean was partially buried but able to get herself free. Injured, but otherwise okay. Micah must've inflated the vest when he realized what was happening, which created an air pocket as the snow buried him. He was closer to the surface because of it, but Trek had been buried too deep.

Chef must've sensed it right away. He'd pawed the door after the first avalanche, looking at the time from the first avalanche to the second one that caught Micah. Zoey played the timeline again in her head. She'd followed him within minutes and gotten the snowmobile immediately. When he pawed the door, to when she got to the site, was no more than twenty to thirty minutes. They'd dug him out in under thirty. It'd been right around an hour. People have survived that and longer. It wasn't the norm, but they had.

A nurse came in and motioned to her. Kyle told her was going to head back to camp since they were busy but would come back that evening. Zoey followed the nurse to the ICU. Micah was hooked up to machines and a saline drip. She touched his hand which felt warmer, yet still cold. His temp was rising gradually but steadily. He seemed so vulnerable in the bed, his face blank. She kissed his cheek and ran her fingers over his lips.

The lips she'd kissed earlier that day. She squeezed his hand, hoping for a response, but it was limp.

"Can I lay with him?" she asked the nurse who was adjusting the saline drip.

They both looked at the bed and Zoey's very pregnant body.

"I think we can make it work," the nurse replied kindly. "Let me get you a stool."

She went out and came back with a step stool. She helped Zoey climb into the bed, moving the tubes and wires over Micah's head so Zoey wouldn't get tangled in them. She scooted Micah over a couple of inches with the help of another nurse, so Zoey had a little more room. Zoey lay next to Micah with her arm over his waist and her legs pressed against his. He was lifeless. If it hadn't been for the machines beeping signs of life, she would've felt he was just gone. She took his hand in hers and started signing to him with the alphabet and words she could do with one hand.

"Micah, I am here. You have to come back to me. I cannot do this without you. That was not part of the bargain. Your daughter needs you. I need you. Please."

He remained unresponsive. She lay with him until her legs went numb and got up to stretch and tell her parents what was going on. She sent them home, promising if anything changed, she'd let them know. When she got back to the ICU, the nurses had brought in a gurney and put it next to Micah's bed, dropping the side next to the gurney, so Zoey could lay next to him without being cramped. They even brought her dinner and made sure she was comfortable. She could see it in their eyes.

The sympathy, the pity. She made sure Kyle was on the list of approved visitors and he showed up a couple of hours later.

"Hey, Zo." He was standing at the door, staring at Micah. It wasn't easy for any of them to see him like this.

"Hey, Kyle. Come on in, there's a chair over there."

"I think I'll just stand for now. No change?"

"His temperature is up, but he's still unresponsive."

"Damn. Do you need anything?"

"I need Micah."

"Fair enough. Chef is stressing out back at camp. I'm going to have him sleep with me tonight if that's okay," Kyle offered.

Zoey nodded. Kyle stayed for a bit and kissed Zoey on the cheek before he left.

"Zoey, you and Micah are the two strongest people I know. Keep the faith."

He walked over and took Micah's hand in his and said softly, "I can't lose you, brother."

He wiped tears away and put his hand on Zoey's shoulder as he walked out.

They'd all started as strangers and now were as close as any blood family. Zoey's thoughts trailed off to her brother Charlie and how the same thing had taken him from her. How could this be happening again? She started to sob, whispering to herself and Charlie.

"Charlie. Wherever you are now, I need you to get Micah back to me. Push him back this way. I can't do this alone. I can't lose him, too. Charlie, losing you almost killed me. I miss you every day. I wanted you to be here to be an uncle to my child. If you have any power over this, please save Micah."

A nurse came in and Zoey wiped her tears, not wanting to be the subject of any more pity. The baby pushed uncomfortably against her rib cage and she groaned, pressing back on the foot shoved under her rib. The baby, sensing her stress, pulled her foot back.

"How far along are you?" The nurse asked politely.

"I'm due in two weeks," Zoey replied flatly.

"Oh! If you need anything, I'm on the night shift. Becky."

"Thanks. I'm Zoey."

It felt weird to get familiar with the staff, as in her job she only saw patients briefly before they were carried away by the ambulance. Becky left and Zoey watched the machines until it made her crazy. Micah's temp was normal now but he was still comatose. She stayed awake as long as she could, then curled up on the gurney next to him, holding his hand in hers. She dreamed she was digging holes in the snow. One after another, but they always ended up being empty. She thought she saw Micah on the edge of a clearing, but he disappeared. As she ran after him, she fell into one of the holes she'd dug, endlessly flailing until she jolted awake.

It was early morning and Micah's hand was still in hers, deceptively warm. She glanced up to his face and into his eyes, which were quietly watching her. She blinked a few times to make sure she was awake and looked around the room. She was still in the hospital on the gurney beside him. She squeezed his hand and he squeezed back. He made the *I love you* sign weakly with his other hand. She sat up shocked. He was awake.

"Where am I?" he asked, his hands moving slowly and clumsily.

"ICU. Kyle and I pulled you out of the avalanche. You were hypothermic."

He nodded, then looked at the machines. "Am I okay?"

Zoey laughed and shook her head. "You tell me."

He tried to sit up but fell back. A nurse came in and paged the doctor.

"No, sit back. We need to run some tests."

Zoey interpreted and the nurse looked surprised.

"Oh, is he hearing impaired?"

"He is deaf," Zoey replied.

The nurse peered at his chart, then frowned. "That's not on here."

"And yet, it is still true," Zoey answered, irritated.

The nurse smiled and blushed, embarrassed. She added a note to the chart. "I'll let the doctor know."

"Thank you," Zoey said, a little softer.

The nurse left and Micah touched Zoey's arm. "That was harsh."

"I know. I am tired. You scared the hell out of me."

"I am sorry."

"Do not ever fucking do that again," she signed and laid down next to him, her belly pressing against his side. The baby kicked and he weakly put his hand on her stomach.

"I dreamed about both of you. I was holding the baby and you were standing with your brother Charlie. He had his arm over your shoulders and was smiling at me. Then he waved and was gone. I looked again and you were still pregnant and I was feeling so much pain. When I opened my eyes I was here and you were sleeping next to me, holding my hand. The last thing I

remember was seeing the snow barreling down on us. We could not escape it."

Zoey rubbed his hand, listening. She knew what was coming next.

"The dogs? Are they okay?"

She sat up and met his eyes. "Chef was who found you. He let me know and I followed him out on the snowmobile. Kyle came from another direction. Bean was wandering around, limping when we got there. We dug you out but did not see Trek. Chef found him but it was too late. I am sorry, Micah."

Micah stared at her and tears welled in his eyes. "He is dead?"

Zoey nodded.

Micah looked away, staring at the wall as the tears fell. "I am so fucking stupid. I should not have gone out. It was too dangerous."

Zoey turned his face to hers. "You did *not* know. We cannot always see what is going to happen. It was a sympathetic trigger, you did *not* do this."

Micah watched her, then shook his head. "He trusted me."

Zoey knew he needed to work through it. Part of SAR was the risk of loss. Dog handlers knew it, but it didn't make it any easier. Trek was a good dog, doing what he loved. But he lost his life because of it. Handlers struggled with putting their dogs in the line of danger, even though it was part of the job. Zoey held him as close as she could and let his tears fall.

Micah needed to grieve.

30

o matter how much they begged, Micah wasn't released from the hospital for over a week. Doctors ran full tests to see what, if any, long-term damage he might've suffered from being buried in the snow for so long. He showed signs of short-term memory loss and frostbite which might, or might not, need surgery. They wouldn't know for a couple of weeks. After the week was up, Zoey didn't feel like they had any more answers than they'd had before and just wanted to get him home with her. Knowing he'd be around medical professionals, they released him with the expectation he'd come back for checkups. Micah would've agreed to anything to leave.

Kyle came to pick them up and helped Micah to the truck. Micah was weak and still had no feeling in some extremities. His feet were the worst, so he had trouble walking but refused a wheelchair. His fingers and toes were swollen and blisters had formed. They'd removed his wedding ring upon being admitted and gave it to Zoey in a bag.

Micah probably should've stayed in the hospital in his condition, but he insisted on being present for the birth of his daughter. Zoey convinced him at least to use canes to get around to try and protect his feet. He begrudgingly agreed when she said she'd tell the doctors he needed to stay in the hospital if he didn't.

The walk to the truck was excruciating and Zoey and Kyle stared at each other, worried. If Micah wasn't careful, he could end up with amputated toes. Kyle braced Micah under the arms and tried to shift his weight as much off of his feet as he could. Micah grimaced with every step and Zoey questioned bringing him home. The baby was due in a week, and she knew she had little chance to convince him otherwise. He was coming home one way or the other. Thankfully Callie and Brandon offered their services to give Zoey some relief. Even if Micah waved off any help prior, the walk to the truck proved to him otherwise. By the time he was sitting in the truck, he'd broken out in a full sweat and was out of breath.

Zoey got in next to him and touched his hand. "Micah, are you going to be okay? Now you have me scared."

He wiped the sweat off his brow and stared at her, shaking his head. "Well, that fucking hurt, I will not lie. I need to be home. Once we are there, I promise I will take it easy. You will take care of me anyway, right?"

He winked slyly at her. She sighed, exasperated. They were a mess and supposed to be responsible adults in a week. He reached out and held her hand. Kyle climbed in, glancing at the two of them.

"Jesus," he muttered under his breath and started the truck.

The whole team was on hand when they got to camp and met them at the truck. The walk from the truck to the cabin seemed like miles and Zoey didn't know if Micah would make it. She made eye contact with Kyle and Jake, motioning her head to Micah. They nodded, knowing what she meant, then picked him up on either side, carrying him like a chair to the cabin. Micah tried to protest but only half-heartedly, relieved he didn't have to try and cross the snow with his frostbitten feet.

The cabin had been stocked with every possible food and necessity. The fire was blazing and the dogs had been moved to another cabin to make sure they didn't trample Micah's feet. Once he was settled, they'd be brought back over and reintroduced gently, so they understood to be careful. Considering distances, Micah was set up in the bed closest to the bathroom to reduce how many steps he took until his feet hopefully healed.

Kyle ushered everyone out, aware Micah and Zoey needed to rest and figure out their areas. Zoey made them tea, feeling the baby trying to move in her tiny space. She was head down, however, Zoey still wasn't dilated. She brought the tea and sat in the bed next to Micah. He was going to get cabin fever not being able to work.

They played cards and Scrabble, then Zoey went to Kyle's to see if he had any other board games. He dug around and found a couple in a cabinet.

"So, you think he should've come home?" he asked, handing her the games.

"Probably not, but you know how Micah is. He'd cut off his arm if he thought it'd get him what he wanted."

Kyle nodded. "You okay?"

"Truthfully, I'm glad to have him home. That being said, I kind of hope the baby comes late, so I'm not taking care of two helpless people. But I'll manage. I'll be glad to reach out and know he's there."

She didn't just mean home and Kyle understood the reference.

"I didn't know if he'd be alright," he said softly. "Anyone I saw in that condition didn't make it, you know?"

She knew. "I don't like to think about it, but when I was with him on the toboggan, I'd started to mentally prepare myself. He was lifeless. Dead cold."

"I guess you brought him back to life," Kyle suggested.

"Kyle, I don't know what happened. Honestly. No one was giving me hope, preparing me for the worst. Then I woke up that morning in the hospital and he was just looking at me, awake and alive. It doesn't make sense. Sometimes I'm afraid I'm dreaming and will wake up, and he'll be gone like Charlie."

"Nah, he's here in all of his redheaded, stubborn glory. He's got a daughter to meet." Kyle chuckled, running his hand through his hair.

Zoey hugged Kyle. He'd called Micah *brother* in the hospital when he was in a coma. He was her brother and Micah's. Every single time she'd called on Kyle, he'd come. He was like their protector. For the rest of her life, she wanted him around. She wanted him to be an uncle to her children. He hugged her back.

"I'm not going anywhere."

Zoey smiled up at him. "Stop reading my mind."

The dogs were circling and sniffing her. She knew it was time to bring them home. Bean was still limping but moving

better. Chef kept staring at her with his sad eyes, afraid she'd leave him again. She scooted them out the door and carried the games back to the cabin. She settled the dogs at the door and opened it slowly. They smelled Micah at once and searched for him, finding him almost immediately. He signed for them to settle and petted them.

Once they had a chance to know he was home and safe, Zoey directed them to their bed by the fire. When she came back to the bedroom, Micah was on the edge of the bed with his head in his hands. Trek. She kneeled in front of him with her hands on his thighs. He lifted his head and the pain in his eyes was almost unbearable. She rose to her knees and put her arms around him. He didn't make a sound, but she could feel the wetness of his tears through her shirt. Finally, he shuddered and took a deep breath. Zoey sat back and watched him. He wiped his eyes and looked at her.

"I am sorry I was not more understanding when Charlie died. I mean, I tried, but I could not understand what you were going through." He leaned forward, resting his elbows on his knees, then reached out to touch her face.

Zoey put her hand on his for a moment. "Micah, you were one hundred percent there for me with Charlie. You have every right to grieve Trek as much as I grieved Charlie. Loss is loss. No one has the right to put boundaries on anyone else's pain."

"Thanks, Z. To some people he was just a dog but we were teammates, he was my family. That day when we saw the avalanche coming, Trek would not leave my side, even though the snow was going to bury us. He tried to protect me right up to the very end."

Zoey got up and sat next to him. She knew no words could make it better and was just there for him. Trek had become a strong leader and did what he was supposed to until he no longer could. She rubbed Micah's back and after a bit, he laid back on the bed.

"I am tired."

"Get some rest. Wait, you need to take your meds first. You want something to eat?" Zoey asked him.

He shook his head.

He had antibiotics, pain pills, steroids, and blood thinners to take. He needed to eat something with them. She opened the fridge to find it packed. She made a sandwich and grabbed a juice. She brought the handful of pills to him.

"You have to eat with these. Do not fight me. I also need to check your hands and feet."

Micah peered at her from under his arm on his forehead and sighed. He sat up, swallowed the pills whole with the juice, and ate the sandwich. He lay back down and she first checked his hands. They had frostbite but would heal since he was wearing thick-lined gloves. She pulled the bandages off his feet and gasped. They were swollen, discolored, and blistered. Some patches looked hardened from the frostbite and would risk needing to be surgically removed if they didn't heal. She made a bowl of warm water with Epsom salt and brought rags over. She had Micah put his feet as much as he could in the water to soak. She instructed him to move his feet and toes while she gently placed the rags on them. She kept alternating the rags in the warm water until it cooled and left his feet uncovered.

When she was done, she let him be because he was tired, and she dumped the bowl. By the time she came back, he was

asleep and she covered him with the blankets. He needed to soak his feet a few times a day. She had a basin in triage she could use. She went over and gathered some supplies. Callie and Jake were hanging out in the warming area and asked if she needed help. She shook her head, waving as she left.

Micah slept for hours. She made English muffin pizzas and vegetable soup for dinner. He stirred by the time she was done and she could see him trying to get up to go to the bathroom. She went to help, but he put his hand out and grabbed the canes. She stepped back and let him do it on his own. She was glad to see him willing to use the canes. He was in there for a while and she wondered if she should go check when he came out. He waved his fingers in the air.

"Hard to do anything with frostbite," he explained.

"I made dinner, are you hungry?"

He nodded, moving slowly to the table, and sat down. Of course, he was going to be hard-headed. She put the pizzas on the table and gave him a bowl of soup.

"Thanks, Z. You are the best." He smiled sheepishly at her, knowing he was being a pain in the ass.

"After dinner, we need to soak your feet again. I think we can heal them and avoid surgery. I was reading up on frostbite treatment."

"You are the boss."

Zoey laughed, then shook her head. "Not likely."

They ate and Zoey made up the footbath. Micah put his deformed feet in and winced. It was going to hurt with the salt until it started to heal. He leaned back in the chair and stared at her.

"You know I came back for you, right?"

"What do you mean?" Zoek asked, confused.

"When I was in the coma. I could feel you next to me. I could feel you holding my hand, signing the alphabet. I just could not get to you. It was like still being buried in the snow, but I kept clawing and climbing towards you. I used your warmth as a guide and then you were there, holding my hand. I did not want to wake you. I just wanted to look at you. You were my beacon."

Zoey stared at him. He shook his head, then brushed her hair off her shoulder and leaned in to kiss her skin. "You do not need to say anything. Kyle told me what you did."

"What I did?"

"He told me when you pulled me out, you took off your coat and shirt and insisted on lying with me on the toboggan skin to skin to warm me up. He said he tried to stop you but you would not listen. He told me you saved me by doing that. I do not know what I would do without you, Z."

Zoey got up and helped him back to the bedroom. She lay down next to him, placing her head on his chest to listen to his heartbeat and the blood rushing through his body. He held her close with one hand and stroked her hair with the other. At some point, they'd both almost lost each other. This fact did not escape their notice. Zoey sat up and looked at him.

"We cannot live without each other, so can we agree to stop doing stupid things which might take us away from one another?"

Micah laughed, his chest shaking under her. "I think that can be arranged."

31

rek was buried by Charlie's memorial, at Micah's request when he was in the hospital. Jake and Kyle made two castings of his paws, one to go over his grave and one for Micah to do with as he wished. Micah put the one by their wood stove where Trek liked to lay. The other dogs sniffed the casting and settled down next to it. Zoey scoured to see if she could find a picture of Trek, eventually finding one where he was sitting, peering up intently at Micah. Micah's back was turned to the camera, his long hair braided down his back. Trek's eyes were clear, a dark shining amber, his face locked on Micah's. Zoey framed the picture and gave it to Micah one morning since she knew it'd be a while before he could visit Trek's grave. She wrapped it in tissue paper left over from the housewarming baby shower and tied a ribbon around it.

He held the present, looking inquisitively. Both of their birthdays were in the spring, and it wasn't a special day. She told him to open it. He slowly untied the ribbon and unwrapped the

paper. His mouth hung open when he saw the picture and he peered at it to get a closer look. He met Zoey's eyes, his own glistening.

"Where did you find this picture? It is amazing."

"I guess I had taken it over the summer. I was trying out the camera we got for our wedding and this is one of the pictures I snapped," Zoey explained.

"I do not know what to say. I am so touched. Look at him. It is the best picture you could have ever gotten. That is my Trek." He put his fingers to his eyes to stop the tears from starting, then hugged Zoey. "You are the most thoughtful person, Z."

Zoey blushed. Micah placed his hand on the picture and closed his eyes, smiling. He was thinking of Trek, a dog he'd raised as a rescue at just a few months old. Trek, who'd been energetic and bright but not easy to train. He'd become a strong rescue dog and Micah's constant companion. His absence was felt by the whole team, but for Micah it was personal. Zoey went to the kitchen to make breakfast, leaving Micah to his memories.

A week passed since Micah came home and it was her due date. The midwives had come out the day before, but she was still only dilated two centimeters; any contractions she was having were sporadic and weak. The baby was going to take her sweet time to arrive. Zoey cleaned the cabin so many times, there was nothing left to do.

She was grateful Kyle had gotten the laundry room set up off the bathhouse because once the baby came, laundry was going to be constant. Kyle continued to add solar panels and they were up to twelve now, which powered the camp with the help

of the backup generators. They used propane and wood to heat and cook as well, reducing the draw off the panels.

Zoey checked Micah's feet again and made him soak them. The swelling was going down and their color was returning to normal. The salts were healing the blisters and he was able to move around the cabin without as much pain, using just one cane. She stayed in contact with the doctors, giving them updates, so he wouldn't have to leave before the baby came. His hands were almost back to normal with just a few spots on his fingers she was watching. She had him soak those as well when he soaked his feet.

Christian was keeping an eye on the training facility, working with the dogs and making sure their areas were cleaned daily. He was a natural dog handler and moved into one of the bunkhouses in the facility. Zoey liked him. He was quiet but dedicated, and the dogs responded to him well. She saw him out working with Razz, and a couple of other rescues, while she was brushing snow off the porch and waved at him. He smiled shyly and waved back.

"Hey, Christian, how's everything going up there?" she yelled in his direction.

"Good! These ones are catching on. Razz is showing them the ropes." He laughed as Razz ran circles around the group.

Razz reminded her of Trek when Micah first came to the camp. Super smart and super wild. She chuckled and headed over to Kyle's to see if she could borrow a screwdriver to hang a shelf in the baby's room. She knocked and stuck her head in to see if he was home. He was at the table with his head in his hand, looking over some building plans. He glanced up, frazzled.

"Hey, can I come in?" she asked, not wanting to interrupt him.

"Hey, Zo. Of course, I need a break from this, anyway." He shoved the papers away and pushed out a chair for her. "Still holding on to that baby?"

"You know it. Due date's today but midwives say it likely will be at least a few more days. Maybe a week."

She sat down and glanced at the plans he was working on. A full kitchen for the lodge. His dream was to make a community center for them to all use and gather at. The lodge itself had the basics built and was waiting for the inside. It was large enough to hold fifty people sitting, with long tables running from the kitchen to the large fireplace at the other end. The tables could be folded and pushed against the walls when they wanted the space opened up. The kitchen would have a full double-door fridge, freezer, and stoves. It was built out away from the cabins, closer to the far side of the bathhouse, with another large fire pit and benches if they wanted to have events.

"Oh, hey, I need to put up a shelf in the baby's room. Can I borrow a screwdriver?"

"Yeah, I have a spare you can have. I saw you talking to Christian. He doing alright with the dogs?" Kyle asked, glancing out the window at his son.

"He's going great! Next to Micah, he's the most in tune with the dogs I've seen. We're thrilled to have him. I saw he was living in the bunkhouse?"

"Yeah. That's okay, right? It's just too small here and his mother kicked him out."

"Of course. I didn't realize he was still living with her. How old is he now?"

"He's twenty. He was going to school, but he told his mother something she didn't agree with, and she asked him to leave. So, school's on hold for now."

"Oh, well, he's always welcome here. He's really helping out while Micah is out of commission. If you don't mind my asking, what did he tell her? You don't have to tell me if it's too personal." Zoey wasn't trying to be nosy, but what could make his mother that upset? Christian was such a nice kid.

Kyle sighed and leaned back in his chair. "Can I trust your discretion? I'm not sure if he wants this public knowledge."

"Kyle, my lips are sealed, and if you aren't comfortable telling me, I won't push."

"No, it's okay. I've had my suspicions for a while, really since he was about fourteen, but figured I'd let him tell me when he was ready. He told his mother he was seeing someone. A guy."

Zoey gazed out at Christian. He was throwing something across the field for the dogs. As a pack they were running towards it, seeing who could get there first. He tipped his head back and laughed as Razz ran under another dog to get the item, then ran back. Kyle was supportive but she felt bad for Christian not having his mother's support. That had to hurt.

"So, she asked him to leave over that? Why?"

Kyle shook his head. "That's just the way she is. Very old-fashioned. Her whole family is that way. They would sometimes say stuff that made my blood boil. A bunch of bigots."

Zoey wasn't all that surprised to hear it. This area had old families that didn't want things to change. She'd experienced their bigotry growing up and still saw it in the eyes of some people when she was in town. The younger people, in general, were more open and embracing, but it would take a generational die-off of old people to change the overall scope of the town.

"I'm sorry to hear that. Is he doing okay? That had to be tough," Zoey asked gently.

"You know, no one wants their mother to kick them out for being gay. He could've hidden it from her but wanted to be honest. Luckily, he has another parent who loves him to the ends of the earth. But yeah, he's pretty torn up about his mother's response."

Zoey nodded. Kyle was just that parent. He loved Christian so openly and honestly and always had. She touched his hand. "He's lucky to have a father like you."

Kyle shook his head. "I'm lucky to have a son like him. He's the best kid."

As Zoey walked back to her cabin with the screwdriver, and a few other tools Kyle insisted every home needed, she felt the baby move and put her hand on her belly. She couldn't fathom a mother going through this, then withholding their love because their child loved who they were supposed to. Then was truthful about it. Christian saw her and waved a little more confidently this time. She smiled and waved at him, sending him all the love she could. No matter what, she'd love her child and any child she had.

"Christian?" she called out to him.

He turned and looked at her with his head cocked. "What's up, Zoey?"

"Hey, we'd love to have you over for dinner tonight. You and your dad."

He grinned, a large wide smile. "I'd love that. I'll let my dad know."

Zoey went in and found Micah with his feet propped up, attempting to put together a baby bouncer chair. He was shaking his head and set it down when she came in.

"Why do they make this so hard?" he asked, exasperated.

"To make sure we know what we're getting into," Zoey reasoned.

Micah reread the directions and tried again, this time slipping the steel bar into the brace, pinching his thumb in the process. He added the attachments and slipped the cover over. What looked like a simple baby chair had taken him over thirty minutes to put together. He placed his pinched thumb in his mouth, then pulled it out to look at it. A purple welt was forming and Zoey sighed.

"Be careful with your fingers, they are still healing. Let me do these things," she admonished.

He pouted slightly and frowned. "I want to help. You are bursting at the seams and I am just sitting here doing nothing."

"Trust me, as soon as this baby comes, you will be helping a lot. You will be the baby holder."

Micah's eyes lit up. "That is a task I will happily do. I cannot wait to meet her."

Zoey sat down beside him and leaned her head against his shoulder. "Me too. Stubborn child."

Micah rubbed her head and chuckled. "The apple does not fall far from the tree, right?"

Zoey laughed. Knowing the two of them, they were going to have their hands full. "Oh, before I forget, Kyle and Christian are coming for dinner tonight. I have a frozen lasagna we can throw in."

"Sounds good. I wanted to run some things by Christian, anyhow, about the training center. I think we are making enough, I can hire him on."

When Kyle and Christian showed up, the lasagna was in the oven and Micah had slippers on his feet so he could move around easier, though it was still a slow and painful process. Zoey made garlic bread and Micah chopped up a salad for the meal. As usual, Kyle brought himself and beer. He offered one to Micah, who looked to Zoey for medical approval.

"One," she replied.

Alcohol was not good for healing and Kyle tended to overdo it. To say the least.

Micah cracked the beer and took a sip, winking at her. Christian had picked up ASL pretty well while training with Micah over the summer, and they got to chatting about him working for the center. They'd always just called it the training center, however, now that Micah was hiring an employee, they officially named it Trek Rescue Dog Training Center. The legal papers were being filed, with Micah and Zoey listed as owners and operators. Kyle was working on a sign to hang out front.

They all conversed over dinner and Zoey was happy to hear Christian openly talk about his boyfriend. He said it cautiously at first, but when Micah and Zoey treated it like they would anything else, he relaxed and opened up. This was his family, too, and they were there for him. Christian came alive talking about the dogs and Zoey noticed the similarities between him and Micah. Kyle helped her put the shelf up and peered around the nursery.

"Very cozy. Now, all you need is to add a baby," he teased.

"You're telling me," Zoey replied, trying to stretch her back.

"Don't worry, it goes fast. One day you're counting the days until they arrive, the next, they're adults, meeting you eye to eye."

They walked back into the living room, where Micah and Christian were in deep discussion about the dogs. Kyle leaned against the door jam, motioning to Christian to make his point. Zoey nodded and thought about it. She wanted to savor every moment. Micah glanced over, meeting her eyes, then turned his head in question. She made an M over her heart and then a C over her heart. He made a Z over his heart and then a C over his heart.

The evening wore down and Zoey excused herself for bed. Micah stayed and chatted with the guys for a while longer, then climbed into bed next to her, putting his arm around her with his hand on her belly. Before long, it wouldn't be just the two of them anymore. Zoey snuggled into him and yawned. She needed to sleep while she could.

Four days later while she was getting out of the shower, her water broke.

32

y the time the midwives came, Zoey was feeling regular contractions, but they were still spread out about eight minutes apart. They checked her and she was four centimeters dilated. It could still take a bit, so they had her walk around the cabin. Micah's feet had healed enough for him to move without much pain and he was by her side with his arm around her waist. Every time a contraction hit, Zoey stopped and leaned her head against his chest, while he rubbed her back until it passed. She told him to dig his fingers in because the more pressure he used, the better it felt. The more she moved, the closer the contractions got. They dropped to under five minutes, then four, then skipped to two. The midwives checked her again and she was seven centimeters dilated. She felt like the baby was already trying to get out and sat down on the couch.

Sitting increased the pain, so she got back up, pacing back and forth. The pain was getting to be too much and she wondered how her mother did this four times. She rested her

head against Micah and cried in frustration. She couldn't do it. She didn't have the strength. The midwives were encouraging, reminding her she was close until she snapped at them to stop talking. Micah massaged her back, holding her when she wanted. She began to feel like she was going to lose it and felt incredible pressure between her legs. Panic filled her and she looked at the midwives for reassurance.

They knew the look, guiding her to the bed and checked her again. She was fully dilated and they could feel the baby's head. They told her with the next contractions to push. She laid back, covered in sweat, not knowing how she'd draw the strength. As soon as the contraction hit, her body went into autopilot and started pushing. She grabbed her knees and put every ounce of energy into the push. The contraction subsided and she rested back, out of breath. Micah pushed her hair out of her face and smiled at her the way only he could. On the next few contractions, she gripped her knees and pushed with all of her might.

"She's coming! We can see the top of her head moving down," one of the midwives exclaimed.

This gave Zoey the encouragement she needed. With the next contraction, she pushed as if she was forcing her insides out and met Micah's eyes. His eyes were amazed and calm, drawing her to a place of focus. The head was out and on the next push the midwives eased the baby's shoulders out. She slid out and Zoey fell back exhausted.

The midwives cleared the baby's air passage and laid her on Zoey's chest as they prepared for the afterbirth and stitched up any tears. They waited until the blood stopped pulsing in the

cord, then asked Micah if he wanted to cut it. He nervously took the surgical scissors and cut the cord.

Charlotte Kylene grimaced and blinked on her mother's chest. Zoey wrapped the blanket around the baby, drawing her close. Micah climbed into the bed and laid down next to Zoey, propping himself on one elbow. He placed his hand on his daughter. They both freely let the tears fall as they stared at the most amazing thing they'd ever seen. She had black hair and blue-gray eyes. The midwives said the blue could fade as a lot of babies had blue eyes or bluish tints to their eyes at birth. The gray was all hers. Micah kept touching her hands and grinning.

"She is perfect," he signed.

Zoey thought about it again. How could anyone do this and not want their child? How could Micah's mother have given him up? She knew her experience was not everyone's, but she couldn't imagine never seeing her child again. She didn't even want Charlotte to be taken from her for the midwives to do a check. They promised she'd be right back, then Zoey could try to nurse. They took measurements and checked Charlotte's reflexes. Charlotte, not wanting to be poked and prodded, squawked angrily, punching her little fist in the air. Micah was in awe and held Zoey's hand as he watched.

"I cannot believe she just came out of you. I mean, I knew she was in there but, wow. I love you so much. I love her so much."

All of the years of not having a family he felt was his own, were blown away in a moment by a seven-pound, eleven-ounce spitfire. The midwives cleaned Charlotte up and wrapped her in a blanket, handing her back to Zoey. Zoey took the bundle and stared down at her daughter resting on her chest.

She was perfect. She unbuttoned her blouse and tried to get the baby to nurse. Charlotte latched on for a few seconds, then turned her head.

"Totally normal. She's still tired from making her appearance. In a few hours, she'll want to nurse, then will never want to stop," the midwife said, laughing.

The midwives sat at the table, finishing up their records, then started to gather their things to go. They filled Zoey in on her self-care to heal and went over cleaning and watching the baby's umbilical cord until it fell off. One of them would be back in a few days to check on everyone. Their work there was done. Zoey was nervous about them leaving but reminded herself that not only was she medically trained, there was always someone on staff who could help if needed. Brandon had already promised a visit since he was now working on Obstetrics.

After they left, Micah made a light dinner and brought it to Zoey. He held the baby and rocked her side to side while Zoey ate, never taking his eyes off of her.

"We did this," he said.

Zoey smiled. He was so comfortable and natural with Charlotte. He got up and walked around the cabin, carrying her and swaying. Zoey laid back after she ate, every muscle in her body aching. Micah noticed and came over.

"Hey, get some rest. I have her. I will bring her to you when she gets hungry. There is no way I am sleeping any time soon." He signed with one hand while rocking Charlotte with the other.

"Thank you. I am exhausted," Zoey replied gratefully.

"Z, thank you. You are the strongest, most beautiful person I know."

Zoey dozed off and woke a few hours later, sitting straight up when she remembered. She glanced into the living room and saw Micah resting on the couch with Charlotte on his chest. They seemed so at peace. His eyes were closed, but when she came around, he opened one of them and peered at her.

"Hey. You get some sleep?"

Zoey nodded and came over beside him, unbuttoning her blouse to feed the baby. He handed her over and got up to go to the bathroom. Zoey rubbed Charlotte's cheek and smiled when the baby opened her small, gray eyes. She placed the baby at her breast and this time Charlotte latched on and began sucking. It was an odd sensation, primal. Micah came back in and watched in wonder. Once Charlotte was done, Zoey switched her to the other breast but she wasn't interested. Zoey put her against her shoulder, patting her gently. Micah sat down and rubbed Zoey's back.

"I am amazed by you," he told her.

Zoey blushed and leaned against him. Charlotte bobbed her head uncontrollably, making a grunting sound. A few seconds later they knew why and Micah took her to be changed. All systems were go. Zoey hopped in the shower and slipped on clean pajamas, feeling a little better from the hot water. When she came out, Micah was sitting at the table, holding Charlotte in one hand and spelling something out on her little chest with the other. Zoey watched quietly.

"Charlie."

He spelled out Charlie and for the first time in a long time, it brought joy to Zoey's heart. She came behind him and brushed the hair awake from his neck, pressing her lips against his skin. He reached up and put his hand on hers. He turned and their eyes met. Everything in the world just made sense. Charlie was sleeping peacefully in her father's arms, so he let the dogs come over and sniff her. Bean sniffed her and went to lay back down but Chef sat beside Micah, staring up with intent round eyes. Micah petted his head and Chef laid down at his feet.

The first night was one of little sleep, with Zoey and Charlie up every hour or so. Micah would carry Charlie around to try and let Zoey sleep. By the time the sun came up, Zoey and Micah were tired, but blissfully so. He let the dogs out and went to let Kyle know the good news. Kyle stopped in a little while later with some home-cooked stew and biscuits.

"Thought you might want to not cook today," he said, setting down the pot. Micah showed him the baby and he grinned.

"Smack dab in the middle of the two of you, isn't she?"

With her dark hair and gray eyes, she was.

"What's her name?" he asked, peering in at her.

"Charlotte Kylene Sanders. But we will call her Charlie after my brother. Kylene was for you," Zoey said softly.

Kyle's eyes got big and round, then his mouth dropped open. "For me?"

"Kyle, without you, neither of us would probably be here. So, yes, her middle name is after you," Zoey responded.

"Uncle Kyle," Micah added.

Kyle turned red and Zoey could tell he was biting back tears. Kyle had been more than a teammate to them. At every turn, he was there. He'd been present for every event, good or bad, which had impacted their lives. She felt closer to him than her surviving siblings, as close as she did her parents. He nodded and grinned.

"Uncle Kyle. I like the sound of that," he said almost in a whisper. "Let me get out of your hair. You know where I am if you need me."

Kyle headed out, giving the baby one last big smile before he shut the door. Zoey looked out and saw Jake outside, then waved. Micah held Charlie up in the window and Jake smiled, giving two thumbs up as he went to the training center. Christian was out working with the dogs and Callie was in triage. Zoey saw Brandon pull up to relieve Callie and for a moment, their whole team was present. Their family.

Zoey thought back to the day Micah came to the camp. It had been Jake, Kyle, and her. Megan was still there then, but had since moved on with her life. Callie and Christian came later. Charlie died and Zoey didn't think she'd ever feel love again. They'd lost Trek. She survived almost drowning. Micah survived an avalanche. Through it all, they kept coming back to each other. They swore their love on the field by the camp in the summer sun.

She let her mind wander back to that first day, seeing Micah drive up and let the dogs out. She remembered meeting his eyes for the first time, having no idea the journey their life would take. Together they'd go through some of the most intensely painful moments of their lives and come out on the other side, having created the most incredible little person either of them had ever seen.

She smiled as she recalled trying to talk to him that first time; how at ease he made her feel. How she fumbled through but was determined to get to know him. How he told her she was beautiful almost immediately and asked to kiss her before they'd even really gotten to know each other.

She watched her husband hold their tiny daughter and wondered for a moment had either of them not made it, how different their lives would've been. Like her brother Charlie. Had he just not been snowboarding that day. Had Michael Andrews walked in front of a truck before he started the avalanche. Had she never begged Micah to let her back into his life. Had he walked away and never looked back, Charlotte wouldn't exist. What if he'd never assaulted the guy in Colorado, losing his job and sending him here?

Zoey didn't like thinking about all of the bad things that had torn them apart, but she realized everything had a trigger point. Micah's anger was his and brought him here in the first place. It also almost took him away. Zoey's was losing her brother, Charlie. It almost killed her, but taught her to fight for what she wanted. Everyone has an avalanche they're running from on some level. For some, they're victims of someone else's actions. For others, they're victims of their own.

No one intends to initiate the slide. Micah's began as a baby given away and turned into a rush of anger he couldn't control. He chose to save himself and put it behind him. Zoey stopped running when she realized it was only herself she was running from. Kyle put his son first and protected Christian from the hatred spewing at him. Zoey didn't know everyone else's, but she could see no one was safe. Everyone was on the slope, living their lives. At any moment, it could all come crashing down.

She came and sat next to Micah, considering this revelation. She wondered if he knew how this was all going to play out from the beginning. He said he knew when he met her, he'd grow old with her. But how could he have known she'd feel

the same? How could he have known they would continually find their way back to each other? She peered over at him as he rubbed Charlie's cheek and smiled down at her. He caught Zoey's eye and paused, reading into her soul. He gave a soft smile and winked.

"I just knew."

Epilogue

---

t was three months shy of three years since Charlie's birth. She was now a rambunctious child with long, wavy black hair, sage-gray eyes, and freckles. She'd covered every inch of ground at the camp and no being was safe from her chubby, grasping hands. She was Micah's constant companion and fluent in ASL. She was also deaf.

Uncle Kyle was her buddy and she'd shriek until he lifted her up on his tall shoulders to carry her around the camp. Zoey and Micah had to screen in their front porch and lock it. More than once Charlie figured out the front door and let herself out, running as fast as her little legs could carry her until her daddy scooped her up and brought her back in, kicking and squealing.

Jake and Callie snuck off and got married at the courthouse one day after the constant questions about them setting a date got on their nerves. They agreed to have no children and if they changed their minds one day, they'd adopt.

Brandon and his wife now had three children and Zoey suspected he volunteered once a month because triage was still quieter than home. Kyle and Marti continued their spacious relationship where neither was looking for a serious commitment and they gave each other company when needed. Christian didn't discuss his relationships but was happy to not have to hide who he was, at least on the mountain. Zoey suspected he was in a serious relationship, as sometimes the same handsome, young guy drove up to pick him up on his days off.

On Zoey and Micah's third anniversary, she surprised him with news of their second child. Not having her mother's stamina for chasing children, probably their last. An ultrasound revealed it was a girl and they looked at Charlie, shaking their heads. They were in for it. They chose the name Isabelle after Zoey's mother Isa and hoped she'd be calmer like Isa was. Charlie was thrilled about having a sister, but her throwing the baby doll they bought her, made them wonder if she even understood what it meant. She'd ruled the camp for years and was probably not ready to share her throne.

Zoey's parents, who already doted on Charlie and stole her away whenever they could, were delighted with the news of another granddaughter. Zoey's father became determined to communicate with his granddaughter and learned ASL in record time after Charlie's birth and revelation she was deaf. Micah and Zoey were told they had a higher chance of having another deaf child, which they were more than fine with.

The training center was so successful, Micah had to hire more staff, rescuing six dogs at a time. He was able to step away from going out on calls and shifted his focus to training people and dogs full-time. Zoey volunteered in triage a few times a week

but stepped into training with Micah, which allowed Kyle to shift her salary to Callie. Callie and Jake converted their cabin into a delightful cottage. Kyle finished building the lodge and added a series of small summer cabins to officially form a kids' wilderness survival camp. They even reached out to deaf schools to let them know they wanted to offer the program to their students.

The once two cabin and two tent base camp had turned into a year-round village. At any given time, a minimum of eight people up to around forty would occupy the space. It became its own self-sustaining community. Gardens were planted in the warmer months and food was preserved for the winters. Kyle created a solar farm to power the buildings. Zoey was grateful to be able to raise her children in such an inclusive and loving environment.

When her parents sold the farm, she never thought she'd feel the same way about anywhere as she had about the farm. As she looked over the land they now owned and would raise their children on, she knew she'd found their forever home.

She found her family.

Resources

National Association of the Deaf
https://www.nad.org/

National Technical Institute for the Deaf
https://www.rit.edu/ntid/

World Recreation Association of the Deaf
http://www.wrad.org/

USA Deaf Sports Federation
https://usdeafsports.org/

Telecommunications for Deaf and Hard of
Hearing INC
https://tdiforaccess.org/

Gallaudet University Laurent Clerc
National Deaf
Education Center
https://clerccenter.gallaudet.edu/

Conference of Educational Administrators of
Schools and
Programs for the Deaf
https://www.ceasd.org/

Acknowledgements

Thank you:

To Marie Peralta for her knowledge of Guam culture and food and for providing honest feedback across the board.

To Justin Sexton for his insight on the criminal justice system and for being a good sounding board for various situations.

To my children for letting me talk incessantly about my storylines, even when it makes me miss my exit.

To my eighth-grade sign language teacher at Oberlin Middle School in Raleigh, North Carolina for making learning ASL fun and pertinent. I never forgot what you taught me, even though I can't remember your name!

To Janet Ericson and her resources for guidance on ASL and the Deaf Community.

To those who serve on Search and Rescue teams, knowing they are putting their lives in danger and doing it anyway.

To dogs who want nothing more than to help humans and be part of our lives. They loyally serve us despite the great risk to themselves.

To all who rescue dogs.

Books by the Juliet Rose

Do Over

We Don't Matter

Prick of the Needle

Trigger Point

Through the Surface

Carrying the Dead

Catch the Earth

In Dreams, We Fly

Stitched Together

Reviews are always appreciated! Thank you for taking the time to check out my books!

Authorjulietrose.com

www.ingramcontent.com/pod-product-compliance
Lightning Source LLC
Chambersburg PA
CBHW022023240626
47154CB00007B/2227